INSPECTOR GHOTE'S GOOD CRUSADE

In the ordinary way it would hardly have mattered. If among the dozens of First Information Reports coming into the office on any one day there had been a suspected case of arsenic poisoning in any ordinary home, he would have been quite happy to let the local uniformed inspector keep an eye on things while he took a quiet half-hour or so to freshen up his store of knowledge. And then he would have descended on the scene and straightaway snapped out those few questions that mark out the C.I.D. man.

But this was no ordinary home he was hurrying towards through the night streets. This was the Masters Foundation. And the victim of the arsenic was Frank Masters, the American millionaire every citizen of Bombay delighted to honour.

Also available by H.R.F. Keating

The Body In The Billiard Room
Go West, Inspector Ghote
Inspector Ghote Draws a Line
Inspector Ghote Hunts a Peacock
Inspector Ghote Plays a Joker
The Murder of The Maharajah
The Perfect Murder
The Sheriff of Bombay
Under a Monsoon Cloud

INSPECTOR GHOTE'S GOOD CRUSADE

H.R.F. Keating

Mysterious Press books (UK) are published
in association with Arrow Books Limited
62–65 Chandos Place, London WC2N 4NW

An imprint of Century Hutchinson Limited

London Melbourne Sydney Auckland
Johannesburg and agencies throughout
the world

First published in Great Britain by
William Collins Sons & Co Ltd 1966
Reprinted 1986 by Constable & Company Ltd
Mysterious Press edition 1989

Printed and bound in Great Britain by
Anchor Press Ltd, Tiptree, Essex

ISBN 0 09 957970 7

I

Inspector Ganesh Ghote came quickly down the wide, well-lit steps of Bombay C.I.D. headquarters. Quickly, but not too quickly. His business was urgent enough. It could hardly be more urgent. But he wanted time to think about it, to hold it in his mind and just a bit to gloat.

So he made himself pause on the bottom step and, before going over to the blue Dodge truck waiting with its engine throbbing, he dug his hand into his pocket, took out his loose change, selected with care the smallest coin and placed it in the ever-ready hand of the broken-legged beggar whose privilege it was even at this hour to occupy this post.

The beggar, without in the least altering his note of monotonous entreaty, darted his dirt-encrusted claw deep into the recesses of the seamy rag round his waist and then turned his head from side to side once more to assess the prospects around him.

Inspector Ghote crossed the broad pavement and clambered into the waiting truck.

" Go to the Masters Foundation, Wodehouse Road," he said to the driver, a new and anxious-looking young constable he had not seen before.

" Very good, Inspector sahib."

The young man let in his clutch with a joyous roar. He had been scared stiff at the possibility that he would be ordered to an address he did not know. But this was easy. Everyone had heard of the Frank Masters Foundation for the Care of Juvenile Vagrants. There had been no need for the inspector to say Wodehouse Road. He knew where it was all right.

He swung the Dodge roaringly towards a coolie crossing the wide road with a great bundle of firewood on his head. The man scuttled to safety in a satisfying scamper of long, bare legs under the light of the tall, craning street-lamps.

"Watch out, you fool," Ghote said almost automatically.

He had hardly noticed what had happened. His thoughts were miles away. Seeing a succession of newspaper photographs of a young, serious-looking American, shaking Ministers by the hand, peering down intently at foundation stones, purposefully snipping lengths of ribbon with large pairs of scissors. Frank Master, the philanthropist. A long, thin-cheeked face with a jutting American jaw and heavy, dark-rimmed spectacles on either side of a long, inquiring nose.

Now dead.

Murdered, if what Deputy Superintendent Naik had told him turned out to be the true state of affairs. Symptoms of arsenical poisoning, the report had said.

Inspector Ghote bit the inside of his lower lip in momentary vexation. He wished he had had time to make a thorough check on arsenic and its effects. He remembered little enough of the single detective-school lecture devoted to poisons, various. And even his trusted Gross's *Criminal Investigation,* snatched up from its place of honour on top of his private filing cabinet, had for once let him down. Not a single index reference.

He frowned.

In the ordinary way it would hardly have mattered. If among the dozens of First Information Reports coming into the office on any one day there had been a suspected case of arsenic poisoning in any ordinary home, he would have been quite happy to let the local uniformed inspector keep an eye on things while he took a quiet half-hour or so to freshen up his store of knowledge. And then he would have descended on the scene and straightaway snapped out those few questions that mark out the C.I.D. man.

But this was no ordinary home he was hurrying towards through the night streets. This was the Masters Foundation. And the victim of the arsenic was Frank Masters, the American millionaire every citizen of Bombay delighted to honour.

The case was going to attract a great deal of attention. The papers would be full of it. There might well be questions in the State Assembly. "To ask the Minister for Police Affairs what steps are being taken in the case of . . ." "One of the Department's most able inspectors is in charge and I can confidently . . ."

Ghote checked himself. He must not think such thoughts. The case would be far from easy. Days might pass with nothing to report, and the affair was the sort of thing that would be talked about at the Centre. The American Ambassador expressing anxiety. All Delhi buzzing with talk of loans being held up. The telephone lines down to Bombay hot with urgent inquiries. And every one of them coming back to him.

"Inspector Ghote, may I ask exactly what progress . . .?"

"Inspector Ghote, the Minister has requested . . ."

"Inspector Ghote, I give you just twenty-four hours . . ."

A sweat broke out on his forehead.

It was a warm night. The clear, brilliant weather of winter had ended with its accustomed abruptness more than a week before and now the sluggish day-heat persisted well into the hours of darkness.

The inspector pulled out a handkerchief and patted at his face.

As the truck was halted for a moment by a tangle of late traffic jockeying its way round the huge, dark, domed block of the Prince of Wales Museum, he forced himself to think rationally about the case. Frank Masters. That was the starting point. What exactly did he know about him? What ought he to know?

He was a millionaire. Or was he? Certainly that was the impression left after reading in the papers about his innumerable benefactions all over the city. But was it exactly true? Was he still a millionaire? What was wanted now were the exact facts.

Well, the Masters Foundation was a fact. It was the crown of Frank Masters's charitable activities. The Masters Foundation for the Care of Juvenile Vagrants.

Its founder could hardly have chosen a more pressing problem.

Ghote looked out into the garishly lighted streets. Sure enough, his glance fell at once on a pack of half a dozen boys, the eldest no more than ten, roaming up and down, clustering round any passer-by with arms held out for money, voices clamouring, eyes darting up and down looking for trouble.

And there were hundreds of them. Some homeless altogether, others who had run away or been chased out. All beggars, almost all petty thieves, many ready to turn to any other form of crime that came to hand.

Frank Masters had taken up a formidable challenge. But then he was the sort of person to do that, or so it seemed. A man determined to do good. Ready to spend all his millions, and himself, in doing it.

And now he was dead. Killed by arsenic poisoning. How had it happened? D.S.P. Naik had had few facts to tell. Just that someone from the Masters Foundation had telephoned and had insisted on speaking to the most senior officer available. They had then reported that Frank Masters was dead, and the word "arsenic" had been mentioned. That was all.

The D.S.P. had summoned him almost at once. He had taken his orders. He had gone back to his office and rung down for a truck, had paused for just that moment to glance at the familiar, comforting, blue, mildew-stained volume of Gross and then had hurried out for the short trip through the still busy night streets.

Had hurried, but had not rushed. This was a case of such importance that he had felt entitled to savour a little the fact that he had been picked to handle it.

"You wanna know who killed him, mister?"

Ghote jumped in his seat.

He almost answered "Yes."

The challenge so exactly matched his very thoughts at the moment the Dodge had pulled up outside the tall front door of the Foundation building.

He looked in fury at the face thrust in at the truck's open window.

Only to be utterly disconcerted. The head at the window was the head of a twelve-year-old boy: the face was the face of a man of sixty.

The startling effect was due, he realised a moment later, to the spread of some sort of infection which had crinkled the skin of the boy's face into a thousand etched and tortuous lines. They gave him a look of extraordinary knowingness.

He was dressed in a ripped and tattered jacket of black plastic hanging open over a bare chest. Ghote could smell the sharp tang of his unwashed body.

"Get down, be off, get away," he shouted.

He pushed hard at the truck door and the boy leapt lightly off the running board and stood dancing on the balls of his feet in the driveway. At the end of an indefinite blur of light coming from above the tall front door of the big, sprawling bungalow, two or three other shapes of children of about the same age loomed indistinctly up.

"Be off, the lot of you," Ghote said sharply. "What are you doing here? This is private house."

The crinkle-faced boy in the tatterdemalion jacket bounced half a step nearer. His eyes were shining with bright malice.

"Live here, mister," he said. "This our private house. You come to visit, eh?"

Immediately Ghote realised who the boys must be. They were obviously some of the vagrants the Foundation catered for. A spurt of anger shot up in his mind at the thought that he had nearly let himself be caught out by that silly remark the boy in the jacket had shouted. He controlled himself sharply before he spoke again.

"You live here, do you?" he said to the wrinkle-faced urchin. "And I suppose you are allowed to go prowling about at such an hour of the night?"

The boy grinned cheerfully back.

"Mister, if they had one half idea there'd be plenty

trouble," he said in a fantastic parody of an American accent.

"Then you had better get back to your beds before I am telling," Ghote said.

The boy sidled swiftly up to him.

"You don't want to know who bumped off Masters sahib?" he asked.

And Ghote hesitated.

Such impudence ought to be dealt with by a quick cuff. Yet the boy knew already that Frank Masters had been murdered. And that was something which had only come through to the Police Department in the last quarter of an hour. It might well be worth getting hold of a possible witness like this before any interested parties found out what he knew and imposed their own views.

He leant forward and looked hard at the dancing boy in the dim light from the window above the door.

"How are you knowing Mr. Masters is dead?" he said.

The boy spat on the gravel of the driveway within inches of Ghote's well-polished brown shoes.

"We got ways of knowing things," he said. "We ain't gonna last very long if we don't know what goes on."

Into the words he contrived to inject another slaughterously powerful dose of American accent.

Ghote decided that his claim was quite likely to be true. An urchin of this sort did indeed need to know everything that was going on in order to survive. There was nothing like gutter life for sharpening the wits.

Though there ought to be.

"All right," Ghote said. "You have been looking where you had no business. This time I would not take any action. But you must tell me what you saw. Everything."

The boy grinned at him more widely than ever.

"Oh, mister," he said. "If we had been doing bad, maybe is better we are not saying anything."

Ghote took a furious step towards him.

But the boy hopped back out of range. All the inspector

could see now in the darkness beyond the light was the white of grinning teeth.

He stood still for a moment and worked things out. He could always call up some assistance and perhaps with some difficulty catch this slippery customer. But that would reduce the boy to total silence. He could always simply turn away and ring at the bell beside the tall front door.

And yet . . .

After all, the boy at least knew that Frank Masters had been poisoned. A little advance information about the circumstances would make up for knowing so few facts about Masters himself and about the effects of arsenical poisoning. The trouble was worth taking.

He dug his hand into his pocket and pulled out a shining nickel twenty-five naie paise bit. He held it up between the tips of his fingers so that it caught the light.

As he had expected, in the pale area lit by the fanlight under the front porch the black-jacketed boy swiftly appeared.

" Now," Ghote said, " let us talk business. You told you knew why Masters sahib had been murdered. You say, and this is yours."

" Oh, mister, mister."

The wrinkled face shook sadly from side to side.

" Oh, mister. You don't think I would be telling for money?"

The boy stepped right up to Ghote and looked at him with an expression of total seriousness.

" Listen, mister," he said, " you know what Masters sahib done for us? You know what life we live before he come along with his pick-up truck and bring us here? You know what is like being pavement sleeper in monsoon time? Oh, mister, if we tell who kill him, is not for money. Oh, never, no."

Slowly Ghote let his hand fall to his side, still holding the despised coin.

" All right," he said quietly, " you just tell me everything you know."

"Mister, it was all those women. All those gay girls."

And in an instant the boy had snatched the coin from Ghote's limp hand and had danced back into the half-light.

"What women? What gay girls?" Ghote shouted.

He advanced a step and then thought better of it. Without help he would never catch a boy who so obviously knew his way about the garden, doubly dark under the shade of faintly seen trees, just as well as he knew his way round the crowded city streets in broad daylight.

"All right," he said in a loud voice, "I should have known better."

He swung on his heel on the loose gravel of the drive and marched up to the front door.

His manœuvre proved completely successful. Before he had even begun to put out his hand to the bell button the black-jacketed, crinkle-faced boy was standing beside him.

"Listen," he said, a lop-sided grin sending the wrinkles twisting in a new direction, "listen, Masters sahib is millionaire. Isn't it?"

Without turning from the door Ghote replied.

"All right, he is millionaire."

"Then he must have gay girls. It stands to reason, isn't it?"

"That is all you have to tell?"

Ghote rang at the bell. Loud and long.

"No, sir. No, sir. That was just story. You wanna hear truth? Whole bag o' tricks? This time I tell. Honest, I tell."

Ghote did not answer.

The boy was obviously an incurable liar. Not a word he said could be relied on. There was absolutely no point in . . . And yet. And yet he had known about Frank Masters being dead. And this time he had promised to tell the whole story.

Ghote turned and walked down the steps to the driveway again. He waited in silence. One by one the whole gang came up. At last Ghote judged it the moment to speak.

"Listen to me, all of you," he said. "If any of you knows anything at all about the death of Mr. Masters, it is your duty to tell. Your duty."

He got a startling enough answer.

II

Out of the half-circle gathered in the patch of light from the house door one of the boys stepped suddenly forward. Without a word, he jumped high into the air, flung up his legs with a quick, strong jerk of his naked torso and stood in front of Inspector Ghote upside down.

It was a good comment on his exhortation to them to tell what they knew about Frank Masters. Perfectly clear, and dramatically expressed.

Do our duty? In our world this duty of yours looks pretty different.

And Ghote could not in his inmost mind deny it. It might be his job in life to see that citizens did their duty and to bring to justice those who failed to. But he had eyes in his head. He knew the sort of conditions the poorest people of the city lived in, the pavement dwellers, the beggars, the homeless like this boy. And he recognised that for them there was only one duty: to stay alive.

Behind him the big door of the bungalow opened abruptly. A swathe of sharp light spread out. The boys in the driveway vanished in front of it like so many sweepings.

Inspector Ghote turned. Standing on the threshold a stately, solemn bearer was waiting to take him inside to begin his investigation into the death of the house's master.

Quickly he climbed the steps.

: : : :

A few minutes later the inspector was being ushered by the solemn, pear-shaped bearer into the doorway of a substantial wooden hut standing at the far end of a big garden partly hidden by a trellis on which Ghote had glimpsed in the soft darkness a gnarled wistaria tree thick with swags of blossom.

"Inspector Ghote, Criminal Investigation Department."

Propped on a hard, white surgery couch, Frank Masters was in no condition to acknowledge any announcement.

His well-cut white shirt and trousers were splotched and stained with the terrible effects of the poison he had taken. The grave, intent face of all those newspaper photographs was limp and finished. The large-lensed, heavy spectacles had been dabbed down at the bottom corner of the couch, one side-piece askew, indispensable a few hours ago, junk now.

The bearer, his introduction performed, had quietly disappeared.

Standing in the far corner of the room, looking into the mirrored front of a white-painted cupboard, was a tall woman of about thirty-five dressed in a stiffly starched white overall. She had not turned when Ghote had been so solemnly introduced. He coughed apologetically towards her.

"I presume this is Mr. Masters," he said.

She swung round with a sharp bark of a laugh.

"Mr. Masters, I presume," she said. "Yes, you're quite right, Mr. Stanley."

Ghote realised, with some uneasiness, that he had to deal with a Westerner. By her voice, an Englishwoman.

"My name is Ghote actually," he said. "Inspector Ghote of the C.I.D."

She made no reply but looked at him steadily.

"You are the doctor who attended the patient?" he asked.

"Dr. Diana Upleigh," she said.

She continued to look at him in silence with a faint smile on her big, pink-complexioned, strongly-featured face and a frankly appraising look in the wide-set eyes under the dark aggressive eyebrows. She was a good six inches taller than

Ghote and was enabled to direct her stare sharply downwards.

When she spoke again it was in the cool, crisp English which sent a prickle of apprehensive irritation down Ghote's spine.

"It's hardly likely that anyone else would have 'attended the patient,' as you put it, is it?" she said.

"Well, no. No, it is not," Ghote said.

He licked his top lip.

"Then you can answer the questions I need to ask," he added.

"Why else do you think I hung about here?" she replied. "I'd have left my dispenser to look after things if it hadn't been that someone responsible had to see you people."

"Yes, yes, of course."

He paused to collect his thoughts, a necessary process, and looked round the room. It was painted shiny white and was dazzlingly clean and firmly utilitarian. Besides the examination couch there was a white, square sink in one corner, a weighing machine with a height measure attached, two green-painted filing cabinets, some hard wooden chairs and a glass-topped table.

At the end of his survey Ghote came back to the surgery couch.

"This is the body of Mr. Frank Masters Esquire?" he said.

"Who else?"

"And—and he is dead?"

The faint, cool smile came again.

"Do you want to make sure for yourself?"

"No, no, of course not. I perfectly trust your judgment. Please do not think I was making aspersion."

"Well, I think I am just about capable of telling whether life is extinct or not. There wouldn't be much point in ten years' study otherwise."

"No. No, I see that. Exactly so."

Once again Ghote had to haul back his mind to the well-learnt pattern of questioning.

" And he died here, in this room?" he asked.

" Certainly."

He straightened his shoulders a little.

" It is essential, you understand, that I should get the whole circumstances perfectly clear. What is the purpose of this hut exactly?"

The doctor answered without any trace of amusement now.

" This is our dispensary. You probably saw as you came down through the compound: it stands all by itself here behind that trellis with the wistaria on it. There's this room, the examination room. And through there is the dispensing room itself."

She jerked a glance at a door leading into the other half of the hut.

Ghote noted that there was no lock.

" Thank you," he said. " That makes it most plain. And now, what was the approximate time of death?"

" The approximate time? I take it you'd prefer the exact figure?"

A fraction of contempt had crept back into the cool voice.

" If you have it, I would prefer," Ghote answered stoically.

" Eleven twenty-four precisely."

" A very exact time."

There was hardly a questioning note in his observation, but the doctor was quick to take it up.

" I happen to have a scientific training," she said. " I naturally realise the importance of exactness in these matters."

" Yes, of course, I see that," Ghote said.

He let his glance slip down and rest for an instant on the doctor's well-made, low-heeled brown suède shoes.

" We come now to the cause of death," he said.

" Arsenical poisoning."

The statement was abrupt and uncompromising. Hardly admitting the possibility of being questioned.

Though Ghote saw the need to put questions.

"You are certain of this?" he said. "Has there been time for tests, etcetera?"

"No, there has not been time for tests etcetera. But you won't find I'm wrong."

"A clinical diagnosis only," said Ghote.

The doctor's heavy eyebrows rose a little at this use of the correct term.

"Yes," she said. "A clinical diagnosis. But you'll find I'm right. The symptoms were very clear."

"There will have to be a check made at the laboratory of the Chemical Examiner," Ghote said.

"Of course."

A jet of abruptness.

"But in the meantime we can certainly proceed along the lines you have suggested."

"Lines I suggested? Now, don't get this wrong. I haven't suggested anything. You've got your job, I've got mine. And, make no mistake, I'm going to leave you to get on with yours just as soon as I can."

It sounded as if the doctor was hardly optimistic about the results.

"Very well," said Ghote calmly. "So will you please tell all the circumstances of the death that you know."

The doctor considered for a moment.

"Yes," she said. "I think I can give you a pretty reasonable account."

She strode over to the glass-topped table and perched on the edge, thrusting her hands deep into the patch pockets of her white overall.

"Frank—Mr. Masters—started to feel ill, I believe, about a quarter past ten."

She looked quickly across at Ghote.

"Oh, yes," she said, "only hearsay, I know. But I don't think you'll find it disputed. I asked him a few questions to get the picture. He managed to say that he'd begun to feel sick about a quarter of an hour before I saw him. The symptoms had developed pretty rapidly—abdominal pain, vomiting, you know the sort of thing."

"Yes," said Ghote.

He would certainly know from now on, anyhow.

"Well, by a stroke of luck I happened to be on the premises when it happened. I was having a talk to a couple of the boys, trying to get into their heads some sort of idea of decent behaviour. We've had a lot of trouble recently."

"I see," Ghote said. "And who were these boys?"

"For heaven's sake, does it matter? You asked me what I knew of the circumstances of the death."

"Where there has been a violent death almost anything may be relevant to the case," Ghote said firmly. "That is an accepted principle of police procedure."

"Oh. Oh, all right then, I'll tell you who your boys were."

But, quite unexpectedly, the doctor looked suddenly almost totally disconcerted.

"Well, that is . . ."

"Yes?" said Ghote.

She gave a short, barking laugh.

"As a matter of fact," she said, "I can't give you their names."

Ghote lifted his head for battle.

"It's quite simple," the doctor went on. "I just don't know what their names are. I could find out, of course, but I just don't happen to know."

Ghote looked at her steadily.

"You must call them something," he said. "You must have heard them call each other something. First names only would be quite adequate."

"All right," said the doctor, "I'll give you them."

Ghote slipped a notebook out of his pocket and waited with ballpoint poised.

"Their names, as far as I remember them, are Edward G. Robinson and Tarzan."

Ghote lowered his notebook.

"Those are the names of film stars only," he said accusingly.

The doctor smiled.

"That's exactly it," she said. "They choose to call themselves by those names: there's nothing we can do about it. It's quite a common thing. When they get any money they waste it at the pictures. And they talk of nothing else."

"Tarzan," said Ghote. "Tell me something about him, please. He is a very acrobatical boy? About twelve years old?"

"That's him. He goes in for not speaking, for some reason or other."

"I think I have met him, and the other boy you mentioned," Ghote said.

"Met them?"

"Yes. They were waiting for the truck to arrive. Outside the front door."

"What did they say to you?" the doctor asked abruptly.

"Say? What do you mean?"

"Oh, come, man. I meant what I said. What did those boys speak to you about?"

Ghote frowned sharply.

There were limits. A police officer in the course of his duties did not have to submit to cross-examination of this sort.

"They did not speak," he said. "I saw only. You told you were called to see Mr. Masters at what time?"

The doctor shot him a quick glance.

"At the time I mentioned already," she said.

"Ah, yes," said Ghote, without acknowledging that he had set the little trap, or that it had been so scornfully leapt over. "At ten-thirty, you said."

"Exactly."

"And what were your preliminary observations?"

"My preliminary observations? I didn't need anything as fancy as that, I assure you. One look and I saw that Frank was in a pretty bad way. For a bit I thought it might be severe food poisoning. But he kept muttering about a feeling of burning. That was when I began to suspect."

"That it was poison, arsenic, you had to deal with?"

"That it was arsenic I had to deal with."

Ghote ignored the elaborate mimicking of what he knew to be an over-preciseness in his use of English.

"You commenced the appropriate treatment then?" he asked. "You administered an emetic or some such thing?"

"Don't be a bloody fool, man."

Ghote was unable to prevent himself drawing back in sudden anger.

"Oh, don't get on your high horse now, for heaven's sake," the doctor said. "When you know me better you'll know I call anyone a bloody fool who says something bloody foolish."

Ghote paused for a moment.

"You were describing the treatment of Mr. Masters," he said.

The doctor leant backwards against the glass-topped table, her hands still pushed deep into the pockets of her white coat.

"I wasn't describing the treatment," she said. "You were. That was precisely what I was objecting to. Emetic. You've got a lot to learn. There wouldn't be much point, you know, in giving an emetic when the patient is sicking up his entire guts every two minutes, would there?"

"I am sorry. I am not very well acquainted with arsenical poisoning."

"No, I can see that. It's a bit of a pity as this happens to be a case of exactly that. They might have sent someone who knew something about it."

Ghote looked at her steadily.

"Such cases are extremely rare," he said. "The police department cannot provide special personnel in such circumstances."

The doctor tilted up her chin.

"Then it won't be much use telling you what treatment I used, will it?" she said.

"Nevertheless I would like to hear," said Ghote.

He turned to a fresh page in his notebook.

The doctor shrugged.

"Very well," she said. "As soon as I realised the likely cause of the trouble I ordered my dispenser to prepare a quantity of ferric hydrate. It's a question of adding alkali to tincture of ferric chloride—a damnably slow business but by far and away the best thing to do, even with only two of us here."

"Did you have no ferric hydrate ready prepared?" Ghote said.

"Wouldn't have been any use if I had. It has to be fresh, you know."

Ghote did not allow himself to be snubbed.

"I have already told," he said. "I am not highly acquainted with the procedures for arsenical poisoning."

"No, evidently not."

"This dispenser you mentioned. What is his name, please?"

The doctor bounced off the table.

"Are you intending to check up on me?" she snapped. "Because if so, you can damned well whistle for his name."

"Yes," said Ghote. "I would naturally ask the same questions to him as I have to you. What is his name, please?"

The tall, white-coated figure stood looking down at him, legs apart, feet planted firmly on the well-scrubbed floor.

At last she spoke.

"His name's Carstairs," she said. "He's an Anglo-Indian. He has a little room over in the bungalow, perched up on the roof. If you want him."

"I will interview in due course. Please continue your account of events."

The doctor slumped back on to the edge of the table.

"There's not a great deal more to tell," she said. "The fact of the matter was that we didn't get the ferric hydrate prepared in time. There's nothing you can do to hurry a scientific process, you know."

"I suppose it is a case where shouting is of no avail," said Ghote.

She darted him a furious look but made no reply.

"And at eleven twenty-four Mr. Masters died," Ghote said.

"Yes. At eleven twenty-four. The time I gave you before. As soon as I saw that death had occurred I left Sonny Carstairs here and went and got in touch with you people. Got hold of a man called Naik eventually. Seemed to understand what I said, more or less."

Ghote decided to pass over such cavalier treatment of the Deputy Superintendent. It might perhaps be best for his own peace of mind if he forgot the remark had ever been made.

"Now," he said, "we come to the possible causes of poisoning."

"Murder," said the doctor.

She sat unmoving on the glass table top. Her hands were once again stuck into the patch pockets of her coat.

"That is obviously one possibility," Ghote said. "However, we must also consider the possibilities of suicide and accident."

"There are plenty of easier ways of killing yourself than swallowing anything as unpleasant as that," the doctor said brusquely. "And besides what would a man like Frank Masters want to kill himself for?"

Ghote pricked up his ears.

"A man like Frank Masters," he said. "What exactly then was Mr. Frank Masters like?"

The doctor gave him a long, steady look.

She got up abruptly and strode across the room until she was standing beside the examination couch where Frank Masters's body lay uselessly propped.

She looked down.

"Frank was a good man," she said. "Simply that. A good man."

She swung away, grasped for the door handle and in an instant was outside leaving the soft night air billowing in through the open doorway.

III

For some minutes Inspector Ghote stood quite still in the clinically harsh examination room alone with the broken body of Frank Masters. He forced himself to breathe deeply and slowly.

Calm, he told himself. That was the first thing. Calm to think out everything he had learnt. He must not allow himself to be swept away by the attitude of this arrogant English doctor. Who was she——?

He stopped himself.

And by standing still in the middle of the room and concentrating hard he did at last succeed in getting calm enough to go over quietly and rationally all that he had heard and seen. He was just thinking how little the doctor had really said about Frank Masters himself when a curious faint scratching noise distracted him.

He checked an impulse to dart out into the darkness of the compound to investigate and made himself stand stock still apparently gazing into space.

Without having to exercise much patience he was rewarded. Down at the bottom corner of the open doorway he became aware of a slow, very stealthy movement. Without turning his head even a quarter of an inch he looked as far downwards as he could.

Second by second there crept into the range of his vision first a small brown hand, grimy and ill-kept, then a thin wrist and finally a section of a ripped-up, ragged black plastic jacket.

Ghote took a long, slow, deep breath.

And pounced.

Successfully.

He felt his fingers grip with satisfying hardness into the lean and stringy flesh of the leader of the boys' gang.

Unable to suppress a faint triumphant smile he hauled the urchin into the hut and on to his feet.

"Well," he said, "and what do you want?"

The boy twisted round in his grip.

"To find out what you are doing, Inspector sahib," he said.

He grinned.

"Inspector sahib," Ghote answered. "So you have discovered that I am inspector. You have been listening at the window, have you?"

"Yes, Inspector," the boy said, hanging his head a little.

Ghote tightened his hold on the thin arm. The boy winced and looked up at him.

"Dr. Diana give you hell all right," he said.

Ghote let the arm go.

"But she spoke truth, Inspector," the boy said.

"Truth? Why shouldn't she?"

"When you were lying, Inspector sahib, she could lie also."

"Me lying?"

But no sooner had he spoken than he remembered how he had denied that he had ever said anything to the gang outside the house.

He put his arms on his hips and faced the boy.

"Now listen to me," he said. "I am investigating the death of Mr. Masters. This is a very important case: there are a lot of things I have got to do, and quickly. You will not watch over me while I do them. You understand that?"

"Oh, yes, Inspector sahib."

"Very well. And if I catch you at it again I would make sure you are locked up where you would not trouble me any more. Do you understand again?"

"Oh yes, sir. Understand very good."

Ghote stepped back. The boy slid gratefully towards the door. In the open doorway he paused for a moment.

"Understand okay," he said. "You don't worry. When

Dr. Diana make it hot for you, you don't want nobody to hear."

Ghote raced out into the garden after him. He caught one glimpse of a swiftly moving shape beyond the wistaria of the trellis and set out in hot pursuit.

The roots of a tree caught his toe and an instant later he was flat on his face with the smell of dusty earth in his nostrils.

: : : :

It was some three hours after this that he came to deal with the Foundation cook and got his next glimpse of real progress. Not that the intervening time had been idle. During it he worked his way steadily over the whole bungalow, finding out just who lived there and exactly where they had been earlier in the evening. With all the boys in the dormitories it was a formidable undertaking, but, aided by reinforcements from headquarters, Ghote got through it with speed.

He poked and pried into every cranny of the big, spartanly furnished house. He set the team with the inkpad to work taking fingerprints wholesale; he supervised the departure of the body on its way to the laboratory; he directed the obedient but unimaginative police photographer in taking shots of every possible relevant scene.

He even went so far as to eliminate the possibility, suggested by the boy in the black jacket, that Frank Masters's death had anything to do with "gay girls." Certainly no one approaching that description had ever been seen at the Foundation.

When he had been at work for about two hours the reporters arrived. The pear-shaped bearer, looking somewhat crinkled at this late hour, came to tell him. He went and met them at the front door.

"No statement," he said stiffly.

There were excited cries of protest.

"I have no time to be hobnobbing with pressmen," he said sternly. "I have investigation to carry out."

"Yeah?" said one of the reporters, a tall, beaky-nosed man wearing a brightly-coloured picture tie. "We got investigation to carry out too, you know."

Ghote turned away.

But just as the bearer, with evident pleasure, was pushing the heavy front door closed he relented. After all, though there was something rather shocking about wearing such a tie, the man was right: he had his job to do.

Patiently Ghote allowed himself to be questioned. But when it came down to it he did not have much to tell. In spite of all he had done up to that point, he knew very little.

The reporters left, looking upset. And Ghote went back to see how the police surgeon was getting on. He conducted a casual conversation with him and succeeded in gathering that the arsenic had in all probability been taken about an hour and a half before Frank Masters had complained about feeling ill. He checked and cross-checked on the time this had happened and came once again to the question of the evening meal and its cooking and to the big gas-stove with its heavy butane cylinders, the gleaming refrigerator and the formidable array of pots and pans of the Foundation kitchen.

And there he tackled for the second time the Foundation cook.

"You cook all the meals in the house?" he asked once again.

The cook, a plumpish, short little man whose skin gleamed and glistened under the light of the single bulb hanging from the middle of the low ceiling, nodded silent acquiescence.

"Did Mr. Masters eat the same food as everybody else?" Ghote asked.

"Oh, yes, sahib. Masters sahib very kind man. He say what good enough for boys from street good enough for him."

"Was it good food?" Ghote asked.

The podgy little cook looked downwards.

" Not very good food, sahib," he said. " Not very good cook."

For a moment Ghote thought about the picture of Frank Masters this evoked. The millionaire from America who was prepared to eat day in day out the indifferently cooked food he himself had provided for the vagrants he had rescued from the pavements of Bombay. The thought of the care and skill Protima, his wife, brought to his own meals rose up in his mind.

" What did you cook this evening?" he asked.

" Oh, very bad food this evening, sahib."

Ghote felt a stab of impatience.

" I asked what food it was," he said.

" Oh, yes, sahib. Very sorry, sahib."

The cook bowed his head. Ghote could see the plump roll of fat on his neck shining as though it were polished.

" Well?" he said.

" This evening mixed vegetable and puris, sahib."

" I see," said Ghote.

Even with a meal sent in at the office, he reflected, he had eaten far better food than the wheat cakes and vegetables that this American millionaire had allowed himself.

" Did Masters sahib eat with the boys?" he asked.

" Oh, no, sahib. He eat own meal as per usual, sahib. In staff tiffin room, sahib."

" His own meal? Then that was something different?"

" Oh, yes, sahib. It would not be right for the sahibs and memsahibs to eat vegetable only."

" Then what did Masters sahib eat as well?" said Ghote.

" Beef curry, sahib, and fish curry. Good curry, sahib."

" Ah," said Ghote, " so you can cook well enough when you want, eh?"

He looked down in triumph at the little cook, whose cringing attitude irritated him more and more from one moment to the next.

" Oh, no, sahib," the little man replied promptly. " Not good cook."

"Then why do you say it was good curry?"

"Dr. Diana come and watch me make, sahib."

Ghote's ears pricked up.

"Does Dr. Upleigh always do this?"

"Oh, no, sahib. Dr. Diana got much more important things to do than make sure how I cook."

Ghote's interest was totally gripped.

"So this was an unusual occasion, was it?" he said.

The podgy little cook looked up bewilderedly.

Ghote tried again.

"So it was special for her to come?"

"Oh, yes, sahib. Most special. Most extra special. Very kind. Very kind."

He rubbed his hands together in writhing gratitude.

Ghote kept the pressure up. This was a piece of luck indeed. The unusual incident, the little difference in behaviour, this was what he had taught himself always to look out for. And now he had really got hold of something.

"Was this perhaps the only time Dr. Diana had ever come to see you cooking?" he asked.

The cook looked up at him anxiously.

"Well, was it the only time?" Ghote said with a jet of impatience.

"Oh, yes, sahib. Only time she come."

"You are sure?"

"Oh, yes, sahib. Indeed, yes, sahib. Only time. Most sure."

Ghote breathed a sigh of relief. When the meal Frank Masters had eaten was being prepared, the doctor had been for the first time ever down in the kitchen pretending to be supervising the cook. And he had got firmly on to it.

"Good," he said. "Now, tell me exactly what happened to the food when it had been prepared. What sort of dishes was it put in? Are they still here? Have they been washed?"

"Oh, sahib, sahib," the cook protested. "Am only poor man, sahib. Not very much brain, sahib."

He looked up at Ghote beseechingly.

Ghote took control of himself. The man's attitude filled him with a desire to march him off to the privacy of C.I.D. headquarters and there to get what he wanted out of him in the most unpleasant way he could. But he was not going to allow himself to think in such a way. The man was a man like any other and he would treat him reasonably, however creepingly obsequious he got.

"The dishes," he said, "they have been washed?"

"Oh, yes, sahib. Most thoroughly washed. Oh, yes, indeed. I know that I must see to that."

Ghote felt a twinge of disappointment.

"That is a pity," he sighed. "However we cannot expect——"

"Sahib, sahib, you want see dishes before they wash?" the cook asked eagerly.

He turned and suddenly scuttled off by the door leading out of the house.

Ghote was after him in an instant.

And, just as he had expected, there outside the door he found the little cook busy picking morsels out of an open-ended oil drum that served as an extra dustbin. With delicate artistry he was placing them one by one in a clean dish.

Ghote felt near to tears. So much for getting hold of the unusual incident, the little difference in behaviour. He had slipped into the oldest pitfall of all: he had virtually told the cook what he had wanted him to say and the squirming creature had promptly obliged with a stream of pure invention.

Ghote stepped forward and with a well-aimed kick sent the half-filled dish spinning away into the darkness.

"Come back inside," he shouted.

The little cook trotted meekly into the kitchen in front of him.

And immediately Ghote regretted his violence. Just because he had been so pleased with himself over his discovery, he had taken out the subsequent disappointment on the person who happened to have provoked it. He made a resolution not to let this happen again, ever.

"The dishes were all cleaned already?" he asked the cook quietly.

"Yes, sahib."

"And was this, or was this not, the only time Dr. Diana had ever come and watched you cook?"

"She had come before, sahib," said the cook.

He spoke humbly as ever, but without any sign of regret at having said exactly the opposite hardly two minutes earlier.

"When did she come?" Ghote said patiently.

"Oh, when Masters sahib was away, sahib."

"When he was away? He has been away?"

"He has been back three weeks only, sahib," the shiny-skinned cook said eagerly. "He was away for three months, sahib. He was in the Punjab, sahib. He was very interested in refugees from Tibet, sahib. Very holy men, sahib."

"Stop. Stop."

By now, Ghote thought, the wretch had undoubtedly entered the realm of embroidery again, adding to his information piece by piece as it seemed to please or not.

"And it was while Masters sahib was away that Dr. Diana came to see you cooking?" he asked.

"Oh, yes, sahib. Came to make sure I cook a little better. She say I was most appalling cook in whole of Bombay, sahib."

The man looked up with something like pride on his plump features.

Ghote's toe itched. But he kept himself calm.

"Why did she not come at other times?" he asked.

"Oh, she was not in charge then, sahib. When Masters sahib go he put Dr. Diana in full charge. She say at least she get some decent meals now, sahib. So she——"

"That's enough."

"Yes, sahib. Certainly, sahib. I stay quite quiet, sahib. You want to think, sahib?"

" No, I do not," Ghote snapped.

He seized on another question before his temper burst the limits he had set on it.

" So why did Dr. Diana come to supervise you to-night? Mr. Masters was here, wasn't he? Why did she come to-night?"

He waited anxiously for the answer. If there was nothing the fertilely anxious-to-please cook could suggest, this was perhaps after all a piece of behaviour well out of the ordinary.

" Oh, sahib," the cook replied, giving him a sideways glance, " that is easy to answer."

He waited, hoping no doubt that Ghote would give him a clue about the reply he would prefer.

Ghote stayed silent, but decided he could let one shaft of angry impatience dart out.

" Well, sahib," the cook said, " it was like——"

Suddenly he stopped short and looked round Ghote as if he had at that moment seen the whole doorway behind the inspector turn into a sheet of flame or a roaring cascade of flood-water.

" Will you tell?" Ghote snapped without taking his eyes off him. " Why did Dr. Diana choose to-night of all nights to come and watch you cooking?"

" I can answer that."

Now Ghote did swing round.

He found himself face to face with a woman about sixty years old, dressed in an orange-toned sari, thin-faced with white hair drawn up on her head and the little mouth and quick eyes of a bird.

" I am Inspector Ghote, C.I.D.," he said. " May I ask what you are doing here?"

" It is rather I who should be asking what you are doing," she replied.

She spoke English with an accent the like of which Inspector Ghote had never heard before. He realised that in spite of her tanned complexion and workaday sari she was some sort of European.

" I am investigating the death of Mr. Frank Masters," he said cautiously.

There could be little doubt that his announcement came as a surprise to her. Of course it was strictly possible that she might have prepared the look of incomprehension and the quick flood of understanding which followed it. He did not know enough about her to tell. But if it was a performance, it was a faultless one.

" Herr Frank. Herr Frank," she babbled now.

" Yes," Ghote said, " I regret to have to inform that he is dead, and that a police investigation is being carried out."

" But Herr Frank. But what happened?"

Ghote kept watching her closely. He detected not a sign of calculation in the rapidly blinking bird-eyes.

" Mr. Masters was poisoned," he said carefully.

" Poisoned? But how? But what happened?"

She darted looks all round the kitchen. At the refrigerator, at the grimy burners of the gas-stove, at the ranks of pallid aluminium *dekchis*.

" There is no poison here," she said.

It was a statement of fact.

She drew herself up.

" But that is a matter which I am bound to investigate," Ghote answered.

" Then tell me how he came to take this poison."

" You had better tell first who you are," Ghote said.

She looked at him.

" Yes. Yes, of course. You would not know. My name is Glucklich. Fraulein Glucklich, citizen of the Republic of India."

She gave a proud glance round. The cook at least seemed impressed. He salaamed deeply.

" Ah, Fraulein Glucklich," Ghote said. " Then you are the housekeeper, are you not?"

He mentally filled in a blank on a list.

" Exactly," said Fraulein Glucklich. " And that is why I am able to answer your question. Why did Dr. Diana come into this kitchen to-night? Quite simple. Because she knew I would not be here. She knew I would be with the new swami."

"The new swami?" Ghote said.

"Yes," said Fraulein Glucklich with a little toss of her crown of white hair, "you do not need to think that only Indians can benefit from the words of a wise man. I am happy to call myself a *sannysini* of Swami Dnyaneshwar."

"And he was holding a meeting this evening?" Ghote asked.

"Of course," Fraulein Glucklich answered. "From five o'clock to midnight. It was advertised."

"It was public meeting then?"

"Swami Dnyaneshwar would turn away no one, however unenlightened."

Suspecting that he was himself one of the unenlightened Fraulein Glucklich had in mind, Ghote persisted.

"And there were a number of people present at the meeting this evening?"

"A number of people? I am happy to state that there must have been at least thirty. And great enthusiasm. We went long past the advertised time."

"And you yourself were there from start to finish?"

Fraulein Glucklich looked at him sadly.

"Do you think I would miss one moment at the feet of such a swami?"

"You were at his feet the whole time?"

A faint blush came up in her withered cheeks.

"I think you misunderstand," she said. "I spoke of course metaphorically. I was not in fact kneeling at the swami's feet the whole evening."

"You left for a little time?" Ghote said.

"No, no. I could not leave. I sat close to the swami every minute. On the ground, naturally."

"Thank you," Ghote said.

He supposed he would have to check with Swami Dnyaneshwar. It would not in all probability be an easy task. Religious figures were apt to show little concern for things of this world. Which was excellent in its way: but difficult for a police officer.

In the meantime he could regard Fraulein Glucklich as having a total alibi as regarded putting arsenic that evening into anything Frank Masters had eaten.

"You were explaining that Dr. Diana had perhaps come down to the kitchen for a particular reason," he resumed.

"Certainly," Fraulein Glucklich replied. "She had come down to meddle. If I had been here, she would not have dared."

Ghote reflected that seven hours and more with the swami did not seem to have made Fraulein Glucklich regard all her fellow human beings with unmixed love. Though it was certainly true, from what he had seen of Dr. Diana, that she would indeed meddle whatever chance she got.

No doubt this after all was why she had come into the kitchen. There almost always was some equally simple explanation for what at first looked like suspicious departures from routine. Ghote felt abruptly tired.

"I tell you, Mr. Inspector, such trouble I had when Herr Frank was away." Fraulein Glucklich chirruped on, "It is all very well for her to say she caught that man Amrit Singh, but she had no business to poke into everywhere like that."

"Amrit Singh," said the inspector.

Thoughts raced suddenly through his mind like racehorses crowding in a blaze of jockeys' silks towards a winning post.

Amrit Singh.

Amrit Singh was a personage well known to every man in the whole Bombay Police. If there was any organised crime happening anywhere at any time, it was safe to say that Amrit Singh, a huge, enormously tough, unshakably cheerful yet plainly ruthless Sikh, was somewhere at the back of it. Burglaries, street robberies, brothel-keeping, bootlegging, trade in forged licences, smuggling, blackmail, protection rackets, anything and everything solidly illegal was meat and drink to Amrit Singh.

And he had never really been caught. From time to time certainly he had been pulled up and even convicted on some minor charge. But even then, thanks to a battery of sharp advocates, he had never had to do more than pay a small fine.

On these occasions he invariably proffered in satisfaction the largest possible currency note. He had every reason to be cheerful.

And now he had turned up here.

It was difficult to pay any attention to Fraulein Glucklich, jabbing her little pointed nose in and out as she detailed her complaints against the formidable Dr. Diana.

"Oh, yes, we had the notorious Mr. Amrit Singh hanging about the Foundation. And, certainly, nobody realised it till Dr. Diana took it into her head to question him. But she did not do anything so very clever. After all, he told her straight away who he was."

The inspector ran over in his mind the information sheets he had seen recently. As far as he could remember there was nothing about Amrit Singh having been notified as causing trouble at the Masters Foundation. If there had been, half the men in the force would have been out looking for him.

"How long ago was this?" he asked.

"Oh, a month or more," Fraulein Glucklich answered. "In any case, it is of no importance."

Ghote was undeterred.

"And since then?" he asked. "Has anything been seen of Amrit Singh in the past few days?"

Fraulein Glucklich sniffed. Delicately.

"Of course not," she said. "He was told the police would be called if he ever showed himself here again, and I suppose he had the good sense to keep off."

Ghote allowed himself a flicker of inward amusement at this withered-cheeked little European woman's notion that it was necessary only to mention the police to the huge Sikh thug to scare him off once and for all. But this was no time for jokes. If Amrit Singh was involved in something at the Foundation, he had to get after him just as quickly as possible.

One or two questions still must be asked however.

He glanced at his watch.

"I would like to know more about what Mr. Masters ate this evening," he said. "Your cook tells that he prepared on Dr. Diana's instructions beef curry and fish. Can you tell——?"

"Fish curry," snapped Fraulein Glucklich. "She ought to have known at least that Herr Frank did not eat that."

"Oh, memsahib," said the cook, "that was special for Mr. Chatterjee. You know how he like."

Chatterjee, Krishna, resident social worker at the Foundation, Ghote noted automatically. He began looking for a way of cutting Fraulein Glucklich short without drying up a possibly useful source of information.

But Fraulein Glucklich's full attention was now turned on the plump cook.

"So Master Chatterjee likes fish curry, does he?" she said.

"Oh, yes, memsahib. All those Bengali fellows like fish."

"And since when have his whims been pandered to in this house?" Fraulein Glucklich asked with a magnificently lofty toss of her little dried-up nut of a head.

"One moment," Ghote said.

Fraulein Glucklich spared him a swift glance.

"Please," he said, "I wish to know with great urgency who exactly ate with Mr. Masters this evening in the staff tiffin room."

Fraulein Glucklich indicated graciously that the cook might reply.

"Yes, memsahib," he said in something near a whisper. "This evening only three in staff tiffin room, please. Masters sahib, Dr. Diana and Chatterjee sahib."

Ghote glanced at Fraulein Glucklich to see if this was likely. She appeared to accept it. He hurried on.

"Now," he said, "when the food is cooked, what happens to it?"

"Oh, sahib, it is taken to tiffin room by Vidur, the bearer."

Ghote stored the name away. He remembered the man, a sullen looking, pointed-nose Gujarati.

"And then?" he snapped.

"It is put on serving table, sahib, till Masters sahib ready to eat."

"Till he is ready? It is there some time?"

"It is generally there a great deal too long," Fraulein Glucklich broke in. "Poor Herr Frank. So many things he has to do. Often I have to tell him several times that the food is waiting."

Ghote decided that this was something he must pursue however anxious he was to get on to headquarters about Amrit Singh.

"And the food is often left in the tiffin room like that?" he asked.

"Much too often," Fraulein Glucklich answered. "More than once it has been stolen."

"Stolen?"

"Certainly. The clients here, you must know, have no very high moral tone. On several occasions they have reached in through the window and stolen food from the serving table. In spite of the excellent supplies they get themselves."

Ghote thought of the vegetables and puris the "clients" had had that evening.

"So that it is most likely that Mr. Masters ate the beef curry," he said. "And almost anyone could have put something in that if they had wanted to."

"Put something in it?" Fraulein Glucklich said. "But you cannot think seriously that anyone would have wished to kill Herr Frank."

She tossed her head.

"That is ridiculous."

It was an edict.

For a moment Ghote wished he could heed it. He was beginning to feel very tired now. If only it was impossible that Frank Masters had been murdered, then he would have done enough for one night. He could even go back home and get to bed.

But the desire lasted only a moment.

If Amrit Singh was involved, there was certainly no time for rest. And Amrit Singh must be involved. He had been on the spot not all that long before, and he was not going to be scared away by a warning about fetching a policeman.

Ghote's heart began to pound.

If he could not only solve the Masters murder but pull in the notorious Amrit Singh for it, then it would be such a triumph as there had never been before. And he would do it. If hard work and patience could piece together a case to stand up in court against the worst the Sikh's lawyers could do, then he was as good as hanged already.

There was a telephone in the stone-flagged entrance hall, he remembered. With scarcely an explanation, he left Fraulein Glucklich and the greasy little cook at a run.

: : : :

Headquarters, it turned out, were not able to help much. Nobody knew where Amrit Singh was now. By no means for the first time he had thrown off the watch kept on him more or less permanently and had vanished into the blue. A number of rackets of various kinds were going on that he almost certainly had a hand in, but he could not be pinned down for certain anywhere.

Never mind, thought Ghote. He has been seen here, and that is enough.

He flung himself into a renewed whirlwind of activity, checking and double checking on every aspect of the affair. This time Amrit Singh was not going to slip out of the net through doubts over the evidence.

Tired though he was, he drove himself and his men steadily on. And all the while the thought of what it was all leading up to grew and blossomed in his head. Even the unpleasant business of emptying the dustbins into sealed containers for analysis was a delightful task. He sorted and picked at the mess of rubbish with his own hands.

"Hey, policeman," a familiar voice suddenly called out. "Don't you know that food belongs to the beggars?"

Ghote leapt to his feet.

That damned boy.

He peered all round in the before-dawn darkness out at the back of the house. But beyond the light of the lantern by which they had been working he could see nothing.

He felt his fury rising.

"If a beggar ate any of this," he shouted into the darkness, "he might find himself good and sick."

"So what?" the boy called back at his most synthetically American. "So what? Then you'd know where the poison was. And a good cheap way."

Ghote found that he had no answer.

A wave of discouragement assailed him.

: : : :

It had not abated when, having done everything at the Foundation he could possibly think of and made his way homewards at last, trudging across the patch of garden in front of his Government Quarters house he saw his wife standing just inside the open door. So, once again she had been unable to sleep while he had been away.

And Protima after a sleepless night was not an easy person.

A raucous cock suddenly crowed loudly from somewhere close by. Ghote shook his head from side to side trying to throw off the weariness.

"A bad case," he said into the chilly, dawn-streaked air. "A terrible business. I was lucky to get away as soon as this."

Protima said nothing.

Ghote found he needed to make an effort to take the last step into the house. Behind him Protima closed the door and latched it.

And suddenly she put her arms round him.

"You would be tired," she said. "Come, there is tea nearly ready. I made it when I heard the truck coming into the Quarters."

And, unusually, Ghote found himself telling every detail of the case to Protima. She was by no means the sort of person to appreciate the need for meticulous checking of samples from dustbins or accurate recording of exactly who was where at what time, and for this reason he never gave her more than an outline of what particular job he was on at any time. But the sudden relief of tension was too much for him now, and out it all came—the sense of bafflement he felt every time he tried to find out enough about Frank Masters to guess why he had been murdered, the almost frightening possibility of bringing in Amrit Singh, even the highly upsetting encounters with the boys' gang. He told her about everything, the samples he had collected, the fingerprints he had had taken, the hopes he put on what the laboratory tests would produce.

He even brought himself to admit how much he hated having to deal with Dr. Diana.

"She was the worst of the whole night," he said. "The way she stood there, so tall and big, like a machine woman, and all the time making her judgments."

He felt better for having brought it out. He tried a small joke.

"No wonder she is not married."

Protima smiled back at him slyly.

He went over to her and took her in his arms. Through the thin cotton of her white night sari he could feel her body, warm, firm, protective.

"Oh, I am so tired," he said.

"Come to bed then," she answered. "Come to bed and sleep."

IV

In the morning Inspector Ghote's hopes of the laboratory tests were answered. They showed that Frank Masters had taken arsenic in the form of arsenic trioxide. And when Ghote read the neatly compiled facts about this form of the poison he felt a growing sense of pleasure. Things were beginning to link up in a decidedly satisfying way.

Arsenic trioxide, he read, was a form of the substance moderately rare but often used as the basis of lotions for the treatment of certain severe skin diseases.

He did not need to dive into his notebook to remember the name of the man he wanted to see next. Sonny Carstairs. The dispenser at the Foundation. He jumped up from his desk.

: : : :

And so it was with the irritating, but necessary, vision of the crinkled face of the boy in the black jacket in his mind's eye that Ghote began questioning the Anglo-Indian dispenser as he sat neatly on a high wooden stool in the back room of the dispensary hut.

"Tell me," Ghote said, "you must have a very big list of complaints to treat here. Is that so?"

"That certainly is so, man," Sonny Carstairs said.

He pulled down the edge of his high-collared, trim white overall.

"Those boys," he went on, "you've no idea, man. They suffer from every disease there is. We have such a time with them. But worth it, worth every minute of it. For Frank's sake, you know."

He looked up at Ghote with a quick smile. His brown eyes were luminous.

"I think I saw one boy with some terrible skin trouble," Ghote said. "Is that the sort of thing?"

"Oh, yes. Him I know well. That's a terrible case, man. We're doing our best for him, but it's hard work, hard work. That trouble has got so engrained."

Sonny Carstairs sighed deeply. He took his left hand in his right, examined it for a moment and pushed down the cuticle on the neatly-trimmed nail of his third finger.

"What treatment do you apply in such a case?" Ghote asked.

"Oh, that's quite simple. We use something called Fowler's Solution. It's a slow business, man, but we have to be patient, you know."

"Fowler's Solution?" Ghote said. "What's that?"

Sonny Carstairs looked up helpfully.

"It's just a solution that a chap called Fowler invented," he said. "It's basically arsenic trioxide."

Suddenly his look of mild benevolence faded away.

"Arsenic," he said. "You don't think . . .?"

"Do you make the solution up yourselves?" Ghote said.

Sonny Carstairs slipped from his stool and went across to one of the big, white-painted cupboards hung all round the room. Ghote rapidly repeated in his mind the exact intonation the dispenser had used when he had said what Fowler's Solution consisted of. He could detect no falsity. Yet . . .

Sonny Carstairs opened the cupboard and selected one of a number of ranged brown glass jars with black screw-top lids and big white labels.

When he turned to face the inspector again his expression was even more uneasy. Ghote was quick to spot it.

"Something is wrong with the jar," he said.

Sonny gave him a quick, worried glance and then looked down at the ribbed jar which he had put on the broad white shelf in front of him.

"Well? Come on."

Sonny looked up from the jar as if reluctant to end a delicate scrutiny.

"I don't know," he said.

"That will not do," said Ghote. "Something is wrong with the jar. What is it?"

He stepped up close to the white-overalled Anglo-Indian and looked at him hard.

Sonny Carstairs swallowed.

"For God's sake, Inspector," he said. "I tell you it may be nothing."

"But it may not be," Ghote said.

"I suppose so."

It was a reluctant, shame-faced admission.

"So what is wrong?" Ghote said.

"Some may be missing. The jar feels emptier than when I stowed it away in the cupboard here."

"And that was when?"

"It was only yesterday, man. When a lot of stuff arrived from the pharmacist's."

Sonny was almost whispering.

"What time exactly?"

"In the afternoon."

The neat little dispenser stared down glumly at his well-kept hands resting palm down on the edge of the shelf by the little, ribbed glass brown jar.

And quite suddenly he brightened up.

"It's okay," he said.

"Okay? You've made a mistake? There is none missing?"

Sonny looked up.

"Oh, no," he said. "I think it is missing all right, but I can tell you for certain. Just you wait a shake-o."

He bobbed down and opened a big, flat drawer under the shelf. Ghote, looking in over his shoulder, saw a handful of stiff-cover exercise books, a couple of chewed pencils and an old box which had once contained Flor de Dindigal cigars and now held three rusty razor blades.

Sonny took out the newest-looking of the exercise books.

"Here it is," he said. "Register of purchases."

Ghote watched him open it. On the first page only there

was a list of items, in precise, rather flowery handwriting, each with the day before's date against it and two bold initials in another hand, in red. "D.U."

That was easy: Diana Upleigh. Who else? Even if he had been unable to read, the totally unhesitant assertiveness of the big capitals would have told him.

"A new book has just been started?" he asked.

Sonny Carstairs straightened up. With pride.

"A new system has just been started," he said. "We are making up a lot of medicines we need now. For reasons of economy."

"Ah," said Ghote encouragingly. "Your idea, I suppose?"

"Oh, no, no."

Sonny seemed shocked.

"We owe this to Dr. Diana," he said. "It takes someone of her calibre, you know, to institute real reforms. She saw that we could make a considerable saving."

Ghote thought of the doctor's descents on the kitchen in the absence of Frank Masters and reflected that the actions of a person of such a calibre did not always receive the acknowledgment they got from Sonny Carstairs.

He watched Sonny's only faintly brown finger, with the neatly pared nail, skim down the column of the register.

"Ah, yes," Sonny said, "there we are. Just as I expected."

Ghote read the entry.

"One 50-gram jar, arsenic trioxide."

"Well," he said, "how much is left in the bottle?"

Sonny Carstairs rubbed his hands together smoothly.

"Just a jiffy," he said.

He quickly brought out a weighing balance, set the poison jar on one pan and a similar empty one on the other with a couple of tiny weights and adjusted the beam.

"Yes," he said, as the indicator waved to a balance, "you can take it definitely, Inspector, that a considerable quantity of this poisonous substance has disappeared."

He put the balance back in its cupboard with an air of satisfaction.

Ghote flipped over a page in his notebook.

" I shall require that jar for the purposes of the police laboratory," he said. " I am making out receipt in due form."

He wrote with diligence.

Without looking up, he let a question slip gently out.

" The keys to the hut," he said, " who else has them besides you and Dr. Diana?"

It was not until later that he properly reconstructed the sequence of events in the next few seconds.

First there came a curious hissing gasp from the little Anglo-Indian. But this was almost immediately blotted out by the sharp crack of breaking glass as the jar of arsenic trioxide slid off the shiny top of the shelf and fell straight on to the cement floor below.

Ghote jumped back with the powder wafting up towards him in a venomous white cloud.

" It's all right, man," Sonny Carstairs said. " It won't do you any harm. It may be poison, but a small quantity on your shoes is not going to hurt."

Ghote bit his lip with vexation.

" Destroying evidence is serious offence," he snapped.

" Destroy—— Oh. No."

The neat little Anglo-Indian subsided on to the shelf and buried his face in his arms.

Ghote took a step forward, gripped him hard by the shoulder and jerked him up.

" Yes," he said, " destroying evidence."

Sonny Carstairs shook his head.

" It was—— It wasn't that—— Look, man, it was the key," he said.

" The key? What key?"

Sonny swallowed.

" The key of the dispensary."

" What key is this? There are many keys. But there was only one jar of poison. And there it is."

Ghote pointed dramatically to the chunky fragments of thick brown glass in the middle of the patch of exploded white powder.

" Do not tell me that you have not destroyed evidence," he said.

The dispenser's smooth face was creased with conflicting anxieties.

Suddenly he darted forward and looked at Ghote with big, pleading brown eyes.

" Look, Inspector," he said, " I'll tell you. I must. I didn't knock that jar off the shelf on purpose. It was shock that made me do it."

" Shock?"

Sonny licked his lips.

" Inspector," he said, " I just realised at that moment what it means. You see, there are not many keys to this hut: there is only one. And I am the one who keeps it."

He thrust an anxious, sweaty hand into the pocket of the drill trousers he wore under his white overall and pulled out a flat key of unusual design with a neat piece of white tape through the hole in the top.

Ghote took it and looked at it.

" You are telling that this is the only key to the whole hut?" he said.

" Yes, Inspector. But listen."

Sonny stepped half a pace nearer till his neat features were within inches of the inspector's face.

" Listen, Inspector, I swear by all that's holy that that key never left my possession."

" There must be other keys," Ghote said, turning irritatedly away.

" No, Inspector. That is a special American lock. It is very difficult to get keys for it. When we had it put on, just after Dr. Diana first came, she said it was safest only to have two keys. One for her, one for me."

Ghote went over to the windows. As he had recalled, they were fitted with heavy metal grilles well fixed to the surrounds.

"These windows cannot be forced as easily as all that," he said. "And not without leaving very plain marks."

"No," Sonny answered. "That was Dr. Diana too. When she came she insisted we improve security all round."

Without replying, Ghote turned and went into the outer half of the hut, the examination room. As he had remembered, the windows there were exactly like the ones in the dispensing room, and equally plainly they had not been tampered with.

He came back.

"Well, what happened to the second key?" he said.

If this man was telling the truth about never having let the key out of his possession, then it was going to be hard to link the theft of the poison with Amrit Singh. And that was what had to be done.

"That key was crushed by a tram, Inspector," Sonny said.

"A tram?"

Ghote took an outraged step forward. Sonny Carstairs stepped back.

"It was, it was, Inspector. Honest to God. It wasn't my fault. I'll tell you what happened."

Ghote looked at him coldly.

"It was like this, Inspector. I had just locked up here one day just after we got the new keys and I was walking up to the bungalow holding my one in my hand when I happened to notice some of the clients in the road outside. I looked to see what they were doing and I found them throwing coins under the trams as they passed the house."

Ghote waited impassively. Evidently Sonny felt that his narrative required some comment.

"Throwing coins, Inspector," he said earnestly.

"Yes, I did the same sort of thing myself as a boy, only it was with trains on the railway."

Sonny's neat features took on a look of faint disdain.

"Well then, Inspector," he went on, "naturally I went

over and pointed out to the boys that they were committing a serious malpractice."

"Oh, yes?"

"Well, first they uttered some obscene remarks, and then one of them ran up, snatched the key I was still holding and threw it under a tram that was just going by. It was the boy who insists on calling himself Edward G. Robinson."

"I know him," Ghote said, seeing the tattered black jacket and the crinkled old man's face.

"Well then, Inspector, you know that that is the sort of unbalanced action he would indulge in."

Ghote did not answer directly.

"You are sure there were only two keys in the beginning?" he asked.

"If you don't believe me, go and see Dr. Diana," Sonny said. "She will tell you all right, man."

Ghote felt a sudden tightening of the muscles in his stomach.

"No," he snapped. "That will not be necessary. Not necessary at all."

He swung round and looked at the neat figure of the Anglo-Indian.

"At the moment I have urgent work," he said.

He hurried out, cursing himself for having shied away from an encounter with Dr. Diana in such an obvious way. He knew he ought to check the keys story with her. If it was true, it was very important. There could be no doubt that the hut had not been broken into. The bars on the windows had plainly not been shifted, the lock on the door had not even been scratched. So that in the time between the afternoon when the arsenic trioxide had arrived and it having been put into Frank Masters's curry before the meal that evening someone must have used a key to enter the hut.

The most likely thing was that the dispenser was wrong about there being only one key. There must be another unknown one, or Sonny Carstairs had convicted himself out of his own mouth.

Ghote thought suddenly of his room at headquarters, of the familiar scored surface of his desk, the familiar walls and furniture. The very labels on his prized, non-issue filing cabinet, "Songs," "Dance," "Piano," "Sacred," "Various," presented themselves vividly to his mind. Half an hour of peace there and he would be ready to tackle anybody.

He passed through one of the gaps in the heavy wistaria trellis and set off across the big lawn at something approaching a trot.

"Inspector."

The voice rang confidently out in the hot air.

Ghote looked round knowing inescapably whom he would see. Sure enough, Dr. Diana had just stepped out of a pair of french windows overlooking the big lawn.

"You called to me?" Ghote said.

"Of course I did," Dr. Diana declared, striding over the dark green grass towards him.

Ghote succumbed to the temptation to play for time. If I can just get away from her for the moment, he thought, until I have got a plan of campaign fully worked out. It is no use rushing into things without a proper plan of campaign . . .

"You have some information to give?" he asked as Dr. Diana reached him.

"If I'd had any information, I'd have given it to you last night," she said. "I merely wanted to know whether you were making any progress. What you might call a friendly inquiry."

She stood, her feet in flat brown brogues planted wide apart, looking down at him.

"Progress is satisfactory," Ghote said.

No, he decided abruptly, to put off asking about the keys even one moment longer would be utterly ridiculous.

He coughed, putting his hand up to his mouth.

" There is one matter," he said.

" All right then," Dr. Diana replied.

She glanced at the little gold watch fastened delicately to her strongly muscular pink wrist flecked with a down of golden hairs.

" But I warn you," she added, " I haven't got all day."

This was a temptation Ghote resisted.

" What I have to ask may take some time," he replied, feeling each word cutting off any means of flight, " but it is most important matter."

" Out with it then," Dr. Diana said.

" Can you then tell, please, how many keys there are for the dispensary hut?"

For a moment Dr. Diana did not answer. She glanced at Ghote with a look of calculation.

" So you've got on to that," she said at last.

" I regret," Ghote replied, " the course of the investigation cannot be disclosed to all and sundry."

Dr. Diana laughed.

" My dear man," she said, " I can think things out for myself, you know. You can't expect me to believe Frank Masters contracted arsenical poisoning from working in a smelter's shop or acting as assistant to an animal stuffer. Is he your idea of an under-gardener? Can you see him messing about with a fruit spray or something?"

" We admit that the case is being treated as one of murder."

" Splendid. And how about admitting, while you're at it, that you were busy just a moment ago asking my dispenser about what arsenics we had in that hut. Well, we had some arsenic trioxide. It arrived just yesterday afternoon. Did he tell you that?"

" As a matter of fact, yes," said Ghote sulkily.

" And is any missing?"

" That is impossible to say."

Dr. Diana put her arms akimbo on either side of her billowing white blouse.

" Listen," she said, " you can carry this reticence business too far. I'm a doctor, you know. I happen to be aware of what the lethal dose of that stuff is. And what's more, it's my stuff, or as good as. So cough up. *Ek dum.*"

"Madam," Ghote said, "you are not in position to give orders. It so happens that the jar of powder in question became accidentally spilt."

Dr. Diana burst out laughing.

She stood with the sun shining steadily down on her in the middle of the big back lawn and hooted with laughter.

"You Indians," she said at last. "How you manage it I'll never know. To get hold of the source of the poison and then to go and spill it all. I suppose it just slipped out of your fingers? You're wonderful, wonderful."

"Please," Ghote said, with an edge of sharpness, "please, will you be so good as to tell whether you formed this opinion of Indians from the behaviour of your dispenser, Mr. Carstairs?"

"Mr. Carstairs? Mr. Carstairs?"

Dr. Diana seemed to find this as funny as anything else. She had to wipe away a tear before she could add to her reply.

"No," she said, "as a matter of fact the ever-obliging Sonny is moderately deft with his fingers. I wouldn't have him about the place if he weren't."

"He is not in any way a clumsy individual?"

"No. I told you. Why do you ask?"

"Because," Ghote said, "Mr. Carstairs was responsible for dropping the poison in evidence."

Dr. Diana suddenly paid attention.

"Was he indeed?" she said.

She thought for a moment.

"Tell me," she went on, "how do you think the arsenic got from my dispensary into Frank's stomach?"

"It is the police belief that he took it unsuspectingly," Ghote said. "But this is not the time to discuss."

He turned resolutely and began to walk towards his waiting truck.

"For heaven's sake, stop waltzing away like that all the

time," Dr. Diana said. "And stop all this 'police belief' nonsense. Everybody knows you took half the dustbins away with you, and a pretty fine mess you left behind too."

Ghote stopped.

He turned back to face her.

"That is wrong," he said. "I personally supervised the dustbin operation. There was no mess."

"Oh, wasn't there? Well, I'm surprised to hear it. There generally is when chaps like you have been around."

"In this case not," Ghote said furiously.

"All right, all right. I apologise. That's what you want, isn't it?"

"Apology was called for," Ghote said.

"All right, you've had one. So now perhaps you'll tell me how you think the arsenic got out of my dispensary. I happen to be interested, you know. Especially as there's only one key and the place is meant to be pretty safe."

"There is definitely only one key?" Ghote said.

Dr. Diana blew out a sigh.

"Yes," she replied. "There's only one. We had two when we started, but that fool Sonny Carstairs went and let one of the boys snatch the second out of his hand and throw it under a bloody tram."

"You had two keys only after the lock was changed?"

"You know all about it, don't you? Why ask me?"

"In a matter of this importance it is impossible to have too many checks," Ghote replied.

He let his glance as he spoke wander back to the door of the dispensary hut. Sonny, he was certain, was still in there. If he suddenly came out and made his way off at speed, could he catch him?

He decided that he could, and gave his attention to what Dr. Diana was saying again.

"All right then, if you're so keen on making checks you can see the correspondence we had with the firm that imported the new lock. They weren't very keen on supplying not more than two keys. I had to point out to them, pretty forcefully as I recall, that to go giving keys to every Tom, Dick and Harry simply defeated the object of the exercise."

"Thank you," Ghote said. "I will send a sergeant to examine, if I may."

He spoke a little absently.

If Sonny Carstairs had the only key during all the time between the arsenic trioxide arriving and the curry being left near the open tiffin room window, he kept thinking, then Sonny must be the only one who could have got hold of the poison. But if so, surely he could not have been so utterly stupid as to stand there and simply state the facts? No one who was guilty could possibly be so senseless, and Sonny was a skilled technician, to say the very least.

He brought his thoughts sharply back to Dr. Diana. She had been saying something in a very loud voice.

"I regret," he said, "I did not quite catch . . ."

"I said, 'Who had the weak-kneed Sonny lent his key to then?'"

Why did I miss it? Ghote asked himself. Why did I miss that Sonny in spite of what he had said must have let the key out of his possession? And at once he knew the answer. Because at the moment he could have worked it out Sonny had suggested that it would be necessary for him to speak to Dr. Diana again. And he had been ridiculously unwilling to face being taken for a fool once more.

"It was his habit to lend this key?" he asked sharply. "I must point out that to allow the key of a building containing a number of poisonous substances to pass from hand to hand in this manner is a highly irresponsible proceeding."

"Thank you," said Dr. Diana. "But let me tell you that if I'd ever suspected he'd done this before, I'd have had him out in less time than it takes to tell. And, may I add, it's not particularly responsible to have missed asking him that question for yourself."

"But if it was not his habit to lend the key," Ghote answered, feeling himself growing hotter, "then why do you say he did this? He may have kept it all the time."

" And sat there and waited for you to find out he was the only one with access to the poison? Sonny may have his faults, but he's not that stupid."

There was nothing else Ghote could do. It was no use claiming now that he had already thought of this. Dr. Diana would simply not believe him.

" Very well," he said, " I would go and ask."

He turned towards the gap in the laden trellis through which he could see the door of the dispensary.

" And you think he'll tell you?" Dr. Diana said.

" He will tell," Ghote replied.

" All right. All right. Don't sound so cross. I dare say you'll have the poor chap beaten up in some out of the way cell or other. He'll talk fast enough then."

" He will talk when I want."

" But will he tell you the truth?"

" I will see he does, however long it may take."

" Even if there's another way of getting to know? A simple and easily made check?"

Ghote swung round. The doctor was standing looking towards him wearing an expression of amused tolerance like a placard round her neck. With an effort he conquered a desire to shout something, anything, at her.

" If you can suggest such a way," he said, " I would be delighted."

" That's better."

Dr. Diana turned and began pacing sternly up and down the big lawn. Ghote walked beside her, adjusting his steps as well as he could to her formidable stride. But beyond that he would not let her get away with anything.

" You told you had something to help," he said firmly.

Dr. Diana looked at him.

" It's just this," she said. " It so happens the dispensary was being watched last evening. On my instructions."

Her announcement, which was made with no little impressiveness, fell singularly flat.

Because, just as she produced it, the inspector became

aware that at that very moment a watch was being kept on him.

All along the top of the wall which hid the house's dustbins discreetly from the garden he perceived a row of heads. Two of them he recognised at once. At one end was the boy who called himself Edward G. Robinson. At the other end was the young acrobat, Tarzan. Between were four other gang members.

And it was plain that every word of Dr. Diana's clear English tones must have fallen sweetly and easily on those six pairs of pricked up ears even from down by the wistaria-laden trellis.

Inspector Ghote took hold of himself. One deep breath, two, three. Then he put a question without the least tremor of the mortified anger that had at first seized him.

"The dispensary was being watched on your instructions?"

He looked intently at the doctor.

"Why was that? Did you expect such a theft?"

Dr. Diana laughed. The short bark of a well-trained English sporting dog.

"No, I didn't actually expect the theft of poison from my stocks. If I had, I can assure you I'd have done something about it, pretty quickly. But as a matter of fact the dispensary was only being watched as a sideline, so to speak."

"Please explain," Ghote said.

He tried by keeping his voice low to influence Dr. Diana to drop her own tones to a point where every syllable at least would not come clearly to the listening boys.

But his quietness seemed only to make her louder.

"It's really perfectly simple," she enunciated. "It so happens I keep my car down in a little shed right at the bottom of the compound. You get into it from a lane at the back. Well, a couple of times recently someone, or some people, have bloody well desecrated it."

Her shocked tones rang through the big garden. From

the quick flurry of movement up by the dustbin wall, Ghote deduced quickly enough that the "desecration" had been the work of the listening gang, and that they were delighted with the reaction it had got.

"I see," he said, in a properly impressed manner.

"Yes," said Dr. Diana, "and I had a pretty good idea who was responsible. So, you know what I did?"

Ghote realised what she would have done: have told off a couple of the gang to watch the car themselves to stop them interfering with it.

"What did you do?" he asked.

Dr. Diana drew in a good breath.

"I told off a couple of members of that particular gang to watch the car," she said. "Stop them interfering with it themselves."

She glanced at Ghote with an air of triumph.

"A most ingenious manœuvre," he said. "And who were these boys?"

Dr. Diana's face hardened.

"The couple I mentioned last night," she said. "The ones they call Edward G. Robinson and Tarzan. The worst of the lot. I've some hopes for Tarzan sometimes, but I utterly despair of the other."

Ghote was interested in this division.

"Why have you hopes for Tarzan?" he said.

They were getting nearer the dustbin wall. But perhaps it would do the boy good to hear something bright about himself.

"Oh well, we happen to have been able to trace his family," Dr. Diana proclaimed. "Fisherfolk, actually. They come from a little village up near Bassein. There's the usual history of a broken home. The father's taken up with another woman. But when we have a few facts to go on we can generally do something."

"That is altogether encouraging to hear," Ghote remarked. "And did your device stop this desecration?"

"No, it didn't as a matter of fact," the doctor said shortly. "But that's not the point. The point is that anyone watching the garage shed would have been bound to see whoever tried to get into the dispensary. Look for yourself."

She wheeled round and pointed down the long garden.

Ghote saw that she was right. The garage was tucked away in a corner of the compound and like the big dispensary was cut off by the wistaria trellis. To watch the garage it would be necessary to use this as cover and from that position anyone trying to approach the dispensary door, however stealthily, was bound to be seen.

"Yes, you are perfectly correct," he said, turning to the doctor.

She took him by the elbow and propelled him swiftly and unexpectedly round.

"Then there's your answer," she said.

She was staring straight at the row of heads along the wall over the dustbins.

V

The boys of the gang, confronted so suddenly with the combined glares of Inspector Ghote and Dr. Diana, grinned fiercely back like so many monkeys.

Ghote turned to the doctor.

"I can find you in the house if I want?" he asked.

Evidently contented with the businesslike note in his voice, Dr. Diana merely nodded briskly and set off indoors.

The inspector strode swiftly across to the boys.

Slightly to his surprise they made no attempt to scuttle away. When he rounded the wall he saw that they were standing in a row on tip-toe on the line of dustbins, which he had so painstakingly sorted through in the early hours of this same day. The boy in the black jacket, with the privilege of a leader, stood astride the open-topped oildrum, one bare foot on either rim.

"Come down off there at once," Ghote snapped.

Nonchalantly the boys jumped one by one and squatted happily on the grimy concrete of the little backyard. Only the one called Tarzan disobeyed. With one flick of his wiry wrists he simultaneously hoisted himself up and swung himself round until in a flash he was sitting perched on the top of the protective wall looking down at the inspector.

Ghote decided to leave well alone.

He placed himself squarely in front of the black-jacketed, wrinkle-faced, squat form of the leader. He noticed with pleasure that, although the boy had risen to his feet, he had succeeded in almost transfixing him to the wall. Perhaps for once the conversation would not end in some atrocious impertinence followed by flight.

He gave him a long hard look.

"Before it was just talking," he said, "but now you have come right into the case. So it is answer up, and speak the truth."

A wry grin worked its way through the boy's wrinkles.

"Oh, sahib," he said, "have you ever know when I not speak truth?"

"Yes, I have," said Ghote. "Now then, name?"

"Edward G., you can call me."

"Edward G. I cannot call. What is your name?"

"Okay, okay. You want my full name?"

"I certainly do."

The boy looked up at him. His eyes were wide.

"Edward G. Robinson."

It was all Ghote could do to stop his hand flashing out and landing smack on the crinkled cheek in front of him. Perhaps it was the very crinkles that saved the boy.

"You are speaking to police officer," Ghote said, banging out each word. "A police officer in the execution of his duty. You have been required to give your name. Your proper name. Are you going to obey?"

The boy's eyes stayed serenely wide.

"No," he said.

Ghote gritted his teeth.

"Do you realise you are committing offence?" he shouted.

"So what?"

The words allowed the boy to give full play to his proudly acquired American. He took the opportunity for all it was worth.

"So you will find yourself in gaol," Ghote shouted.

"For just not giving a name you like?"

The eyes in the crinkled face widened again.

"For obstructing a police officer in the execution of his duty."

The boy abruptly held out his arms towards Ghote. His two thin wrists protruded far beyond the sleeves of the tattered black plastic jacket.

"Okay," he said, "put on the bracelets."

Ghote looked down at the pair of hands under his nose with baffled fury. It would be utterly ridiculous to lug a boy like this along to the station in handcuffs and solemnly charge him with an offence. But he was not going to let his authority be flouted. He was dealing with an important case, perhaps the most important case that would ever come his way. And this pip-squeak of a gutter urchin was holding him up.

He felt a wave of red rage come spurting up ready to burst in a deluge of frenzied action.

And suddenly in the middle of it the picture in front of his eyes registered. The two thin wrists held close together, looking as frail as the legs of a bird. Two stalks of grass almost that you could snap between your fingers.

This was only a boy.

What had he been himself at such an age? Nothing like as serious as he was now. The seriousness had come only when he had had to transform his desire to be a policeman into the slow slog of learning the job and taking its constant damping frustrations. He had been long enough sobering down, too. There had been the years at college when in the early days at least it had been touch and go whether he got through the course. And in his schooldays the teachers he had cheeked, the hours he had played truant.

He remembered himself running one day at the tail end of some political procession. He had had little idea of what it was all about. It had been enough that it was a chance to make all the noise he could. To run with his shirt tails flying and his bare feet shooting up the dust behind him, to wave a ragged piece of flag and to shout the worst insults he could think of at anyone who looked staid enough.

"Yah, ravisher of your own sister. Yah, imperialist dog."

In a flash he pointed his finger straight out at the black-jacketed boy in front of him.

"Stick 'em up, wise guy," he said.

And it worked.

A slow grin spread itself on the boy's wrinkled old man's face.

"So you wanna play it tough?" he answered.

"You tell me what I wanna know," Ghote said, "or I'll fill you so full o' lead you'll never know what hit you."

All the lore of boyhood afternoons spent in the cinema came flooding back to him. Those long, hot, thirsty mornings of marching through the streets carrying an advertisement placard to earn a free ticket for later on were paying unexpected dividends.

"Now, talk, buddy," he said, "and talk fast. Were you watching that dame's car last night?"

"Sure was," said the boy. "Me and Tarzan."

He looked over at his almost naked friend perched on top of the wall.

"Okay," Ghote said. "And whaddya see?"

But this time the boy did not answer. A wary look flicked back into his eyes.

"What did you see?" Ghote said. "Come on, this is important. I want to know just what you saw down there."

"I tell you what I saw," Edward G. answered suddenly.

"All right."

"Saw a parrakeet," the boy said. "Parrakeet with green feathers."

Ghote's fist tightened.

And then he realised his mistake.

"Okay, kid," he said. "So you saw a boid. But what else did ya see? See any guy hanging around the dispensary?"

For a moment Edward G. calculated. Ghote could see it happening. Then the boy spoke.

"Yeah," he said. "I saw some guy."

"You did?"

"Sure thing."

"You knew this guy?"

"Sure I knew him."

"He know you were watching?"

Ghote risked taking his eyes off Edward G. long enough for a quick look at Tarzan on the wall. He just noticed the boy glancing down at the ground on the far side. There was nothing he could do to stop him if he made a bolt for it, unless he wanted to lose Edward G. as well.

He decided to stick to what he had got and shifted a quarter of a pace to the side to be in the best possible position for a quick grab. Edward G. did not seem to take much account of the manœuvre.

"Nah," he said, "when I keep watch on a fella he don't know there's nothing there."

"Smart guy," Ghote said. "You gonna say what this fella did?"

"Maybe."

"Fill you full o' lead if you don't."

He bunched his fist into a gun shape again and crouched over it menacingly.

"Okay, okay. I talk."

"Go ahead, buddy, and make it good."

"This guy he visit dispensary," Edward G. said.

"Sounds a kinda clever guy get in there without a key."

"This is a double clever kinda guy. He got a key."

"Mister," said Ghote, "you kinda making things up. Only one key to that hut."

"Sure thing," said Edward G. with a professional shrug. "And this guy got that key off the guy that keeps it."

"Off Sonny Carstairs?"

"Off that two-timer. Just like we got the other key off him."

"The one you threw under a tram?" Ghote asked.

The boy's eyes went bright with delight.

"Guess he told you," he said. "He ain't gonna forget that in a hurry."

Ghote's mind was cramming in the facts and assimilating them like a high-powered vacuum-cleaner.

"Okay, buddy," he said, "so who was this guy you saw go in the hut?"

But however American the question sounded, and Ghote fondly believed it might have been concocted in Hollywood itself, it was one too much for Edward G.

Ghote saw the sparkle die out of the boy's eyes. The lips in the thickly wrinkled face closed hard. He shook his head.

"No dice?" Ghote said.

"No dice, mister."

Ghote began making his fist gun again, but the boy shook his head before the forefinger had had time to point.

Ghote thought rapidly.

He had to know who had managed to get hold of that key at just the critical time. But obviously the limit of cajolery had been reached. And now a tough line was not going to help. The boy would deny everything. He could always be taken down to the station and handed over to a certain sergeant. But, although he would probably talk fast enough then, there was no knowing how much truth he would tell.

There must be some other way.

A bribe? Ghote's hand went to his pocket. He could not be sure. The boy would take the money all right. But would he——?

Then he relaxed.

"Say," he said, still in his best American, "you wanna come for a ride in the police wagon?"

There were two seconds while the success of his stratagem was in doubt. Ghote looked into the eyes in the crinkled face and tried to read what was going on there. A tiny upward flicker, as if seeking escape, indicated fear. But then there came a sparkle. Pure joy.

"Sure," said Edward G., "I could take a ride."

He jerked a nod in the direction of Tarzan, still perched on the wall. Just.

"Can he come too?"

"All of you. So long as you spill the beans, and fast."

There came a movement from the top of the wall. Ghote risked another glance. But Tarzan still lingered. The bait was powerful.

"Okay," Edward G. said lazily. "I'll tell, mister. You know who I saw? I saw a big-time guy called Amrit Singh."

Ghote's heart thundered in triumph. He had done it. He had got witnesses who had actually seen the big Sikh thug enter the place where the poison had been kept. And he had done it without in any way suggesting that this was what he wanted to hear.

Well, he thought, there are after all other ways of doing a policeman's job than twisting arms and landing out with kicks.

He looked down at Edward G. again.

"You ever work for Amrit Singh?" he asked with great casualness.

With too much casualness. He entirely forgot the Hollywood note and at once the gang in front of him froze into blankness.

He stood looking at the row of distant, incurious eyes and cursed himself. He had done it again. He had stopped to luxuriate in thoughts of his own cleverness, and he had lost touch at once.

He thought hard. And an idea came to him about what

the boys' link with Amrit Singh might quite possibly be.

"Listen, fellas," he said, back in his broadest American, "so you helped that guy out with something. A bit of smuggling maybe?"

He caught an instant of calculation in the wary eyes in front of him and hurried on.

"So what? Who cares? Smuggling's something the Customs guys can take care of. Smuggling never meant a thing to me."

Edward G. grinned.

"Okay," he said, "you win, I guess. That guy Amrit's working a big racket in gold. Could be we help him out sometimes."

"Like last night?" Ghote said.

He held his breath.

"That's what he was here for," Edward G. said. "Heard some of his gold had been pick up. By Frank Masters. Came to look. Pronto."

Ghote felt himself getting nearer and nearer the heart of the matter with every word he heard. Frank Masters. Here was the beginning of finding out how the good American was linked with the Bombay bad man.

"Amrit Singh was looking for gold?" he asked cautiously.

"Sure. The big boss locked the gold he found in the dispensary hut. Best place to lock anything. Is one place we can't get in. We tried, but we can't."

Inwardly Ghote recorded with pleasure the advanced state his relations with the gang had reached. When Edward G. could happily admit to attempted theft in this way, things had certainly improved.

"So Amrit Singh was coming to get the gold back?" he asked.

"Guess so."

"How did he hear it was there?" Ghote asked. "From one of you? Who passed on a message? Was it you?"

He looked at the black-jacketed figure in front of him.

"Nope. Not me. Guess the news was all around the joint. Even they knew."

"They?"

"The other big shots. Them."

Ghote nodded.

"Why did the big shot himself hide the gold?" he asked, feeling his heart beat faster with every mention of Frank Masters.

Edward G. began to shrug this one off.

Then suddenly his attitude changed. He looked up at Ghote with eyes bright in his old man's face.

"You want me to tell?" he said. "I could tell good."

Ghote had control enough of himself to smile.

"Not interested in any more of those stories of yours," he said.

Edward G. laughed.

"Was a honey," he said. "Went down a wow before."

"Not for me," Ghote said.

The boy looked up to the washed-out blue of the sky.

"We gonna hit the road yet?" he asked, nonchalantly flicking one of the many buzzing flies off his taper-thin thigh.

"Soon enough, soon enough," Ghote replied. "Maybe you'd care to tell where this Amrit guy is hanging out right now?"

Edward G. shrugged.

"Right now the guy's on the trail," he said.

Ghote experienced a sudden vision, triggered off by this unlikely jumble of film talk, of the big Sikh loping along a dust track dressed in a ten-gallon hat, smoking a big cigar and with a sub-machine gun tucked under his arm.

"You wanna see the guy?" Edward G. asked.

"Sure thing."

"Be right here to-morrow round about this time," the boy said.

Ghote snatched a hungry glance at his watch. Ten o'clock. At ten to-morrow morning he would have Amrit Singh under his hand.

He took a deep breath.

This time he would not exult. He had been very lucky,

and the luck might not hold. Besides could he really trust Edward G.?

He looked at the boy coolly.

"You're mighty ready to talk," he said.

"Sure am," said the boy.

The crinkled face looked up at him. The familiar twisted grin manifested itself.

"With all you policias around, you'd pick the guy up pretty quick. So why not spill the beans? And besides . . ."

A dangerously thin hand was held out.

Cupped.

: : :

Ghote knew better than to take his new friends completely on trust. Hardly had the police truck disappeared down Wodehouse Road in the direction of the Afghan Church with the gang clustered in the rear and the rigid back of the young driver signalling utter disapproval, than he had turned and sprinted for the telephone.

C.I.D. Records confirmed that Amrit Singh was still nowhere in sight. Yes, it was most likely he was out of Bombay.

So far so good.

He asked to be transferred to the Fingerprint Bureau. Yes, they had got a lot of prints from the dispensary at the Masters Foundation, and a bloody waste of—— Amrit Singh? The tone of the conversation changed rapidly. There was a remarkably short pause, and then an excited voice.

"Yes, sir. Definitely yes, Inspector. Prints of Amrit Singh's in the dispensary. Quite definitely. Thank you very much, Inspector."

Ghote asked whether the Sikh's prints could also be found on the packet of broken brown glass or the black screw-top he had brought in later. They would check. It would take time but they would check. If it wasn't that the defence would insist on every precaution, they would find them there in five minutes.

No, all right. They would play it the inspector's way.

Ghote banged down the phone and stood for an instant thinking. What next? Yes, another of the facts he had stored away during his productive talk with Edward G.

The key. Amrit Singh had entered the dispensary with a key. A key he had got from " that two-timer " Sonny Carstairs.

Ghote thought about Sonny for a few moments, and evolved a plan of action.

: : : :

About an hour later, an hour spent mostly in allowing the reporters waiting at headquarters to extract a cautiously optimistic statement, Ghote watched two constables march into his little office in a great clatter of heavy boots and swinging brawny arms. Between them hung the neat figure of the little Anglo-Indian dispenser.

Ghote dismissed the constables and waited till the door had shut. Then he asked Sonny to sit down on the square-looking, heavy little wooden chair in front of his desk. Sonny sat with his knees close together and one hand clutching the other.

For an instant he looked down and flicked his fingers straight so that he could see the nails.

" I asked you to come to see me because a very serious matter has been brought to my notice," Ghote said slowly.

Sonny looked at him across the lined and blotched surface of the desk.

For a little while Ghote kept silent.

After the hours of steadily burning sun the day was by now decidedly hot. Sonny began gently to sweat.

" In the course of inquiries," Ghote began again at last, " it has come to light that a certain person obtained unauthorised access to the dispensary at the Masters Foundation."

He left it at that once more. Sonny clearly felt obliged to say something.

" How——? How did this person do—do that?"

" You know the answer perfectly well."

" No, Inspector. Really I don't. I think perhaps you

must have got a false impression. I'm afraid I can't help you on this. Yes, yes. I'm sorry, I can be of no help at all. If you'll excuse me. So, if you'll excuse me . . ."

Sonny stood up.

Ghote recalled once again how when he had begun to question Sonny sharply about the arsenic trioxide he had in a panicky gesture swept the jar to the ground. Perhaps that had been just acting so as to get rid of incriminating evidence. But he had not thought so then, and nor had he when he had decided to haul Sonny into the intimidating atmosphere of headquarters. Now was the time to prove it.

He glanced sharply up at Sonny.

"Sit down," he shouted.

For half a second Sonny stood stock still.

Then slowly he subsided on to the squat wooden chair.

"So you cannot help me on this," Ghote went on. "So you would like to be excused. I will bet you would. No wonder you cannot help me. You cannot help me because you are to blame."

"No, no. Really, no. Honest to God, man, it isn't so."

"What happened to the key of that hut?"

"Nothing did. Honestly, nothing."

"It is the only key, is that not so?"

"I don't know."

"Of course you do. You admitted it to me. It is the only key to that hut. Is that not so?"

"I—I suppose it is."

"And someone else got hold of it. I want to know how."

"I can't say. I can't say."

"Can't you indeed?"

Ghote allowed a gleam of malice to come into his eyes.

"Can't you indeed?" he repeated slowly. "Then we will have to see what we can do to help you, will we not?"

"No."

He knew then that he had been right. The note of fear was too plain.

"Oh yes, we will," he said, leaning forward across the desk till his face was only a couple of feet from Sonny's.

"You know that we have ways of helping people's memories in this department?"

"But—— But it isn't allowed."

"No, it is not allowed."

He paused.

"But that does not mean it is not done. Now, that key. Who did you let take it? Answer now, or we will go downstairs."

It was the last, innocent enough phrase that did the trick. Sonny went grey under the sheen of the sweat. He licked his lips.

"You know Amrit Singh, Inspector?" he said in a half-whisper.

Ghote nodded.

"He made me give it to him. You won't understand."

Ghote thought he understood very well. Sonny was not a difficult man to make do what you wanted.

"When did he take it?" he said, not letting the pressure up.

"It was going on for eight o'clock last night, Inspector. I was just up in my little room on the roof. He suddenly came in. It was through the window. I knew him. He'd been consorting with the boys. I'd heard them talking about him. I knew what sort of man he was. Of low moral character. He demanded the key. What else could I do, Inspector?"

"So you handed it to him?"

"Yes."

A total whisper now.

"And later he gave it back?"

"Yes. I begged him to. I said that, if he did, no one would ever know he'd had it. So after I'd given it to him I just sat there on the edge of my bed and waited. And after about quarter of an hour I heard a bit of noise out on the roof. And then suddenly the key came whizzing in. It hit me, Inspector. Look."

Sonny quickly began tearing at the buttons of his jacket.

Ghote thought with amusement that it was exactly like

Amrit Singh to have returned the key by throwing it good and hard at the poor dupe he had got it from.

" Undressing will not be necessary," he said sharply.

Sonny fumbled for a bit trying to do the buttons up again. Then he stopped.

Ghote stood up.

" You can go now," he said. " Though I must warn you that you have not heard the last of this."

He walked over to the door and held it wide.

He was longing to see the back of the wretched Anglo-Indian. Only then could he indulge for a few moments in pure exultation. This was enough. He was sure of it. Amrit Singh's fingerprints in the dispensary. Some evidence to come about a consignment of gold seized by Frank Masters. It should be easy enough to tie that up. And finally this plain, incredible statement that Amrit Singh had obtained the key of the dispensary where the poison was kept only a short time before Frank Masters had eaten the fatal meal. This time he had got the big Sikh. Good and proper.

Because this time the master thug had made one mistake. He had misjudged his catspaw. He might have guessed that Sonny would be as easy to break as a wisp of straw. But he must have relied on him keeping quiet at all costs about letting the key out of his possession. He ought to have known better than to trust such a soft creature for anything.

" Out you go," Ghote said.

Sonny got up from the heavy little chair with reluctance. He approached the door Ghote was holding open as if what lay beyond was bound to be unpleasant.

For a moment he paused and looked at the inspector.

" Go on," Ghote said impatiently. " I have a great deal to do."

" But don't you want me to tell you who else made me give them the key last night?" he said.

Sonny looked up at him.

VI

Inspector Ghote's tower of exultant thoughts collapsed in an instant about his head. He could hardly believe that the despised Sonny Carstairs had said what he had. Yet the words had been clear enough. He had let the only key of the dispensary out of his keeping, not once but twice. The evidence against Amrit Singh was suddenly totally dubious.

Ghote stared at the neat figure of the Anglo-Indian dispenser. Perhaps if he had not treated him so contemptuously, he would have been alerted to the fact that there was more evidence to come. He sighed and resolved not to despise another witness ever again.

"You gave that key to two people?" he said.

Sonny Carstairs, smarting still from the treatment dealt out to him, evidently enjoyed Ghote's present discomfiture.

"Of course I gave it to two of them, man," he said.

Ghote was not going to stand this.

"And who was this second person?" he snapped. "It was bad enough to let Amrit Singh have it. Who else did you give it to?"

Sonny Carstairs gave him the hint of a smile, quiet and self-satisfied.

"I gave it to Mr. Chatterjee," he said.

"To Mr. Chatterjee, the social worker at the Foundation?"

"Of course."

"And what was this for? Does he have access to the dispensary? Was there some special need?"

Sonny Carstairs shrugged.

"He wouldn't tell me what it was for, man," he replied. "It was only a little while after Amrit Singh threw—after he gave me back the key. A knock came at my door. It was Krishna Chatterjee. He said he desired to speak to me urgently. I let him into my room and he asked me for the key."

"And you just handed it over?"

The dispenser looked a little put out for the first time since he had produced his bombshell.

"Well, no. No, I didn't," he said.

"But you told you let him have the key."

"Yes. Yes, in the end I did."

"He threatened you like Amrit Singh?"

Ghote thought of the social worker, whom he had seen on his tour of the Foundation the night before. He formed physically a complete contrast to the big, tough Sikh thug. He was a smallish, round-faced, slightly plump Bengali with a gentle, bubbling manner and big, soft almond-shaped eyes for ever flitting here and there. It was difficult to imagine him threatening to batter the life out of anybody at all, even the neat little Sonny Carstairs.

"No, Inspector, not threatened really," Sonny said.

"What then? You gave him the key. He was not meant to have it. Did he give you reason?"

"No, Inspector. That was the hell of it. He refused absolutely to say why he wanted it. That was when he said he would tell—— That was when I refused to let him have it."

Sonny drew himself up with a touch of pride.

"You refused to let him have it," Ghote said. "Yet he went away with it all right. What happened?"

"I just sort of changed my mind, Inspector."

"When he said he would do what? Come on, out with it. You are in trouble enough as it is."

Any tendency to resistance in the dispenser had been well and truly rolled out of him in the earlier part of the interview. Now he simply swallowed once.

"He said he would tell Mr. Masters about the drugs," he muttered.

It did not take Ghote long to realise what this must mean.

"Oh," he said, "so we have the misapplication of drugs to take into account also."

He took a longer look at Sonny.

"But you are not addict, I think," he said.

"Honest to God, no, Inspector," Sonny babbled. "But just sometimes I used to take a sniff of ether or something. Till Mr. Chatterjee caught me one day. And he said if he ever suspected I was doing it again he'd have me sacked—dismissed."

"I see. And he threatened to have you sacked again if you did not hand over the key?"

"Yes, sir. Yes, Inspector."

"But he did not tell you why he wanted it? Not at all? Not a hint even?"

"No, Inspector, honestly."

"Then I will have to ask."

: : :

But before Ghote put his question to Krishna Chatterjee he got a chance to ask another which had worried him perhaps even more. If the social worker had gone to the trouble of bullying the key out of Sonny Carstairs, surely he must have used it. After all, he had returned it in time for Sonny to open the dispensary up again when Frank Masters had had to receive treatment. So two people would have entered the hut that evening. But Edward G. and the gang had said nothing about a second visitor.

Ghote felt let down. After all that he had done to come down to the level of these boys, after all those silly games, they still had not been fair with him.

As soon as he had got rid of Sonny he had rushed down to his truck and told the driver to get round to the Masters Foundation as fast as possible. The Dodge drew up in the gravelly drive with a great screeching of brakes. As Ghote had half hoped, the noise and dust of their arrival immediately conjured up the familiar apparition in tattered and torn black plastic jacket.

The boy evidently believed that his relations with Ghote were still in the same comfortable state as when he had set off on the promised jaunt in the police truck. He sauntered carelessly up. Behind him the gang approached in an equally happy-go-lucky way.

"Hi," said Edward G.

Ghote waited till he came right up close. Then his hand shot out and closed firmly round the battered black jacket.

"You," he said. "You are just the one I want."

The boy blinked at him in utter astonishment. There could be no doubt that this time the inspector had the upper hand.

"Now," Ghote barked, "just what do you mean by not telling that Mr. Chatterjee went in the dispensary also?"

For an instant the question really worried the boy. Then the old, wry half-grin sent the deep wrinkles of his face off into new convolutions.

"You never ask," he said. "You wanna learn that, fella. Don't ask: don't get."

"I'll teach you to fella me," Ghote shouted suddenly.

All the rage at his disappointment over having had Amrit Singh so neatly trapped boiled unexpectedly up. He gathered up the tattered black jacket in his fist.

But Edward G. had enraged too many people in his short life not to know the signs to a hairsbreadth. And in a moment Ghote found himself holding the filthy old jacket while its owner danced back to the edge of the gravel and stood on tiptoe looking at him, wearing only a grimy pair of shorts.

Ghote glowered.

"You knew it was important if anyone got into dispensary," he said. "I asked you specially about Amrit Singh, and you had the damned cheek to say nothing about Mr. Chatterjee."

His reply did not come from Edward G. himself. As if by some signal, he deputed the task to his lieutenant, the boy called Tarzan. And the reply was characteristic.

With a sudden wild whoop the boy launched himself high into the air and with the tips of his outstretched fingers caught hold of the edge of the beam supporting the roof of the front-door porch. From there he swung forward without a break. His legs were extended, his bare toes pointed. He came flying towards Ghote before the inspector had time to realise what was happening. A long, sharp, extremely dirty, big toe-nail just perceptibly flicked him on the nose. And then the boy was swinging back, and a moment later had dropped lightly to his feet and had darted off with the others out of sight round the back of the house.

Ghote stood forcing himself not to put up a hand and rub the place on his nose.

: : : :

So when he had found Krishna Chatterjee, resident social worker at the Masters Foundation, it was with no very subtle method that he went to work.

The door of the office had a wooden nameplate on it with " Krishna Chatterjee " painted in spidery black letters on a white background. Ghote gave the panel just underneath one perfunctory bang and opened the door.

The room was very narrow and long like a cupboard, except that at the far end there was a tall window. The cupboard-like look of the place was added to by the shelves along both walls running from the door down to the window. They were crammed with books, new and old, tall and squat, some fat and glossy, others thin, starved and paper-covered. They pushed and strained against each of the partitions fitted at intervals along the shelves.

For some reason the sight of them only inflamed Ghote the more.

What would anyone want with so many books? Spending a whole lifetime with their head buried in useless old tomes? What was the point of that? There were things to be done in this world. Frank Masters had not wasted his time reading books.

A figure stooping over an enormous sheet of paper spilling over the edges of a rickety typist's table looked up. In the dim light of the tall, narrow room Ghote could make out little more than a pair of enormous brown eyes glistening like some disturbed night animal's.

And as frightened.

So he began in a fashion that surprised even himself.

"All these tomes," he said, "all these tomes."

He gestured towards either wall.

"What do you want with all these tomes?"

Krishna Chatterjee stood up, still stooping slightly as if the position was habitual.

"Well, it is Inspector Ghote," he said.

He seemed relieved.

"Yes, it is Inspector Ghote. And Inspector Ghote is wanting words with you."

Mr. Chatterjee bustled round his desk, which in the confined space between the two book-lined walls was not an easy thing to do.

"Come in, come in, Inspector," he said. "Won't you sit down? The chair is not unsafe. I can guarantee that. Absolute, unconditional guarantee. You see, I have evidence. This chair is regularly sat upon by innumerable small boys while I talk to them in very imperfect Marathi or Gujarati. What better evidence of essential stability could you have than that? Eh?"

He held the chair in front of him with both hands and looked up at the inspector with his big eyes bigger than ever.

Certainly the chair did not look strong. It was a plain wooden one with a crude pattern of a lotus stamped on the seat. The rungs of the back were tilted slightly out of true.

"Never mind chairs," Ghote snapped. "We have more important matters than chairs to talk."

Mr. Chatterjee lowered the offensive chair to the ground, peered at it for an instant and shrugged his rounded shoulders.

"Yes," he said, "the books. All the books. The tomes. You want to discuss them. Well now, Inspector, I must confess that you strike me on the raw there. Yes, definitely on the raw. I do not need so many books. I realise it. And yet, you know, I cannot seem to help myself buying them.

And really there is very little room left for new acquisitions. Very little indeed."

He turned to examine anxiously the long rows of shelves.

"But I promise you one thing, Inspector," he said, "bibliophile that I am, I think I can say with perfect honesty that I do not let my passion interfere with my work. Indeed, it sustains it. Yes, sustains it, I think I can say. You see, Inspector, it is absolutely necessary in a profession like mine to have the widest possible grasp of human nature. And what can enlarge one's grasp of the infinite peculiarities of one's fellow creatures than the study of the many and varied books that have been written about them? What indeed?"

Inspector Ghote caught hold of two words in all the spate.

"Perfect honesty," he repeated. "Perfect honesty. I do not think you can talk to me about that, Mr. Chatterjee."

The two big brown eyes in the round face in front of him suddenly were flooded with pain.

Mr. Chatterjee held out his two hands wide.

"Inspector," he said, "that is an accusation I hoped never to hear. I am dishonest, of course. I recognise that. I talk of perfect honesty, but I recognise that there are states to which we can never attain. But, Inspector, I promise you, without one iota of unnecessary self-praise, that I do make an absolute point of keeping the ideal of honesty always in the forefront of my mind. It is not easy, you know, not easy at all. But dealing with the sort of young people who fall to my daily lot I believe it is absolutely essential. Absolutely."

"So you practise honesty with the sweepings of the pavements," Ghote said, "and forget all about it when you are talking with a police inspector."

"But no, my dear sir. Are you saying that I have been dishonest with you? Inspector, there has been some dreadful error."

The big-eyed Bengali was every bit as voluble as before,

but Ghote thought that somehow he was beginning to lack the full torrential flow of assurance.

"Nevertheless," he said, "I am accusing."

Krishna Chatterjee looked round his book-lined retreat in plainly growing dismay. He reached up and pulled a tall volume from one of the higher shelves, peered at the title on its spine as if he expected it to have suddenly altered, put the book down on his little desk, trotted round to the far side, stooped and picked up a scrap of paper from the floor, examined it, shrugged, went to the window and lifted the catch, pushed at the two tall frames, realised after a little that they were held fast by the bottom bar, released it and eventually turned and faced the inspector again.

"It seems most appallingly hot all of a sudden," he said.

Ghote marched up and stood in front of the desk.

"Mr. Chatterjee," he said, "why did you lie to me in those few minutes that I saw you last night?"

The big, brown eyes clouded over.

"Inspector, why should I lie?"

"Mr. Chatterjee, your employer, the late Mr. Frank Masters, has been murdered."

"Inspector, I know it. I know it. Inspector, this is a very terrible thing. That man was an immense benefactor, Inspector. An immense benefactor. He poured out money into this city. I cannot begin to enumerate the causes that gained from his generosity. It is a totally terrible thing that he has been done to death in this appallingly violent way. Inspector, all my life I have striven to put into practice the principles of non-violence. To me, Inspector, this is catastrophe. Absolute catastrophe."

"The principles of non-violence," Ghote said. "You seem very concerned to emphasise those. Can it be that you have ceased to obey them?"

A look of penetrating pain overwhelmed Krishna Chatterjee's roundly mild face.

For once he was deprived of speech.

"Now," said Inspector Ghote sharply, "I think it is

time you told the whole truth. What did you want with the key of the dispensary yesterday evening?"

Krishna Chatterjee clasped his hands tightly together. He swallowed.

"Inspector, I do not know what you are saying. What key of the dispensary is this? I am a social worker, Inspector. That is a very different kettle of fish, I assure you, from a medical worker like my good friend Carstairs. Carstairs is the medical man here. And of course Dr. Diana. Though not a man. Of course."

"Your good friend Carstairs?" Ghote said.

"Well, that is of course only a manner of speaking. Yes, only what you might call a polite fiction. Not that I haven't the highest esteem for Carstairs. Don't misunderstand me, Inspector, I beg. No, I have the highest esteem for the good fellow, but I must admit in all honesty that he is not my friend. There are no common interests, Inspector. That is the whole trouble. And I do not think without some community of interest one can hope to achieve any really satisfactory relationship with a person. Except on a purely superficial plane, of course. Except purely superficially."

"Then Carstairs is not a friend of yours?"

"Well, regretfully, I must admit it. No."

"So that you had to use methods of blackmail to obtain that key from him?"

"Inspector, I do not know what you are saying."

"Mr. Chatterjee, you know very well. You obtained the sole key to the dispensary from Carstairs. You entered the hut and you took from it the poison that was subsequently found in the body of Frank Masters. You administered that poison."

The round-shouldered Bengali glanced desperately from side to side. He opened his mouth to speak but no sound came. He clutched his stomach as if he were going to be violently ill.

"Inspector," he said. "Inspector, you must understand. I will make an admission."

Having got the word out at last he seemed happier. He stood up straighter and let his hands fall to his sides.

"Yes, Inspector, I see that I can no longer attempt to hide the truth. I see, indeed, that it was foolish of me to contemplate doing so. I hope you will believe me when I say that I think it was truly the first time in my life I have ever attempted to practise flagrant deception. And I fear I was not particularly adept. Well no, I suppose I am grateful for that. In the long run."

"The truth," said Ghote implacably.

"Yes, the truth. I must tell it. Very well."

Krishna Chatterjee stroked at his round cheeks with the tips of his fingers to brush away some of the beads of sweat that had collected there.

"Terrible humidity," he said.

Ghote looked at him unblinkingly.

"Very well then, Inspector, I must confess that I did indeed obtain that key from the unfortunate Sonny Carstairs. I am afraid I took advantage of a piece of inform——"

"All right," Ghote cut in. "I know all about what you said to Carstairs. We need not go over all that."

"Yes. Yes, I see that a person in your profession must avoid unnecessary and repetitious statements. Time is of the essence, doubtless."

"It is. Come on."

"Well then, you know that I had the key to that hut."

"Yes."

"And that in due course I returned it."

"Yes."

"Well then, I think that is all I can tell you, Inspector. Yes, with the greatest possible good will I do not think I have the right to add a word to that. No, not a word."

"You took the key from Carstairs, and what did you do with it next? You went to that hut, did you not? And you took the poison. And then what?"

"No, Inspector. I can give you an assurance that I did no such thing. Though, of course, I realise that in the light of my past actions you cannot be expected to extend any great degree of credence to my unsupported word. No, I realise that. But that is the most I can give you. Yes, definitely the very utmost."

"Mr. Chatterjee, I want to know what you did with the poison. Your exact course of action, Mr. Chatterjee."

"No."

Krishna Chatterjee was sweating more profusely than ever now. He turned to the window and pushed it open wide.

"No," he repeated, "not another word."

"The whole truth," said Ghote.

He stepped sharply to the side of the desk.

And with a cumbersome, curious wriggling sideways lurch, little Mr. Chatterjee was out of the window.

For a moment Ghote stood and gaped. The sudden physical action seemed so totally out of keeping with the scholarly Bengali's whole mode of existence that he could hardly believe that it had taken place.

For a moment only he stood and gaped.

And then he was after him. Three long strides took him to the window. In one vault he was through. He looked to left and right.

The window gave on to the side of the big bungalow. There was a narrow cement path running alongside the house wall and then a wide flowerbed full of big unkempt bushes, their leaves wilting a little in the hot sunshine. If Krishna Chatterjee had darted into these and then had stood quite still, it was going to be impossible to tell which way he had gone. And if Ghote happened to choose wrong, then before he could get back there would be nothing easier for Mr. Chatterjee than to walk quietly away.

The sunlight glared down, too, just here and made it difficult to see anything more than the varied green masses of the bushes and the dense purple shadows under them.

Ghote blinked.

There was only one thing to do.

He began shouting.

"You there, come out." "Come out, you." "You'll pay for this." "Just wait till I get you down to the station." "Come out, you, I can see——"

And it worked.

Like a startled mouse Mr. Chatterjee broke from cover not ten yards away. He ran ducking and blundering through the bushes with the dry earth under them sending up a wavy column of whitish dust. Ghote ran along the cement path until he had nearly drawn level and then plunged sideways.

"You stop," he shouted once again.

Mr. Chatterjee stopped.

"Run, sahib. Run away."

A sudden shrill voice darted out from just behind Ghote. He turned in fury. Krishna Chatterjee began to run again, with little waddling steps hardly faster than a walk.

As Ghote had expected, standing at the corner of the house, once again clothed in the abominable black jacket, was Edward G. Robinson.

"You wait," Ghote shouted at him.

He turned to pursue Krishna Chatterjee.

And suddenly went sprawling into a prickly, wiry-branched flowering shrub. He rolled, cursing, out of it and looked down to see what he had stumbled over.

A thin noose of rope was neatly caught round one brown shoe. He followed its length back. And there was Tarzan, grinning with great cheerfulness.

Ghote jumped to his feet.

In a flash Tarzan disappeared round the side of the building. Ghote tugged at the rope till it came off and set out in the direction Mr. Chatterjee had bumblingly taken.

A few quick steps brought him to the driveway. The Dodge truck was standing there in a patch of shade. The driver was sitting at the wheel, bolt upright and quietly snoozing. Krishna Chatterjee, for all the ineffectiveness of his run, was just leaving the house gate.

In Wodehouse Road outside a bus was slowing to a stop. There was nothing to prevent the little Bengali jumping on board and then getting off again wherever it pleased him.

Ghote ran a pace or two forward. But it was hopeless.

" Stop," he shouted.

And abruptly Krishna Chatterjee stopped.

He stopped, turned round, saw Ghote and began coming towards him. He was bending a little at the waist from the violence of his exertion.

Ghote did not have the strength of will even to go to meet him. He just stood, hoping the round-shouldered Bengali would not change his mind.

He did not.

In a few moments he was standing in front of the inspector.

" My dear sir," he said, " I owe you a most profound apology."

VII

Krishna Chatterjee apologised. He stated at length how wrong it had been of him to try to run off. He hinted that it was only the unusualness of his situation which had made him act in this way.

But he did not offer the least explanation of why he had persuaded Sonny Carstairs to hand over the key of the dispensary. Nothing Ghote could say would budge him.

" I am very sorry, Inspector, but I just cannot divulge my reasons. I can only state as positively as possible that I did not in any way harm Mr. Masters. It was the very last thing that I would wish to do."

" But you took the poison?"

" Inspector, I did not."

" But you went into the dispensary?"

Mr. Chatterjee hesitated.

" Yes," he said, " I did."

" Then, if it was not to take the poison, what was it for?"

" Inspector, I regret profoundly but I decline to say."

" I could arrest you on the evidence I have."

" Then you must arrest me, Inspector."

" But if you say you did not kill Frank Masters."

" I do say so. Most emphatically. But I realise that you cannot, in the nature of things, proceed to act on my unsupported word alone. You would be perfectly within your rights in carrying out my arrest."

But, thought Ghote, I will not do it. Not however much I can see how, in spite of your strangely honest denials, you could really be the murderer of Frank Masters, a man of truth until the moment comes for the one lie. But I cannot bring myself to arrest you because I no more know for certain you are guilty than I know that Amrit Singh is. The evidence balances up. To a grain.

Amrit Singh forcing Sonny Carstairs to hand over the dispensary key. Krishna Chatterjee blackmailing him into doing the same thing. Amrit Singh hurling the key back after keeping it for just the time needed. Krishna Chatterjee returning the same key before it was wanted for the emergency of Frank Masters's illness. Amrit Singh's fingerprints discovered in the dispensary. Krishna Chatterjee confessing to having been there himself.

The balance was exact.

There remained one hope. The Fingerprint Bureau were still testing the mess of brown glass fragments that had been the arsenic trioxide jar. If they could definitely find one of Amrit Singh's prints on one fragment . . . Or one of Krishna Chatterjee's . . .

But not both. Not both, Ghote prayed.

: :

Nor did a rare evening at home, spoilt only by four separate phone calls from newspapers, none of which Ghote now found easy to answer, do anything to resolve his dilemma. He arrived at the office next morning, Sunday, hoping passionately that the report from the Fingerprint Bureau might be there to provide the answer.

And as soon as he opened the door he saw it. A single

sheet of foolscap paper in the familiar style with a dozen lines typewritten on it. And the heading "For the attention of Inspector Ghote." He crossed the little room in two strides, picked up the sheet, twirled it round, and read.

His spirits slumped.

Sonny Carstairs's prints had been identified on the glass fragments, and so had Dr. Diana's. There was one other set, unidentified, doubtless belonging to someone at the pharmaceuticals factory. But not a trace of Amrit Singh's.

And equally not a trace of Krishna Chatterjee's, since the bureau had his prints along with all the others taken at the Foundation.

There was worse to come, a little. Underneath the bureau's report lay another one. It was from the sergeant detailed to check the key business, and it entirely confirmed what Dr. Diana had said. The sergeant had seen her correspondence with the lock importers. Something of the awe with which she had come to be regarded by the firm seeped through even the formal words of the report. And the facts were clear: only two keys to the dispensary had ever existed. Only one now did.

So it would all depend on what could be got out of Amrit Singh at ten o'clock. There were a great many things Ghote wanted to ask him: details of his movements during and after the time the poison had been taken from the dispensary, what exactly he had been doing hanging around the Masters Foundation, and, above all, what his relations were with Frank Masters himself.

Nor did a third report, brought in a few minutes later, advance matters. It was on the check made to see whether Fraulein Glucklich had in fact spent Friday evening with Swami Dnyaneshwar. The swami had been unexpectedly precise. He was prepared to swear his *sannysini* had been well and truly at his feet the whole time. Definitely.

Ghote looked at his watch. A long while to go yet before it got near ten o'clock.

He went over in his mind arrangements made the evening before to have the big bungalow in Wodehouse Road surrounded at the appropriate time. It would be a tricky business. Put too many men into the area before Amrit Singh was due, and it was almost certain he would spot something and be scared off; on the other hand, if it came to an arrest, there could never be too many hands waiting to grab a character like the big Sikh.

Resolutely Ghote set himself to tackle what routine work he could find to do. But it lasted all too short a time.

He picked up the telephone and spoke to Chavan, the uniformed inspector in charge of the ambush party. Chavan simply made it clear that he resented being fussed over, and Ghote put down the receiver with a sigh.

He looked at his watch again. It would still be absurdly early to set off.

He took out his copy of the *Times of India* Sunday edition. He had already read the meagre report of the case and the long obituary of Frank Masters. For all its length the latter had not helped him one little bit to understand the American. There had been the lists of charities which had benefited from his wealth. There was a reference to his education in America, but the names of the school and college he had attended meant nothing to Ghote. There was a more detailed account of the origins of the Masters fortune, but what use was it to know about how Frank Masters's grandfather had added acre to acre and oilwell to oilwell? There was a sonorous passage about India's poverty. It had not helped.

Ghote removed the paper's week-end supplement for women and children and put it in the top drawer of his desk to take home later. He closed the drawer firmly and with conscious virtue. He had resisted the lure of the colour comic page.

He turned to the political news.

Pak inhumanity to women. Even hard-boiled, old-time reactionaries burst into tears in the Lok Sabha to-day while referring to the plight of the large number of women who were recently abducted in East Pakistan.

Ghote shook his head. There was a limit to the amount of that that he was prepared to read. Something a little more down to earth would be needed to take his mind off Amrit Singh until the moment he could decently set off.

Opposition Parties Accused. Stating that the Congress to-day was as strong as ever, a party spokesman said Opposition members were magnifying small differences to vilify the organisation. Party members should not be frightened by such tactics of the Opposition, but work with redoubled energy and in a selfless manner for the good of the people.

Ghote looked up. Was there something he should be doing with selfless energy at this moment to make certain of pinning that enemy of the people, Amrit Singh?

He looked all round his little office. A flicker of movement caught his eye down in the dark corner by the filing cabinet. He got up and went over.

Sure enough, at the bottom of the small glass-fronted bookcase in which he kept copies of current information circulars a tiny lizard had contrived to get itself trapped. As he approached, the little beast flung itself into a maniac whirl of activity trying to penetrate the thin sheet of glass that cut it off from escape. But within a few seconds it had fallen on its back on the bottom of the shelf, palpitating and exhausted.

Ghote took a sheet of paper from the top of his desk, rolled it into a tube, opened the drop-front of the bookcase and flicked the little creature out.

For an instant it lay on the floor, its beady eyes still. Then suddenly it appeared to realise what had so mysteriously happened to it. With a twist of its tail it righted itself, paused just long enough to gulp once, and darted straight into the safety of a small crack between the floor and the wall.

Ghote walked back to his chair, picked up the *Times of India* again and flapped over the pages. For a few seconds he lingered at an advertisement showing four women grinning frantically over a naked baby with a fifth looking soulfully away out of the picture with firmly shut mouth. "A friendly tip to the fifth woman," he read. "Use our toothpaste and smile like the others: brush your teeth with it every night . . . and every morning, of course. More confidence in company . . . more fun!"

He found himself wondering whether his own breath was up to standard. He tried jutting out his lower lip into a sort of vent shape and puffing upwards. It seemed to be all right but it was hard to tell. And with a convenient neem tree just at the bottom of the garden at home it was surely a waste not to use its twigs as he had always done.

He puffed upwards again.

His hand stretched out to the notebook lying on his desk ready to be slipped into his pocket when he left. He flicked through it until he came to the first blank sheet and scrawled a couple of words.

"Buy toothpaste."

He looked at his watch again. Half an hour more and he could leave without upsetting Chavan's plans.

He made up his mind to settle down to the book reviews page. It was at least a way of catching up with all those things he wanted to know about, and should just occupy the right time.

He lowered his head and plunged in.

The door opened briskly.

It was Deputy Superintendent Naik. Hastily Ghote thrust the paper down behind his desk and stood up.

"Good morning, D.S.P.," he said.

The D.S.P. came and stood on the other side of the little desk peering closely at Ghote.

The inspector tried to withdraw his eyes from the round, softly moustached face so close to his own. He could detect a slight asthmatic note in the D.S.P.'s breathing and it was evident too that here was someone who was thoroughly modern in the matter of dental care. A faint minty tang in the air was quite unmistakable.

"Now then," the D.S.P. said, "are you making progress, my dear fellow?"

Ghote quickly debated the wisdom of telling the D.S.P. his exact dilemma. He decided to say nothing. So much still depended on what he was able to get from Amrit Singh. If he could screw just one admission out of him, then he could justify pulling him in. But there was no point in handing the defence points on a plate by acting without enough evidence. And unless he had something concrete to put before the D.S.P., it would be much safer to say nothing. Rouse no expectations, bring no recriminations. You learnt things like that after a while in the C.I.D.

"I think we are doing well, D.S.P.," he said. "There are several possible leads."

He launched into an account of all the groundwork he had gone through at the Foundation.

After a little he gave up. It was obvious that the D.S.P. was not listening.

Instead he was leaning forward over the narrow desk and peering with an extraordinary tenseness. For a few moments neither said anything. Then the D.S.P. spoke.

"Inspector?"

"Yes, sir? Yes, D.S.P.?"

"Inspector, there is a pimple on your neck. A small pimple, but distinct. I cannot make out whether it has come to a head yet."

Ghote swallowed.

"No, sir," he said. "Thank you, sir."

"You must watch such things, Inspector. I cannot have my officers being unhealthy. It won't do at all."

"No, sir."

"Are you taking plenty of exercise, Inspector? Exercise is very important. Are you playing hockey?"

"No, sir. Actually, no. I would like to, sir. But the work takes up a great deal of time, sir."

"You must not let it interfere with proper precautions over your health, Inspector. And one more thing."

"Yes, sir?"

"All these men Inspector Chavan is sending out for you. What is that about?"

Caught.

Ghote drew a deep breath.

"I came across a lead up at the Foundation on Amrit Singh, sir."

"Amrit Singh. Amrit Singh. Those men are for Amrit Singh?"

"Yes, sir. I thought it best to take pretty full precautions. You cannot be too careful with a fellow like that, sir. I had this tip from some of the young boys up at the Foundation. They said he would be there again at ten a.m., sir. So I shall tackle him myself then, and Chavan will give me backing."

"You will go up there at ten a.m. and tackle him, eh?"

"Yes, D.S.P. I managed to get the confidence of those boys, sir. They are a bit mixed up in Singh's smuggling activities, I think. But I will sort it all out at ten o'clock."

"You will not, Inspector. You certainly will not. A pack of pavement sleepers choose to tell you that Amrit Singh will be up at the Foundation at ten a.m., and you sit on your backside here and wait for him. He'll be there and gone this moment, Inspector. Get after him. Get after him, you damned fool."

Ghote felt the sweat spring up from every pore in his body. What if the D.S.P. was right? Amrit Singh warned and . . .

His heart thumping, his mouth dry, forebodings of disaster screeching like sirens in his brain, he tore from the room and flung himself down the stairs.

VIII

The blue Dodge truck skidded to a halt on the loose gravel of the drive at the Masters Foundation. Inspector Ghote leapt out. He took one look at the big, slightly shabby bungalow. Nothing different as far as he could tell. Still, silent and asleep in the hot sun.

But Amrit Singh would hardly be in the house itself. The compound was the place.

Ghote ran.

There was nothing for it but a frontal approach. To go round to the lane at the back would take too much time now. And help him no more. Amrit Singh could go out this way just as easily as by the back.

Darting glances to left and right, the inspector pelted over the dark green grass of the big lawn, dodging trees and flowerbeds and all the time searching along the line of the trellis ahead for the least sign of telltale movement.

Nothing.

The garden, the dispensary hut, the garage shed, the whole place seemed to be asleep. Ghote conscientiously examined every corner, but with growing despair. He ought not to have relied on what that boy had said, even though at the time they seemed to be getting on so well. Obviously since the incident of Krishna Chatterjee's panic flight they had found a way of warning Amrit Singh. If he had come here at all, it had been earlier. And now he was safely away again. Lost somewhere in the teeming vastness of the city.

He came to a dispirited halt. Hot, sweaty and profoundly miserable. Why, oh why, had he been so self-confident in front of the D.S.P.? It was all very well to feel he had done everything possible on the case so far, but there was no need to have boasted like that.

"You looking for someone?"

As he might have guessed, it was Edward G. Robinson. He chose moments like this to appear from nowhere. Ghote hardly looked up from the matted grass at his feet.

"You looking for a guy called Amrit Singh?"

"You know that."

"You think a guy like Amrit Singh going to be caught by a policeman only?"

Ghote's eyes flashed in anger.

"Not when he has friends like you to warn."

But the boy simply grinned.

"Look," he said softly.

Ghote turned and followed the line of his glance.

And there, happily swinging over the tall, barbed-wire-topped wall in the far corner of the compound, was the burly figure of the Sikh himself. He landed lightly enough, for all his size, on the balls of his feet on the soft, dusty ground. Ghote could see his great, black beard shining lustrously under a heavy blue and red turban.

With one quick look at the black-jacketed boy at his side, Ghote stepped forward.

"You, Amrit Singh," he said in a loud, clear voice. "Stay where you are. This is the police."

He saw the brawny figure stop and look towards him. Then there came a quick second of calculation. A glance back to the tall wall behind him, a look forward to the big empty garden.

"Hallo, Inspector Ghote."

Amrit Singh strode forward to meet the inspector, his hand outstretched, a smile showing the white teeth in the depths of the luxuriant black beard.

Ghote found that the boy by his side was no longer there. He took the big Sikh's outstretched hand. His grasp was as steely as the quietly glinting bangle that circled his wrist.

"And why would as great a man as Inspector Ghote want to see a poor travelling salesman?" Amrit Singh said.

"There are some questions to ask," Ghote said.

He felt that he had been a little more rushed into his

interrogation than he would have liked. But there was something to be said for holding it here in the deserted garden. If the big Sikh tried to get away there was plenty of time to shout a warning. And Chavan's men, with any luck, would soon be taking up their positions round the house.

"Questions?" Amrit Singh said. "It is sad that I can never talk to my friends in the police just like two men talking. Always they want the talk to be questions and answers. Their questions, my answers."

"If you had less to hide, perhaps there would be less to ask," Ghote replied.

The big, thickset Sikh laughed till his beard shook.

"How can you think that I have things to hide?" he said. "You know me. I travel about selling here, buying there, making a poor living."

"And what were you selling or buying in this compound on Friday evening?" Ghote said suddenly.

"In this compound? You are joking only, Inspector. This is no bazaar. How should I be buying and selling here?"

"You do not deny that you were here?"

Amrit Singh opened his great hands wide in a gesture of simple amazement.

"Why should I deny? You have seen me here now. You know how I know my way here. And what is there to deny after all?"

"Then you admit trespassing on private property?"

"Oh yes, I admit."

The big Sikh laughed.

"Oh, I have committed very terrible crime," he said. "No wonder it is a C.I.D. inspector himself they have sent to arrest me. Trespassing. Will it be hanging matter, do you think, or seven years R.I. only?"

Ghote felt the sting of a defeat.

"It is not rigorous imprisonment matters only that I am wanting to talk," he said. "How did you get the key to the dispensary hut there?"

He glanced over at the long, low hut with its criss-cross of heavy wires at the windows and stout wooden walls.

The Sikh laughed again.

"Hanging matters, is it?" he said. "To have a key to an old hut. Oh, you policias, you are getting more strict every day. Once they did not want to hang you for every little mistake. But now the least thing you do and already a policeman is there with a rope ready to put round your neck."

"You have not answered my question," Ghote said. "How did you get that key?"

"There are so many keys," Amrit Singh said with a shrug of his broad shoulders. "How can I remember each one?"

"There are not so many keys. There is one only. The lock on that door is no ordinary one. It is American-type. There is one key only for that, and you had it."

"Perhaps it was given to me," Amrit Singh replied.

His eyes were bright and dancing under the jutting black eyebrows.

"And who should give you the key to the dispensary at the Masters Foundation, you a notorious thug?"

"Who knows who might give it?" the Sikh said. "Masters sahib himself it could have been."

Ghote felt his blood begin to race. Was there really some link between the Sikh and the mysterious American millionaire? Or was it, after all, only the big thug's particular brand of humour?

"Masters sahib," Ghote said cautiously. "What do you know of Masters sahib?"

"Oh, he is a very generous man," the Sikh replied.

"Everybody knows that," Ghote said. "You have to read the papers only to see that."

"Then if he is so generous, why should he not give me key?"

Amrit Singh leant back on his heels delighted with this simple piece of wit.

"What did Frank Masters know about you so that you had to make sure he could not speak?" Ghote snapped suddenly.

But Amrit Singh was too old a hand to be caught this way.

"How should I know a man like the great Masters sahib?" he asked. "I, a poor travelling salesman?"

"What were you doing so near his house on Friday then?" Ghote said.

A dark glint of humour came into the Sikh's eyes.

"I suppose you have witness who saw me, Inspector sahib?" he said.

"It is not for me to tell you of the nature of the evidence that the police department has," Ghote replied.

"Perhaps you are not sure yet that your witness will say the right things?" Amrit Singh answered quickly. "Perhaps he has not yet had enough teaching in his part?"

"I do not find it necessary to use evidence of that sort," Ghote replied stiffly.

"Ah, no, I beg your forgiveness," said the Sikh. "I forgot I was speaking to the great Inspector Ghote, the one who never bribes his witnesses, the one who can never be bribed himself."

Infuriated as he was by the big thug's cheerful contempt, the inspector could not help feeling at the same time a quick-running vein of pleasure. So he had got a reputation for not rigging the evidence, for not taking any sort of bribes. It was a tribute.

The Sikh laughed.

"Though it is pity that you will always be so poor," he said.

"If it is necessary to be poor I am happy to be so," Ghote said, the words tumbling out before he had time to check them. "My rate of pay is enough to live on. There is no need for luxuries and refrigerators and air-conditioning and all those sort of things."

The Sikh inclined his head in solemn agreement.

"Oh no," he said, "no need, no need at all. But it is pleasant to be cool, and to drink beer from the ice and to have your own car to ride in."

"That is nothing to do with it," Ghote stormed. "I am asking you questions. Important questions. What food did Mr. Masters have to eat on Friday?"

"Iced beer he had to drink, that I will bet," the Sikh replied.

"I asked what he had to eat."

The Sikh shook his head from side to side till his big beard wagged.

"Oh, Inspector," he said, "I have heard the news, you know. Masters sahib is dead. They say he was poisoned. Am I going to tell you what food he had, even if I knew?"

"Then you do know?"

Amrit Singh stepped a pace back and held up his right hand as if he was taking an oath.

"I am not knowing one thing," he said.

"I think you are. Tell me, did you have to open the window, or was it open already?"

The Sikh's eyes widened enormously.

"What window is this, Inspector sahib? I know of no windows."

"The curries on the serving table," Ghote said, "how many were there?"

"What table, Inspector? What curries?"

"You refuse to answer?"

"Inspector, how can I answer? I am knowing nothing of all this."

"Then what were you doing in this compound on Friday?"

The Sikh bowed his great turbaned head.

"Inspector, I was trespassing."

"But I asked why. Why were you trespassing?"

"Inspector, I am a very bad fellow. A deplorable fellow, Inspector."

"Why were you in the garden?"

"Such a bad fellow, Inspector."

Ghote looked at him in silence for a moment.

"There are ways of making you answer," he said.

"Oh yes," said the Sikh promptly. "Very terrible ways. I know. Many have been tried on me."

He leant forward a little and winked. Hard.

"But not by the good Inspector Ghote," he said. "Inspector Ghote does not do such things."

And again Ghote felt the little quicksilver dart of pleasure. But he did not let it deter him from his object.

"Did Dr. Diana eat the fish curry or the beef?" he snapped.

"Ah now," said the Sikh, "that Dr. Diana I am knowing. A very fearful person, Inspector. Is it not? Most terrible. Enough to make the heart of a man tremble."

He filled his lungs with air, letting the big muscles swell.

"But with the curries," he added, "I cannot help. You would have to ask the memsahib herself, Inspector. Though I can feel for you if you do not want. Even I am a little afraid of Dr. Diana."

Inwardly Ghote fumed. Had Amrit Singh really divined his own timidity about Dr. Diana? Or was he just striking at a venture?

"There is nothing to be afraid," he snapped out. "Dr. Diana is just resident medical officer at Masters Foundation. What is there to be afraid in that?"

Under the tangle of bushy black eyebrows the thickset Sikh's eyes gleamed with sudden dark lights.

"Oh, there is nothing, nothing at all," he said. "Only it is not given to everyone to be as brave as a police inspector. It is not everyone who would face a gun and think nothing of it."

His hand slipped down towards the heavy sash round his waist. Ghote calculated that he almost certainly did have a gun concealed there.

"What is this facing of guns?" he demanded. "Do you think Dr. Diana threatens me with gun?"

Amrit Singh laughed.

The picture of Dr. Diana as a gunman seemed to amuse

him a great deal. He laughed with a deep, rich chuckle that shook his entire brawny frame.

At last he wiped the back of his hand across his eyes.

" Oh, Inspector," he said, " that Dr. Diana does not need gun. But it was not her I was talking."

He was no longer laughing now.

" No," he said, " it is not her who would be threatening the good Inspector Ghote with a gun. Not her at all."

He looked steadily at the inspector and quietly patted the folds of his cummerbund. The motionless, intent eyes.

Ghote felt a flicker of pure apprehension down in his stomach. An uncontrollable flicker of apprehension.

" Enough of this," he said with sudden briskness. " Amrit Singh, I am asking what you were doing in this compound on the evening of Friday last?"

" Inspector," said Amrit Singh, " I am not telling."

" What were you doing in that hut?"

Ghote pointed at the long dark brown shape of the dispensary.

" Inspector, you would have to prove for yourself."

" Why did you kill Frank Masters?"

" Inspector, are you going to arrest? I am quite ready, Inspector. I am quite happy to go to your station and be locked up in one of your little cells."

A faint smile curled the wide mouth hidden in the luxuriant beard.

" But watch out, Inspector. Watch out when we come to court."

: : : :

Ghote knew that he had to let him go. If he was going to get him in the end, he must not rush in and spoil everything. No doubt, Amrit Singh had realised from the drift of his questioning that there was still something needed to make a reasonable case. Otherwise he would have more likely made a bolt for it than have offered himself so happily for arrest.

It would be a bad moment when he got to know about

Krishna Chatterjee. His defence team would make a terrible amount out of that.

Ghote resolved that, come what may, he would get at the truth quickly. But until he had got out of his dilemma he was hamstrung. And the balance was still exact: on one scale the quiet little man who could so easily have been pushed by his own virtues into murder, and on the other scale the big bad man, a real killer for all his joviality.

Ghote went home for something to eat rather than face Inspector Chavan and explanations about why the careful net of uniformed men had not been called into play.

He was still thinking about what he would say eventually as he stepped into the little square of garden in front of his small white house. The smell of cooking tickled his nostrils. He hurried in, suddenly devouringly hungry.

Protima was busy kneading dough for chapattis, her bangles jingling rhythmically.

"Have you made enough for a husband to have some?" he said.

She did not look up from the soft, whitish slack piece of dough.

"Oh," she said, "you thought I would not know you were back, you policeman with your thumping shoes. Already I have put in more flour."

Ghote smiled.

"I am ready to eat all you have made," he said. "What a terrible morning I have had."

"And so I am going to hear all about it," Protima said. "All about how this old fingerprint matched that one and that there was some dirt of a most interesting colour under the toenails of some poor man you have hauled into your big headquarters."

From where he stood Ghote could just see the smile lifting the corner of her cheek. He stooped and put his arm round the curve of her bending back.

"Oh, stop your nonsense," she said. "You see I have work to do."

Ghote stepped back.

He thrust his arms out in a great stretch.

"Well," he said, "some fingerprints would have been useful to me to-day."

And he told Protima what hopes had been dashed by the lack of Amrit Singh's prints on the ribbed brown glass of the broken jar.

This time she did turn away from her dough.

"But my clever Mr. Policeman," she said. "So near to catching a man like that Amrit Singh. In no time at all they will have to be thinking of promotion for Inspector Ghote."

"No, no," said Ghote hastily. "I tell you I am far away from catching Amrit Singh. And beside I am very low in seniority. There is no question of promotion for a long time."

"But they do promote out of turn," Protima replied. "You were telling only three days ago of all the talk because that Inspector Nimbalkar has been made Acting-D.S.P., you know that."

"But Nimbalkar is quite a senior man," Ghote protested. "That is not the same thing at all."

"We shall just see," Protima said, with a slight, secretive smile.

She began to cook the chapattis with great concentration.

Ghote sat on the edge of the gas cylinder and watched her in silence. Suddenly he sighed breathily.

"If only I could get into my mind a clear picture of him," he said.

"Oh, but you have a very good brain," Protima replied a little absently.

"But he is so far from anything I have ever known. It is so difficult with a man like him," Ghote said.

Protima looked round from the whining flame of the gas-burner for an instant.

"What man is this?" she asked.

"But Frank Masters," Ghote said. "Who else could it be but Frank Masters? If I had a clear picture of him, then perhaps I could see why either Amrit Singh or Krishna

Chatterjee wanted to poison him, whether it was the bad man because he stood in his way or the good man from some twist in his goodness."

"Oh, Frank Masters is only rich," Protima said. Rich people are like all the others underneath."

"But it is not that he is rich," Ghote said. "If it was that only . . . But, you see, that man was good too. All that money he gave up, to live on just the same food as he provided for those vagrant boys he took from the pavements."

He checked himself.

"Or nearly the same food," he added.

"Well, if it pleased him to do such things."

Under her dark blue and green sari Protima shrugged her invariably elegant shoulders as she rose from the gas-rings.

"Come along with you," she said. "The meal is ready now."

"But do you understand such a man?" Ghote asked.

Protima looked him full in the face and smiled a slightly mocking, provocative smile above the wide brass dish she had put the food on.

"I understand the man I have got," she said. "And I would rather have him than all your millionairing, vagrant-rescuing ones put together."

In spite of his anxieties Ghote smiled back.

"Then you do not want more money, little Hindu wife," he said. "You do not want, for instance, refrigerator?"

Before she could set down the dish and get at him he dodged nimbly away out of the kitchen, giggling like a schoolgirl after a mild reference to the difference between the sexes.

: : : :

Not a minute later than his due time, Inspector Ghote was back at headquarters. He felt he owed that to himself.

But he waited till he heard voices in Inspector Chavan's room and went past the glass-panelled door in a swift glide.

When he was seated at his own familiarly blotched little

desk a sudden wave of discouragement swept up on him. He thought over the whole Frank Masters affair. And whichever way his thoughts turned, they seemed in no time at all to run up against a blank wall. The fact of the matter was that he had done everything there was to be done. He had been utterly conscientious. He knew it. And all that his every effort had been able to turn up was this appalling balance between the possibility that Krishna Chatterjee, a man whose very goodness might have turned somehow sour, was the one he was looking for and the simple desire to fix the business fairly and squarely on Amrit Singh, who had already got away with murder more than once.

There must be something he had forgotten.

He pulled open the lowest drawer on the right hand side of his desk where he kept his supply of paper and took out a hefty wad. From the little enamelled brass tray he took a pencil. And with the utmost care he set himself to write an account of the whole business from start to finish.

It must show some new line somewhere.

About an hour later, just as he was getting to the end, the door opened.

Ghote looked up quickly. It might be Chavan.

But it was Deputy Superintendent Naik. Hastily Ghote put the sheet he was writing face downwards on the pile in front of him and stood up.

" Sit down, sit down, Inspector. I am just looking in to see what progress you are making. You are letting him cool off a bit?"

Ghote felt he had no time to think. If it had been Chavan, he knew some reasonable excuse for not picking up Amrit Singh would have come to him in time. But the very sight of the D.S.P., entering so unexpectedly, had driven every coherent thought from his head. He only knew that his careful account of the case, so nearly finished, had not done a thing to give him a new lead.

The D.S.P. plumped down on the squat little chair in

front of the desk, puffing heavily. He cocked an eye up at Ghote.

"Cool off, D.S.P.?" Ghote stammered. "Well, that is—— In a manner of speaking, yes. Sir."

The D.S.P. leant slowly forward.

"That pimple," he said. "It does not seem to be getting any better. It is larger than when I saw it before."

Ghote smiled uneasily.

"You are not having digestive troubles?" the D.S.P. asked. "That is often the root cause of blood disorders, you know."

"No. No, thank you, sir. Really my digestion is very good, considering."

"Considering?"

The D.S.P. slewed round in the heavy little wooden chair and gave Ghote redoubled attention.

"Considering what?" he said. "You have some chronic complaint? A duodenal, perhaps? I have often thought you were underweight, Inspector."

"No, no. No, it is nothing like that, D.S.P. It was just a joke really."

Ghote swallowed.

"It was just a joke, sir," he said. "I meant I have a very good digestion considering how often a detective officer has to snatch what food he can from all sorts of eating places."

The D.S.P. looked grave.

"Yes, that is a very serious consideration," he said. "Very serious."

His hand strayed out to the papers on Ghote's desk. For an instant Ghote contemplated putting something down quickly on top of the pile, something heavy. But it was too late.

D.S.P. Naik picked up the top sheet, turned it over and began reading. He made no comment. He picked up another sheet, and another and read through them rapidly.

"Inspector," he said thoughtfully, still reading, "you have checked on other possible sources for arsenic trioxide?"

Ghote breathed a sigh of relief. This was a question he could answer with a good conscience.

"Yes, sir," he said. "I have had most thorough checks made. And I can trace no leakages. And think of this, sir: you have a man poisoned with a substance like that in one place, and enough of that substance to kill him is stolen not a hundred yards away. Well, sir, the chances of the two being unconnected are most remote."

The D.S.P. looked up at the ceiling fan for a moment.

"Yes, Inspector," he said, "I think we can dismiss that possibility altogether."

Ghote let a feeling of relief begin to creep over him. Perhaps the D.S.P. would be satisfied with having made one cogent observation.

But, no, he returned to his reading with renewed vigour.

Suddenly he jumped up.

"What was that about leaving Amrit Singh to cool off?" he said. "It looks from this as if you even think he may not be guilty."

Hot surges of blood ran up and down Ghote's back. Did the D.S.P. realise he had not actually arrested Amrit Singh?

"But, sir," he managed to say, "there is Krishna Chatterjee. Sir, it might just as easily have been him."

The D.S.P. put his hands on the front of the desk and leant over towards Ghote.

"Inspector," he said, "I am surprised any officer working under me could be so ridiculous."

"But, sir, it is fact that Chatterjee went into the dispensary at just the crucial time. Sir, social workers can be killers too."

"I dare say they can," said the D.S.P. "So you must just take very good care to see no one ever finds out about your Mr. Chatterjee. That is all."

Ghote made no reply. He was not shocked. No one could have been in the service as long as he without realising that at times likely evidence was suppressed. But one way and another he had drunk too deeply at the springs of different approaches to crime and justice to feel that the D.S.P.'s attitude was one that, when it came to it, he could ever copy himself.

Up till now he had always succeeded in letting his acquiescence be taken for granted and had avoided compromising himself. But now, thanks to this silly business of allowing the D.S.P. to think he had actually brought in Amrit Singh, he had let himself get caught fast.

The D.S.P. wheezed more loudly.

"Inspector?" he said.

"Yes, sir?"

"You don't seem to agree, Inspector."

"But, sir," Ghote said, "I am as keen as anybody to see Amrit Singh on the end of a rope."

"I should hope you are, Inspector."

The D.S.P. looked at Ghote with an unexpected twinkle of kindness in his eyes.

"Listen, my good fellow," he said, "just because everything points to Amrit Singh don't start trying to convince yourself he is somehow or other not the man you are looking for. It is a terrible temptation to be too clever, you know. In time you will learn that."

Ghote suddenly saw how it was that a man like the D.S.P. had got to where he was in the force. He was right. The obvious answer did often somehow look too easy.

"Come on now, man," the D.S.P. said. "Get down to that cell and beat it out of him."

Ghote sat upright in his desk chair.

"D.S.P.," he said, "Amrit Singh is not in a cell."

For three wheezes out and two wheezes in D.S.P. Naik was silent. But under his cheeks the colour gradually spread and darkened.

And at last the pent-up feelings splurged out.

"Inspector Ghote. I have just been sitting here reading your account of this most important case. You have summed up the situation with admirable clarity. Every word you have written points to only one thing. For the first time in the history of this department we have got that bastard Amrit Singh just exactly where we want him. And now I hear from your own lips, from your own bloody lips, that you have let him go."

His tautly spread right hand swept round and clutched in agony at his solar plexus.

"Let him go. Let him go."

He moaned the words over again as if they were too completely awful to be assimilated at one swallow.

Slowly he crossed to the door and held it open.

"Inspector," he said, "you will go out now and first of all get hold of those damned urchins at the Foundation. Then you will drill into each and every one of them such facts as we need to make sure that Amrit Singh hangs. And when you have done that you will stay out of this office until you have brought that unutterable Sikh back here on the end of a pair of handcuffs. Do you understand that?"

"Yes, D.S.P.," said Inspector Ghote.

IX

Inspector Ghote was too sensible to defy D.S.P. Naik's orders then and there where he had been given them. He at once grabbed his telephone and with a great deal of shouting ordered a truck to take him round to Wodehouse Road.

The D.S.P. stood beside the open door, still wheezing hard, and stared at him in silence.

Ghote wished he would go.

He wanted a few moments to think. He had had to say he would obey orders, but there must still be a way round. Only, unless he had a little time to himself, he would not be able to sort things out. And now he had been pressured into calling for transport to take him to the Foundation. He could always stop the truck outside and sit and think on the spot, but if he did the driver would begin to wonder why he had been sent out at a moment's notice and now was being made to hang about at the kerbside. And nothing must distract him from thinking this through properly.

There must be a way out.

Ghote collected a notebook and put it in his pocket. Still the D.S.P. said nothing, and still he remained exactly where he was, leaning a little bit forward and wheezing ever more slowly with each breath.

Ghote turned towards the doorway.

And down in the corner where he kept his filed information sheets he saw that the same little lizard had contrived once again to imprison itself in the glass-fronted bookshelf. If he left it in there in the shut-up office it might die. He might be away all the rest of the day if he did have to try and pull in Amrit Singh.

He hesitated.

And then he quickly picked up one of the sheets of paper on which he had so painfully written out his account of the case and rolled it into a cylinder.

As he did so, his eye fell on the words he had written at the top of the page. "From information received from Dr. Diana Upleigh, resident medical . . ." And suddenly he knew that there was after all something that he had left undone in his investigation. He had not got all that he should have done out of Dr. Diana. She, more than anyone in the Foundation, knew Frank Masters. And it was in the character of the young American that the reason for his death must lie. Once he had a firm idea of what that was, then it should surely be obvious whether he had died at the hands of a stop-at-nothing thug or at those of a talkative, pedantic, over-the-edge little Bengali intellectual.

Ignoring the still expectant figure of D.S.P. Naik, Ghote stepped swiftly over to the glass-fronted bookcase, opened it, flicked up the little lizard with his paper cylinder, slid it off near to the crack at the edge of the floor and tossed the paper into the wastepaper basket.

"I am going now, D.S.P.," he said.

The D.S.P. made no reply. He was staring at the empty

patch of floor where an instant before a tiny lizard had blinked its two beads of eyes twice and had darted incredulously to safety once again.

: : : :

The stately, pear-shaped bearer at the Masters Foundation showed Ghote, when he asked for Dr. Diana, into the doctor's private sitting-room. Ghote had glanced into the room when he had made his first tour of the bungalow just after the crime, but now he stood in the doorway and looked with care.

It was cool and quiet for all the unrelenting brightness of the sun outside. At each of the windows a heavy split cane blind hung, letting in only broken and jumbled bars of light. They caught the flowered pattern on the material of the soft armchair in which Dr. Diana sat. They caught too the real flowers in a blue pottery bowl on a low table of dark wood, carved with heavy scoops in a curious rough pattern. Ghote had seen such work in the homes of other Britons: it always made him feel it came from somewhere very distant, where the people were as brutally decided as the thick strokes of the carving.

He looked up from the low table with its bowl of soft-bloomed flowers. On the walls there were a mirror and two photographs. Each was in a dark frame carved in the same fierce style. He looked away.

Dr. Diana, who had been reading an illustrated magazine sent from England, laid it down. Ghote registered the smell of the thick, shiny paper and the sepia brown squares of the photographs of clumps of Englishmen and women standing about in ungainly but determined poses.

" Well," Dr. Diana said, " and what can I do for you?"

She looked up at him from the billowing mass of her flower-covered armchair. She was wearing a frock in much the same pattern as the chair material though the flowers were smaller and more tightly bunched. Her face was aggressively pink and white. The rather coarse eyebrows were raised in an attitude of direct inquiry.

Ghote braced himself.

" I have come to you," he said, " because I think you are the one who can most help me in the next stage of my investigation."

" Oh," said Dr. Diana, " then your investigation has got past one stage, has it? I'm glad to hear that."

" My inquiries have revealed a great deal," Ghote said.

" But not anything on which you can actually take action?"

Ghote made himself ignore the rebuke.

" My problem is otherwise," he said. " I have discovered too much in many ways. Too much about what has been going on at the Foundation here, and too little about the person who suffered from it."

Dr. Diana sat up straighter in the billowing, flower-covered armchair.

" What nonsense," she said. " If you've discovered anything that's been going on here, it can't have any bearing on Frank's death. And you don't need to go poking your nose into his whole life history to find out who killed him either."

" Excuse me," said Ghote, " but I think the opposite is the case. I have found that there were people in a position to obtain the arsenic trioxide, but until I know more of their relations with Mr. Masters, I cannot decide whether they would want to administer."

" Well, there isn't any mystery about Frank's relations with anybody," Dr. Diana declared, flopping back in the big chair. " Frank was as open and straight as anyone in this world."

" That is something to have learnt," Ghote replied. " But I would like to learn more."

" All right, learn more if you want to. But don't come bothering me for it. I've got the whole of this place to run now, and I really haven't got time to attend to inessentials."

" Of course I understand that you are very busy, but——"

" I'm more than very busy. If the Foundation's to go on without Frank it's absolutely essential that I should take hold of the reins firmly right from the start. Otherwise the whole place'll go to pot. I know, I've seen it happen to other places before."

"Then you are taking over permanently?" Ghote asked, seeing how he could discuss what Frank Masters had done in a way acceptable to Dr. Diana.

"Yes, yes, of course. That was always understood," she said brusquely.

"And you are to carry on with the same policy?"

"Naturally. Frank Masters set the pattern. We shall always honour his memory. His plans will be carried through to the last detail. Except where circumstances alter, needless to say."

"Of course," Ghote agreed. "And how would you describe these principles?"

"My dear man, I should have thought they would have been obvious to anybody."

Ghote said nothing. And, as he had hoped, Dr. Diana after a short pause did go on to explain the self-explanatory principles on which the Masters Foundation had run during the lifetime of Frank Masters himself.

"Frank was a very rich man," she said. "He had had great advantages. But he knew that he must share them with those less fortunate than himself. You've got to give sometimes in this world, you know."

She looked at Ghote challengingly.

The thought came into his head that he himself gave very little. He remembered the beggar on the office steps. The last time he had given him anything was when he had wanted a few moments to think about the Masters case the night he had come out here for the first time.

But Dr. Diana was continuing with her exposition of the principles behind the Foundation. She rose like a lioness from the big chintz-covered armchair and strode up and down the cool, dark room.

"We in the West have got to give to those countries that need help," she said. "We have all the advantages: we have got to share them."

She swung round.
"Of course, you have your own way of life," she went on. "We respect that. Frank respected that. He went up to the Punjab, you know, a month or two ago and did a lot of work studying the religious outlook of the Tibetans, and all that sort of thing."
"Yes," said Ghote, "I had heard."
Dr. Diana looked at him briefly.
"Yes," she said. "Well, that was all very well, but of course there were a great many practical things that needed doing here too."
"It was then that you discovered that Amrit Singh was making a nuisance of himself in the Foundation?" Ghote put in quickly.
He was delighted that a chance to introduce the Sikh's name had come up so easily. Perhaps he could get on to mentioning his possible links with Frank Masters.
"Oh, him," Dr. Diana said shortly. "Yes, I dealt with him. But, as I was saying, Frank did more than simply give money. He could have stayed at home in America and done that. Or, I could have stayed back in the U.K. and organised a few raffles and things for the Church Missionary Society. But Frank was not just a giver: he was a doer. He came out here and got down to a spot of good hard work."
Ghote bowed his head slightly.
"That's the trouble out here," Dr. Diana went on.
Her pacing of the cool darkness of the room had grown swifter now. She covered its length in a few long strides, came up against a wall, halted as if affronted, swung round, and set off again.
"That's the trouble with so many of you," she said. "You haven't got the simple bloody guts to get on with the job. That's all that's needed, you know. Roll up your sleeves and get down to it."
She came to a full halt again in front of the mirror in its dark coarsely carved frame. She looked at her reflection in

it for a few seconds. Her muscular pinky white arms were bare to the elbow.

"Yes," she said, "people out here are mostly in a damned appalling muddle. What they need is a swift leg-up. Over the stile."

She swung round sharply and marched up to the inspector.

"But don't you go thinking that we aim to help them every inch of the way," she said. "That's not it at all. Help them to help themselves. That's what Frank believed in."

"A most excellent principle," Ghote observed.

He felt he was at last beginning to get a grasp of the hitherto totally enigmatic figure of Frank Masters. It was not helping him to see why he had been killed yet. But it was filling him with a certain awe. He himself was so much below this.

"Well, there it is," Dr. Diana said tersely. "That's what Frank believed. Heaven knows, I don't want to be a nurse-maid to anybody myself. It just so happens I've a good clear mind, and I can see what has to be done. And when I do, I go ahead and do it."

She had come up against the mirror again. She swung away from it after a few instants.

"And that was what Frank was like too," she said. "He had a clear mind. He saw what was to be done and did it. And this city has a lot to be thankful for because of that."

Ghote could only agree.

"That is most true," he said. "Most true."

A niggling thought reared up.

"But Amrit Singh," he added. "Mr. Masters did not realise that Amrit Singh was bad influence?"

Dr. Diana looked shocked.

"Now, just you listen to me," she said. "Frank Masters had the widest open eyes of anybody I ever met. He was no sloppy, sentimental fool, all think beautiful thoughts and do nothing. When he saw that something was wrong he got up on his two feet and darn well did something about it."

"Yes," said Ghote.

: : : :

He left Dr. Diana seated once more in her billowing chair turning over again the thick, odoriferous leaves of the English magazine. He felt doubly oppressed now. To begin with nothing that she had said seemed to indicate clearly one way or the other whether Krishna Chatterjee or Amrit Singh was most likely to have poisoned Frank Masters.

But, more than this, the thought of Frank Masters himself was oppressive. The picture of someone with so much, not only giving and giving abundantly of what he had, but getting up, in Dr. Diana's expressive phrase, "on his own two feet" and doing what needed to be done in this world, made him feel simply inadequate.

He decided, in spite of D.S.P. Naik, to seek refuge in his office and try to pull himself together and decide what to do. As the truck approached the headquarters building he leant forward and told the driver he would get out where they were. The man shrugged and stopped for him. Ghote waited on the pavement till the Dodge was well out of sight and then set off towards the office on foot. It had occurred to him that he stood a much better chance of reaching the sanctuary of his own little room if he went in by the back way.

He made his way through the jostling crowds on the pavements thinking over and over the details of Frank Masters's life as Dr. Diana had recounted them to him. And suddenly he stopped in his tracks.

A thought had struck him. By going round this back way he was once more avoiding the beggar on the front steps.

He turned and marched back the way he had come and round to the front of the building. At the steps he stopped, took out all the coins in his pocket and selected the largest. He went up to the monotonously whining figure crouched at the edge of the wide steps. And then he stopped again. He plunged his hand into his pocket and brought out a second coin. Quickly he thrust them both into the beggar's grimy paw. The man swept them away out of sight even more quickly.

He did not look at the inspector. His begging whine continued unchanged and unabated.

Ghote crept into the building and up to his room. Although the D.S.P. was nowhere to be seen, he still did not feel very happy. He sat at his desk, but he could not bring himself even to contemplate the complications of his life. He knew that in fact once he did begin to think there was only one thing to work out. D.S.P. Naik had ordered him in the clearest possible terms to prepare a number of witnesses with false statements as a preliminary to getting up the case against Amrit Singh. Well, Amrit Singh might well be guilty. He probably was. But equally——

He stopped himself going on. He must not think about the dilemma. The two equal blank walls would oppress him to desperation.

Almost stealthily he fished the newspaper out from behind his desk. It was at least a way of preventing himself thinking of anything else.

West Silent on Pak Guilt. Many members of the Lok Sabha referred to-day to the sad fact that the world had displayed an incredible indifference to the sufferings of the East Pakistan minorities. There had been some stirrings only when it became known that Christians were also being persecuted by the Pakistanis.

He lowered the paper.

This did not seem to be in the spirit of Frank Masters. On anybody's part. He wondered what he would do about it if he was actually faced with the problem. Ought he perhaps to face himself with it? He could give up his job, give up everything, go to the Pakistan border and by example and exhortation . . .

He thought of Protima and little Ved at home. How would they live if he went off? And were there not problems enough in Bombay? Perhaps having a proper police force in the city was a help even.

Except that the police force was not being at all successful in the case of the wanton murder of Frank Masters.

He tried the paper again.

Guerrillas Active in China. Reports reaching Western capitals speak of serious anti-Government unrest in China. Trouble has broken out in various parts of the country.

If only it was as easy as that. If only your problems really did solve themselves. If only something would happen in the mysterious land on the far side of the Masters case which would solve his problem.

But that was not the way things went.

He skimmed indifferently down the rest of the column.

A group of 400 guerrillas has been causing trouble in Yunnan, according to . . . Corroborating reports of unrest in Canton the Hongkong Tiger Standard *said . . . According to an eye-witness report a special meeting was held.*

"Inspector."

He looked up.

D.S.P. Naik was standing right up close to his desk, looking down at him coldly. Slowly he lowered the paper and tried to stuff it away under his chair.

"Inspector, I do not expect to find my officers idling with the papers and such trash in working hours. A policeman must be a dedicated individual, Inspector. He should be above such trivial nonsense."

Ghote slowly stood up with head bowed.

The D.S.P. regarded him in silence.

Now comes the moment when he asks why I am back here, Ghote thought.

His stomach muscles tightened. He felt sick.

"And Inspector."

"Yes, sir. Yes, D.S.P.?"

"You do not look at all well. There is a distinctly greenish tinge to your complexion. I spoke to you before about the need to take regular exercise. Have you made any arrangements yet? Have you asked the Sports Officer when he can find you a place in a hockey team?"

"No, sir. Not yet, sir."

"Then see to it, Inspector, see to it. There is one thing I will not stand and that is unfitness among my officers. That I will not stand."

And to Ghote's amazement, with those words D.S.P. Naik turned and, wheezing like a dynamo, stumped out of the room.

Ghote straightened his shoulders as the door shut. There was nothing else for it now. He would have to go and see those boys.

: : : :

He hoped he would not find them. The Foundation's clients were supposed to take jobs when they could, and Ghote hoped that this would be a day when all the boys of the gang would be employed somewhere in the city, and that no one would know where. It was possible. It was possible even that they would all choose just this day to drift mysteriously away from the temporary security the Foundation offered. This was something that could happen. He knew that much from his first long, patient night of investigation.

But it had not happened to-day.

The pear-shaped bearer took him with great solemnity round to the boys' dormitory. He did not throw open the door and announce him, but not being able to do so obviously left him feeling uneasy. He salaamed to Ghote with extra deepness as if to put the situation to rights.

The dormitory was simply a large room in the big, rather old, bare bungalow. It may once have been a drawing-room. It would have needed a large, very expensive carpet to cover the big area of floor. Now the heavy tiles were bare, with here and there a black crack snaking jaggedly across them. The only furniture was two ranks of serviceable string beds running down the two long walls. Once there must have been a lot of chairs, sofas, tables to fill the empty echoing space.

On the bed in the farthest corner the whole gang was assembled. At the head, squatting smoking a stub of cigarette, was Edward G. Robinson in the dignity of his tattered black jacket. At the foot, comfortably upside down, was Tarzan, resting on the nape of his neck with his bare legs running up the wall. The others lounged between them, half on the floor, half on the creaking bed.

Before Ghote said anything he held a quick debate with himself. Should he or should he not talk in the film American he had used before? It had worked then, but he had a strong feeling that he had over-rated its success. After all, Edward G. had behaved very badly over helping Krishna Chatterjee when he had attempted to get away. It was no thanks to the boy that he had not disappeared entirely.

On the other hand, there was the fact that Amrit Singh had not been warned off. Edward G., with his mysterious appearance when the big Sikh had entered the compound, had even seemed to be on Ghote's side.

Ghote abruptly came to a decision.

It was not good enough. He was a police officer. He was not going to hang on every whim of a dirty, cheeky little street urchin like that.

"Yes," he said sharply, "you are the boys I wanted to see."

Edward G. removed the butt from between his crinkled lips with finicking care and blew out a cloud of rank smoke.

"Now, you listen to me carefully," Ghote said. "It seems you do not realise what has happened in this house where you are treated so well. Mr. Masters has been murdered. That is no joking matter."

He looked at them severely.

It was difficult to be sure whether Edward G. did or did not make some tiny movement of command. Possibly Tarzan simply took it into his head himself. But whichever way it was, he lazily but with plain intent swung his wiry legs round and moved them pointedly apart in a gesture which could only indicate the lewdest contempt for the inspector and everything he had to say.

Ghote ran forward and delivered a stinging blow with his open palm on the boy's lean thigh.

Tarzan took absolutely no notice.

"Now, look——" Ghote began to shout.

And then he pulled himself together. After all, what he wanted from these boys was co-operation. And this was certainly the wrong way to go about it. Whether he really did want them to co-operate as fully as D.S.P. Naik had ordered, he did not know. But he was at least going to do everything he ought.

He decided to approach the matter obliquely.

"You must tell more about the message to Amrit Singh," he said. "It is not clear how he came to know that Mr. Masters had found the smuggled gold and locked it in the dispensary."

He reflected that this was true enough. That whole part of the business, he had hoped, would have made itself clear after Amrit Singh had been arrested. Now it would form a very useful introduction to the subject of "witnessing" the big Sikh actually take the poison from the dispensary.

He glanced at the boys. For the most part their faces were stony. He might as well have not been there. Only Tarzan appeared to react at all. He slowly lowered his legs and swung himself round till he was sitting upright with his back to the inspector. That was something.

"Come on," Ghote said sharply. "I want answer."

Still the boys said nothing. Edward G. puffed intently at the stub of cigarette. Ghote addressed him directly.

"And from you," he said, "I want explanation. Your behaviour when I was questioning Mr. Chatterjee was deplorable."

"I had to give the sucker a chance," Edward G. said casually. "Guess I had my fun with him. So now I help."

"What do you mean 'sucker'?" Ghote said. "Mr.

Chatterjee is a very important person. He is charged with great responsibilities for your welfare. How dare you speak of him in such terms?"

"If the guy's a sucker, he's a sucker," Edward G. explained with tired patience.

"He is social worker."

"Brother, you said it."

Ghote tried another tack.

"When I have gone to great trouble for you boys," he said, "that is hardly the reward I expect."

Edward G. slipped off the bed and walked across the room. Ghote turned to watch him. The boy kept silent. He crouched on the floor in the opposite corner and began scuffling at the broad tiles. Ghote could not quite make out what he was doing. He spoke sharply.

"Well, I am waiting for explanation."

Edward G. answered without turning round.

"Listen, fella, you are a cop. You don't get treated nice. Get it?"

"But I have been better to you than a policeman might be," Ghote argued.

For a little Edward G. did not bother to reply. Ghote saw that he had succeeded in prising up one of the tiles. Now he dipped his hand into a hole under it. Only when he had secured a crisp and shiny packet of American cigarettes did he say anything.

"Listen, fella, when the cops have got something to give, they get something too. When it's nix, it's nix."

"In this world it should not be get, get, get only," Ghote said fiercely. "Sometimes it should be give. I am going to ask you to give."

Edward G. replaced the tile and tapped it into place with the heel of his bare foot.

"Mister," he said, "for give you have come to the wrong guy."

He dropped his hands to his sides and stood in front of the inspector. Ghote looked at him. The bare feet, the bare thin legs, streaked with dirt, the battered and filthy pair of shorts hardly kept up round the desperately thin waist, the bare chest with the remains of the black plastic jacket hanging from the shoulders above, the diseased and wrinkled old man's face on the boy's head. No, he had indeed come to the wrong guy for giving.

He felt confused.

All he could do was to plough on. He was a policeman. He had received clear and categorical orders from his superior officer. All he could do was to carry them out to the very best of his ability.

"I have come to discuss your evidence when we make arrest for the murder of Frank Masters," he said.

The boy could not prevent a quick dart of interest.

"You must know who it is we are going to arrest," Ghote went on.

"It would take more policemen than you have got to get Amrit Singh out of the Morton Road place," Edward G. said.

"We shall see about that," Ghote answered quickly. "You boys need not think that the police come out worst every time. Your friend Amrit Singh may be pretty tough, but we are not so weak."

He puffed out his chest a bit. It was important that the gang should be taken in by this boast. Otherwise they would realise they had let slip where Amrit Singh was hiding.

"Oh," said Edward G., his crinkled face splitting with delight, "I would like to see Amrit Singh taking you apart, Inspectorji. Oh, that would be good to see."

"But you will not," said Ghote. "You will see your friend Amrit Singh in handcuffs before too long. We shall find him all right wherever he is."

The boy was after all only a boy. Ghote had no difficulty in detecting the faint look of relief in the wrinkled face at the thought that he had not really given away the Sikh thug's hiding place.

"Now," Ghote went on, "it is when we have arrested

that you boys will come into the picture. It is a question of evidence."

He saw them look at one another with open uneasiness.

"Well," he said sharply to Edward G., "you have important evidence to give. You were the one who saw Amrit Singh go into the dispensary where the poison was kept. It will be your duty to state that fact in court."

"Mister," said Edward G., casually taking out one of the American cigarettes, "I ain't going to court."

"You are," Ghote said. "You will be called as witness. It is too late now."

"You call away, mister."

"We would do more than call. If you did not come by yourself, you would come in handcuffs."

Ghote thought again of how he had threatened to use handcuffs before and how ridiculous he had felt when the boy had held out his stick-like wrists. But perhaps he had been wrong to have allowed himself to be influenced by the thought of the ridiculousness of the situation. After all, D.S.P. Naik expected him to get his witnesses and if this was the only way . . .

"You would have to find first," Edward G. said.

"We would find," said Ghote. "But now it is a question of just what you would say in court."

"I would say nothing, mister."

Ghote decided to ignore this persistent line.

"You know," he said, sitting down on the edge of the string bed next to the one the boys were lounging on, "you know, we have to be very careful about the way we tell the truth when it comes to court. This is one of the difficulties a policeman faces."

The boys received this insight into another kind of life with stoicism.

"Yes," Ghote went on, "it is all very well to come out with the simple truth. But the defence employs lawyers. Very clever lawyers. If we are not careful, they can make the simple truth look like simple lies."

"That is bad," Edward G. stated.

Ghote began to wonder if after all he was not beginning to make contact again. Perhaps all that was needed was to show that even a policeman had his difficulties.

He sighed.

"It is hard for us," he said. "Very hard. We would like to tell the truth just as it happened. But if that will not be believed, what are we to do? That is why sometimes we have to——"

He stopped and searched for an analogy which might make it clearer to his audience.

"Sometimes we have to polish up the truth a bit," he said. "You know, like you polish up a brass ornament so that it shines and everybody can see that it is what it is."

Edward G. Robinson puffed out a long conical cloud of tobacco smoke. The rich smell of best American tobacco.

"Hey, Tarzan," he said, "go and polish the ornaments, boy. They ain't shining too good."

The joke was extremely successful with the other members of the gang. They lay on their backs, kicked their legs in the air, and roared with laughter.

Ghote frowned.

"That was to give you a general idea of what I meant," he said. "You do not have to have ornaments to understand."

But the boys went on laughing. Only when they had stopped did Edward G. answer.

"You want me to fake some evidence?" he said. "How much you going to pay, copper?"

Ghote's heart sank.

He had not expected this. Somehow it had been in his head all along that he would have the greatest difficulty in persuading Edward G. to agree with the Deputy Superintendent's plan. And now it looked as if he had known from the start what Ghote would be bound to ask and would be only too pleased to agree, if the price was right.

"It is only a question of stating what we know to be true," Ghote said. "We know Amrit Singh poisoned Mr.

Masters. You yourself saw him go into that dispensary. You were too far away to see him take the jar of poison down and take some of the powder out, but if you had been looking through the window you would have seen."

"Oh, but I did see, mister," Edward G. said.

X

Inspector Ghote stood on the bare tiles of the clients' dormitory of the Masters Foundation and gaped. On the string bed in front of him the boy called Edward G. Robinson sat with his legs tucked underneath him and his half-smoked, fat American cigarette dangling from the puckered lips of his raddled and diseased face. There was a look of utter candour in his eyes.

"You saw Amrit Singh take the poison?" Ghote said incredulously. "You actually saw in the dispensary hut and Amrit Singh went over to a cupboard and took some of the poison?"

His thoughts were wild. Shooting through them all was the feeling of maddening irony. He had contemplated disobeying the orders of a superior officer so as to avoid persuading this boy to say falsely he had seen the Sikh thug steal the poison. And all along the boy had actually watched him do it and had chosen to keep silent.

Mixed with this were surges of plain fury. Why had the little devil taken it into his stupid head to say nothing about going up to the window of the dispensary hut when he had been on watch at the bottom of the compound?

The fury might have over-ridden everything else, except for one thing. Amid all the inconsequent jumble in his head, Ghote could not entirely suppress a strain of growing triumph. Never matter how it had come out, the fact remained that he had now got his evidence against Amrit Singh. And he had got it without cheating. Here was something he could put up in court without the least hesitation, and it was something which by all the laws of reason and justice should hang Amrit Singh. At one stroke he would have ended the career of the biggest thorn in the side of the police department and at the same time have solved the murder of the biggest foreign benefactor in the whole city of Bombay.

But under the whirl and tumble of these thoughts another strain lay.

Ghote took a step nearer the boys on the bed and looked hard down at Edward G.

" You saw him take the poison," he said, " the poison in the little blue jar?"

Edward G. looked up at him, candid-eyed as ever.

" Oh yes, Inspector sahib," he said, " from the little blue jar. I saw with my own eyes."

Ghote stepped back.

The smashed fragments of the brown glass jar on which the Fingerprint Bureau had failed to find a single print belonging to Amrit Singh formed a picture in his mind as clearly as if they were laid out at that moment on the cracked tiles of the dormitory.

: : : :

Ghote might have persisted. Edward G.'s evasion had not solved his dilemma. If anything it had sharpened it. It was plain that, if the boy was happy to invent a story about seeing Amrit Singh steal the poison just to annoy, then in fact he certainly had not crept up to the window of the dispensary when the big Sikh had been in there.

So D.S.P. Naik's orders to secure witnesses who would swear to seeing this happen were all the more difficult to obey.

Ghote had just reached this conclusion when the stately bearer who had escorted him to the dormitory reappeared.

" Inspector sahib," he said, with a salaam worthy of the bare room's days of former glory.

" What is it?" Ghote snapped at him.

The man's unvarying solemnity invited insults.

"Telephone, Inspector sahib. If you would be so good as to step this way."

Unpuncturable, it seemed.

As the inspector followed him through the bungalow, he turned to hoping it was so.

He picked up the telephone.

A fearful wheezing could be heard on the other end of the line. D.S.P. Naik. Ghote's heart sank. If I was unpleasant to that bearer, he reflected wryly, I have been punished for it soon enough.

"Inspector Ghote here," he said into the telephone.

"Ah, Inspector. You have got the boys all right?"

Ghote hesitated an instant.

"I have just been interviewing, D.S.P.," he said.

Two prolonged wheezes. And then the D.S.P. spoke again.

"Interviewing, yes. But making sure of evidence, what about that?"

It was at this moment that Ghote took a decision.

"I do not think you would have to worry about that, D.S.P.," he said.

He spoke the words with every ounce of conviction that he could muster.

"Good man. Good. Then get after Amrit Singh and bring him in."

"I am seeing to that, D.S.P."

"And, Inspector."

"Yes, sir?"

"Do not forget I would like to hear you are getting some decent exercise. Hockey, Inspector."

"Yes, D.S.P."

Ghote put down the receiver.

There was nothing else for it now. He would have to find out who had murdered Frank Masters before D.S.P. Naik realised that the boys were not going to provide doctored evidence. And his next step in that event was clear. Thanks to what Edward G. had let slip he could at least get hold of Amrit Singh.

And he now had a weapon to use, of a sort. If D.S.P. Naik was prepared to have the Sikh arrested on the evidence as it stood, then at least the threat of using that arrest was ready at hand.

Ghote straightened his shoulders.

: : : :

It was late that day, however, before the inspector came face to face with Amrit Singh again, and when he did so it was in circumstances that he would have preferred to have been different.

He had the name Morton Road to go by and nothing else. He could have asked around at headquarters to find out whether Amrit Singh had a known hide-away there. But he had learnt his lesson from D.S.P. Naik discovering his proposed plans over the ambush at the Masters Foundation. It was no use talking: he had to act on his own.

Morton Road, for all its solid English name, proved to be a very ramshackle thoroughfare in North Bombay. It ran in fits and starts for nearly half a mile north from Foras Road. Ghote set off to walk its whole length, keeping an eye wide open for any sign of Amrit Singh's presence. One trip along its length convinced him that he had set himself a hard task. There were dozens of tall, narrow houses with dark uninviting doorways and little open-fronted shops on the ground floors, their high shelves crammed with a huge miscellany of cheap goods and little boys scrambling up monkey-fashion to serve the customers. Here and there were courtyards, which could reasonably come under the description of "the Morton Road place," even if they were not strictly on the street. Amrit Singh could be anywhere. It was all disreputable enough.

From decaying balconies from which fluttered long strips of many-coloured drying saris, street-girls looked down calling to likely customers. At doors here and there stood heavily-muscled men idly swinging hefty sticks and interrogating the occasional hang-dog visitor.

When he got to the far end Ghote almost decided to give up and go and see what was known about Amrit Singh's

Morton Road place at headquarters. But the thought of how easily the D.S.P. might get to know that his orders had not been carried out finally persuaded him to try again.

There was a small hotel on the top corner of the street, an uninviting place smelling of South Indian food and stale coffee, obviously designed to catch the unwary arrival at the nearby Central Station. The proprietress, a big, shapeless, very dark woman with bright betel-stained lips, made no objection to him taking a room for the rest of the day. As she shut the flimsy door and left him he heard her chuckling hoarsely as she waddled downstairs. He quickly took off all his clothes except for a cotton vest and his trousers. It was easy enough to find plenty of dust to smear over these two garments to make them look inconspicuous enough for the area.

He located a back way out and a minute later was idling down the crowded and dirty street with the acrid smell of smoke, spices and ordure in his nostrils and in his ears the clashing sounds of shouted conversations in half a dozen languages, blaring radios and assorted musical intruments.

He stopped at a small eating stall and ordered tea. Sitting on the creaky wooden bench, nursing his brass tumbler between his two hands, he listened to the talk of other customers. And sure enough he had not been there much more than twenty minutes when he heard the name Amrit Singh.

He turned slowly and looked at the stall owner, a tall bald-headed man with the predatory nose of a vulture. It was evident from the glitter in his close-set eyes that he knew who was being talked about and was following the conversation with interest.

The two customers who had mentioned the Sikh were at the far end of the stall from Ghote and he could not, without drawing more attention to himself than he would have liked, get near enough to hear more than a murmur of what they were saying. But he was happy enough to have got a smell of the trail as quickly as this.

Some ten minutes later he called the stall holder over

and asked for something to eat. When the man came back he beckoned him close.

"I have heard that this street is a good place for certain things," he said.

The bald head ducked a little nearer him.

"I have a friend who has a friend somewhere near here called Amrit Singh," Ghote went on.

Into the close-set eyes came a look of calculation. Ghote put his hand into the pocket where he had put all his money and other possessions before leaving the corner-hotel. He took out two rupees.

"I would very much like to see Amrit Singh," he said. "I hear he would have something for me. But unfortunately my friend is away and I do not know where to go."

The bald-headed, bird-of-prey stall holder shook his head. Ghote tried a little more money.

"Amrit Singh is a very dangerous man," the stall holder said.

Ghote shrugged his shoulders.

"Perhaps I shall find what I want somewhere else," he said.

"It is very likely," said the man.

But in the several hours that followed Ghote got no further clues. Then as he was leaving a paan-shop, where he had spent a good deal of time negotiating over a twist of black tobacco before bringing Amrit Singh's name into the conversation, a beggar reclining propped on the shop's stacked wooden shutters with a great balloon of swollen leg laid out in front of him plucked at his trouser leg.

Ghote nearly went straight past. But the memory of Frank Masters and his new resolves stopped him. He felt for a coin small enough not to attract attention and put it in the man's hand.

"You want Amrit Singh?" the beggar said, a meandering grin appearing on his puffy and blotched face.

Ghote's heart thumped.

"You know where he is?" he said. "I have been sent with a very important message, but I cannot find him."

The beggar laughed for a little bit.

"Many messages for Amrit Singh," he said.

A trickle of saliva escaped from his loose lips.

"Where can he be found?" Ghote asked.

He was beginning to be afraid that the man was not intelligent enough to give him a clear answer.

But his fears were unjustified.

The beggar pointed with the length of gnarled stick he had to act as a crutch.

"In that courtyard just past the street tap."

Ghote looked in the direction the wavering stick was pointing. The courtyard entrance was dark as pitch although the sky, or what could be seen of it in the gap between the tall houses, was still filled with light.

Ghote gave the beggar another coin, a large one, and hurried off. The man's hiccuppy chuckles followed him.

At the entrance to the courtyard Ghote stopped. He was in something of a quandary. It was a good bet that Amrit Singh was there to be found, and he very much wanted to be sure of him. But when he had him he wanted to have the upper hand, and, dressed the way he was, by now a good deal grubbier and sweatier than when he had left the little hotel, he could not see himself playing the assured police inspector. Yet if he went back and got his clothes the beggar, or someone else, might warn the big Sikh. And even approaching a house in such a district looking like a policeman was liable to send all the inhibitants scuttling out by a back way.

It was this last thought which decided him. He plunged forward into the thick darkness of the courtyard entrance.

Beyond, the place was lighter again. The pale blue sky looked down into the yard and it was easy to see the several doorways that led into it. Ghote chose the first and made his way over to it. There was a narrow hallway with the slumped figure of a man wrapped in a whitish cloth fast asleep on the floor. Ghote pushed at him with his foot till he stirred. Then he crouched down beside him and spoke sharply.

"Amrit Singh? Where is Amrit Singh?"

"What do you want with Amrit Singh?"

It was not the stirring figure wrapped in the sheet that spoke. The voice came from behind Ghote and at the same time he felt a hard hand clamp firmly down on the nape of his neck.

He slipped forward over the half-sleeping figure and attempted to wriggle to the side.

An instant later he was dangling upright, his feet off the ground and a pair of locked arms tightly round his waist.

But for all his slightness of build, Ghote was not the sort to be caught like this. One sharp, well-judged backwards kick and he was free. He wheeled sharply round, crouching lightly on the balls of his feet ready for a throw.

And without the least warning felt another pair of arms clamp round his chest.

He was lifted up and suddenly jabbed hard down. The force of the unexpected jerk sent a spasm of pain shooting up from his left heel. For an instant he lost consciousness.

When he came to it was to find that the sleeping man at the foot of the stairs had disappeared. In his place stood his first attacker, a huge creature wearing only a loincloth and a turban. Ghote could see his bare chest gleaming in the dim light, with the muscles standing out like great coils.

The man thrust his face close up to the inspector's in a wave of bad breath and garlic.

"What do you want with Amrit Singh?"

"I have business with him," Ghote said. "Private business."

Behind him the man who was pinioning him gave him a sudden sharp shake.

"What business?" said the big, bare-chested man.

"I want to see Amrit Singh," Ghote repeated.

The big man drew back his clenched fist. His eyes, sunk in the heavy flesh of his face, were shining with sharp excitement.

"What is this? Why, it is my old friend, Ghote."

Behind the heavy face and glittering eyes there appeared

the luxuriantly curling beard, the jutting eyebrows, the bulky turban of Amrit Singh himself.

"Hallo, Inspector," he said. "This is most pleasant You have come to visit only? I did not know you knew my poor home."

He gave a little flick of his head and Ghote found himself standing on his own feet again. A dull pain spread up from his left heel.

"But I have found you out," he said to the big Sikh.

Amrit Singh laughed.

"Come up, come up, Inspector," he said.

He turned and marched easily up the stairs. Ghote followed. He was limping badly, and at the turn of the stairs when he put his foot down awkwardly an involuntary groan escaped him.

"I hope those fellows did not treat you badly," Amrit Singh said. "They are rough men only. But good-hearted."

He chuckled to himself in the ever-increasing gloom of the stairway.

Below Ghote could hear the two good-hearted fellows grumbling to each other in mutters.

Amrit Singh opened a rickety door. A beam of light came out. Ghote blinked.

"Come in, come in," Amrit Singh said.

Ghote entered. He saw at once that the place was a speakeasy. The room was bare except for two hard wooden chairs placed almost in the middle of the floor and a sagging bed in one corner. Protecting an inner doorway was a crude wooden counter on which stood half a dozen thick, dirty glasses and a hair-oil bottle half full of heavy brown liquid. Behind the counter was a weary-looking man with a thick growth of beard and a little bright blue Christian medal hanging from a thin chain in the gap where his stained red check shirt was open to the navel. Sitting on the floor beside the two chairs were three young men. They looked a good deal cleaner than their surroundings. Two of them wore *kurtas* of fine white cloth and the third had a bush-shirt of dull blue silk and a gold chain round his neck. As Ghote entered he was leaning forward towards his two companions with a dreamy, ecstatic look on his face reciting poetry.

None of the three took any notice as Amrit Singh strode round behind the rough counter, shouldered the bar tender aside and led Ghote through a jangling glass-beaded curtain into the inner room.

This was as bare as the outer one, furnished only with two beds facing each other on opposite walls about six feet apart. A small electric light bulb dangled from the ceiling. There was no fan. By way of decoration there was a religious motto in a wooden frame painted silver.

Amrit Singh flung himself back on one of the beds and lay resting his thickset frame against the damp-patched wall. He said nothing, but rested there uttering an occasional grunted chuckle. Ghote sat on the edge of the bed opposite. He decided to leave the Sikh to make the first move.

He read the motto on the wall. " Love thy neighbour as thyself." The frame hung askew.

Eventually Ghote came to the conclusion that there was no point in not speaking after all the difficulties he had had in getting there.

" Why did you poison Frank Masters?" he said.

Amrit Singh did not stir a muscle.

" Inspector," he answered, " I hoped you would have decided not to speak more about that."

" You were in the compound of the Masters Foundation the night Mr. Masters died," Ghote said.

The Sikh's eyes twinkled.

" But will your witnesses say that in court?" he asked.

Ghote paused for an instant. The time had come.

" They will say more," he replied. " They will say they watched you enter the dispensary hut. They will say they crept up to the window and saw you go to the cupboard where the poison was kept, open the jar and take out enough to kill Frank Masters."

The Sikh's eyes ceased to twinkle.

"And who will say that?" he demanded.

Ghote smiled a little.

"Do you think I will tell and let you threaten them into silence?"

"There would be no need. They would be lying. In court they would break down."

"We will see."

Ghote felt a flicker of the hunter's excitement. Amrit Singh was coming up with the predictable responses. He would hardly expect him to go down on his knees and babble out a confession straight away. But along this path lay what might amount in the end to an admission. Certainly enough of one to let Ghote feel that the Sikh was being arrested with good cause.

He stayed silent. And as he had expected Amrit Singh was unable to let the conversation drop.

"So you have witnesses that I was seen to go into that hut?" he said.

"One of them you know," said Ghote. "We will take steps to see Sonny Carstairs gives evidence that you made him hand over the key."

The Sikh gave a single grunt of a laugh.

"Sonny Carstairs," he said. "I would like to see him in court."

"You will."

"But evidence I had the key is not evidence that I went into the hut."

"We have that."

"And evidence that I went into the hut is not evidence that I took the poison."

Ghote could not stop himself hesitating fractionally. But it was fractionally only.

"We have that evidence also," he said.

A faint smile lifted the Sikh's full lips in the deep jungle of his beard.

"That is strange," he said. "Because that at least I did not do."

Ghote pounced.

"You entered the hunt then?" he said.

Amrit Singh's eyebrows rose.

"You had evidence?"

"We have evidence for more than that."

The Sikh shook his head.

"Not for me taking the poison," he said.

Suddenly he swung to his feet. Ghote instinctively tautened up.

The Sikh laughed.

"Oh, Inspector, if it was going to be like that, would I have told my man downstairs to let you go?"

He paced up and down the little room a few times.

Then he stopped and looked down at Ghote.

"I will tell you what happened," he said.

He shrugged.

"Why not? You can be sure later I will deny."

He sat down on the bed opposite the inspector again. This time crouching eagerly forward.

"Last Friday afternoon," he said, "I came back here from some business in Hyderabad and there was a message waiting. It said that that Frank Masters of yours had found some gold in his bungalow and that he had taken it and locked it in the dispensary hut."

Ghote leant forward another inch.

"I knew Frank Masters," the Sikh went on. "I knew he might lock away the gold while he thought whether to tell that his favourite boys were smugglers only. So, although I did not expect gold there that day, I went."

Ghote's brain was seizing on each driblet of this story, especially these hints about Frank Masters himself, and pounding at them like a hammer.

The Sikh shrugged his massive shoulders.

"It was possible," he said. "That boy may be very good at standing on his head but he is not very sensible. No matter. I went to the Masters Foundation. I knew all about that hut and that it was the one safe place to lock away anything. So I slipped up to the house, climbed a drainpipe, went along the roof and had a little talk with your good Sonny Carstairs in that room of his."

He found the recollection very amusing.

At last he went on.

"Then I went back and went into the hut. I did not think I was seen, but it is never possible to be sure. That is why it is important to have good lawyers, even though it is expensive."

He laughed again.

And suddenly sobered up. He got to his feet and stood towering over the inspector.

"I went into that hut," he said. "I looked everywhere for the gold. There was nothing there. I went out of the hut."

His deep-set eyes were glowing fiercely.

He turned away.

"I thought the message must have been a mistake," he said. "Such things happen. And when I asked it was indeed too hard to find who had sent it first."

Ghote felt a gradually spreading sense of depression. Why had the Sikh told him all this, unless it was actually the truth? Or was it just some of the truth? Some, but not the vital last piece? Had Amrit Singh detected that hesitation before he claimed that the police had evidence for the actual theft of the poison? And then had he invented this plausible tale?

"That was a very interesting story," he said slowly.

"Oh, Inspector," said the big Sikh, "you are not going to arrest me, a confessed gold smuggler?"

"A confessed smuggler and not a confessed murderer," Ghote said.

"You want a lot, my little inspector."

Ghote urged himself on a step.

"I have got good evidence," he said.

The Sikh smiled.

"No evidence is good that is made for the occasion," he replied. "It may look good now, but after it has been dragged through the courts it will look different, I can tell you."

"We will see," said Ghote levelly.

Suddenly a deep glint of malicious humour appeared in the Sikh's eyes.

"And we will see how Krishna Chatterjee looks in the witness box," he said.

Ghote's heart felt filled with lead. So Amrit Singh had somehow found out that shortly after his own visit to the dispensary the little Bengali had followed in his footsteps. And it was easy to imagine what a poor showing someone as timid, scrupulous and suggestible as Mr. Chatterjee would make at the hands of the sort of lawyers Amrit Singh used.

In no time at all they would have him plainly labelled as a murderer. And they might well be right. After what the inspector had just heard from Amrit Singh he really believed at this moment that the almost painfully good social worker had for some reason seen Frank Masters's death as a lesser evil and had put him out of this world from sheer excess of kindness. If only some clue to what that reason was would appear.

And yet, he said to himself, the man standing in front of me here is in real fact a killer. Jovial, happy-go-lucky, but proven in all but the processes of law a murderer.

Ghote let the waves of gloom roll over him.

And, quite unheralded, a flash of light appeared. One single, incautious phrase that the thickset Sikh had used came back into the inspector's head. There might be a way out yet.

XI

It took Inspector Ghote some time to get away from Amrit Singh. The big Sikh offered him the pleasures of an evening at his speakeasy. Ghote found them easy enough to refuse. Amrit Singh suggested his house of ill-fame farther along the street. Ghote pretended to be shocked. At last he consented to take one drink, not from the bar room next door, but from Amrit Singh's personal supply of guaranteed American bourbon.

He endured patiently a number of jokes about policemen drinking smuggled liquor in an illegal drinking den. And at last he got away.

By consent, nothing more was said about the murder of Frank Masters.

Ghote took a risk as soon as he got out of the Sikh's house. He had an unpleasant feeling that the moment his back was turned Amrit Singh would slip out and disappear once more. So he went into the first likely shop he saw and asked if they had a telephone. He rang headquarters and in the most discreetly garbled way he arranged for a new watch to be put on the Sikh. As he had expected, the duty telephonist was incredibly slow to understand, and before the talk was finished it must have been plain to the listening shop man that Ghote was not the grubby passer-by he seemed.

Growing more anxious with every minute, he waited outside the shop till he saw a pair of constables, looking distinctly apprehensive, appear some way down the ill-lit street. Then he hurried back to the seedy corner-hotel, so tired now that he could hardly stand. Luckily the place also ran to a telephone. He called Protima and said briefly that he would not be home that night. She sounded sleepy. But before the latent anger in her voice had had time to spark out he rang off.

Something more to attend to when he had time. There was the matter of D.S.P. Naik's game of hockey, too, if it came to that. He flopped down on the grimy bed, felt the pain in his left heel ease a bit and fell fast asleep.

: : : :

He woke early next morning. As he had expected, he was pretty badly bitten by bugs. But nothing worse had happened. His clothes were still there. His pockets had not been rifled. His heel hurt much less. He bathed and dressed and went out.

He made his way as quickly as he could to the Masters Foundation and presented himself once more at Krishna Chatterjee's little narrow book-lined office.

The Bengali social worker had his head studiously bent over a hectically jacketed American work. He looked up as Ghote came in and at once grew very serious.

"Inspector," he said.

His face got steadily more sombre.

"Yes," he said. ""I am ready to come."

He stood up. For a second or two he searched over the cluttered surface of his desk and then he picked up a piece of white card closely covered with notes in black ink, underlined here and there in red. He put it down carefully on the open page of the wide-margined American book. Then he took it up again.

"I suppose it will be no use marking the place after all," he said. "A gross superfluity."

He looked down at the card with its close lines of neat handwriting. His big, almond-shaped eyes seemed to fill with tears.

Ghote suddenly felt wretched.

"It may be a long time before—before this whole affair is over," he said. "These things often take years even. Put in your bookmark."

He coughed.

"But nevertheless I must do my duty."

"Yes," said Krishna Chatterjee.

He stood silently by the crowded desk. After a moment

or two he picked up the card of notes, slipped it hurriedly into place and slammed the book closed. Then he stood silent again, looking at the book-crammed larder shelves of his cubbyhole almost caressingly.

Ghote cleared his throat.

"Perhaps you would prefer to tell here," he said.

"Tell?" said Mr. Chatterjee. "What is there to tell?"

Ghote looked at him.

"But it is necessary to make a full statement," he said. "If you want to confess."

It was Mr. Chatterjee's turn to look surprised.

"To confess?"

"Yes. You said you were ready to come."

Suddenly the round-cheeked Bengali's face was transformed. From a picture of utter dolefulness it changed in an instant to one of helplessly lost, giggling merriment.

"Good gracious me," he said. "Oh, my dear fellow, what a mistake I have made. A most comical error, most truly comical."

Ghote felt a surge of irritation.

"What error is this?" he said sharply.

Krishna Chatterjee wiped his eyes with the back of a plumpish hand.

"A quite simple error," he said, "but of major proportions, I assure you. You see, I was not offering to make a confession: I was saying simply that I thought you had come to arrest me, and that if I had to go I was ready."

The simple misunderstanding appeared to break in on him again in its full ludicrousness. A new fit of high-pitched giggles assailed him.

Ghote looked at him.

And bit by bit his irritation succumbed. Abruptly a giggling laugh welled up in his chest. A moment or two later he had his arm round the Bengali's bent shoulders laughing almost as heartily.

"You were quite right," he said, drawing breath hard. "Quite right. A ridiculous misunderstanding. I came for quite another reason too."

" You did not come about the murder even?" Mr. Chatterjee asked.

" Not directly about the murder," Ghote said.

" Oh no, this is too much."

Once more the plump little Bengali was reduced to helpless tittering.

" What was it then?" he asked, looking up at Ghote expectantly, as if whatever he said was bound to be even more ridiculously amusing.

" Oh, it was nothing. A small thing only."

Mr. Chatterjee managed to subdue his giggles almost to silence.

" Inspector, if there is anything I can do to help, you have to ask only."

Ghote pulled himself together.

" It is a small thing," he said. " But it is to a certain extent important."

Into his mind came the line of hard thought that had led him here. The casual remark made by Dr. Diana that she had hopes of reforming the boy Tarzan because they knew his home background, that he was from a fishing family. Added to this Amrit Singh's presence here at the Masters Foundation, and Amrit Singh's interest among many other illicit occupations in smuggling. Tack on to this that Ghote knew, as every Bombay policeman did, that the city was one of the big routes for bringing gold from the Middle East, where a little tola ingot might be worth fifteen American dollars, into currency-starved India, where the same tola would be worth the equivalent of forty dollars. Then add one thing more. The incautious word that Amrit Singh had let slip the day before. The phrase about it being possible that gold had been brought into the Foundation without his own knowledge because the boy who was good at standing on his head was not also very sensible.

And now had come the time to play for all it was worth this hunch that Tarzan and his fishing family were a key link in the gold smuggling chain.

" Just a small thing," he said. " I happened to hear that you know where the boy they call Tarzan lives. You know the boy? It would be most helpful if I could have his address."

Krishna Chatterjee had stopped laughing too.

" Certainly we have his address, Inspector," he said. " There is rather an unfortunate family situation there. The boy's mother died and the father took——"

Mr. Chatterjee looked the inspector full in the face.

" Well," he said bravely, " there is no point in mincing words. He took a paramour."

He sighed.

" There was considerable ill-feeling, of course," he said. " But at least we have the facts to work on. Facts which I know on this occasion to be true. Yes, on this occasion."

Again he sighed heavily and contemplated the difficulty of arriving at facts which would in the end prove true when dealing with the half-world of young vagrants.

Ghote coughed and looked pointedly at a cluster of card-indexes on one of the long shelves. Mr. Chatterjee followed his glance.

" Yes, quite so," he said.

He sat down at his desk.

" Unfortunately, however, Inspector," he said, " I cannot let you have the address."

" But you said you had it."

" Quite so, yes. Yes, we have it. It is there in that index. Under 'T.' We have been reduced to filing it under the name the boy prefers to use. Lamentably unscientific."

" Yes, yes," Ghote said. " But did you say I could not have the address?"

" But of course I did."

" But why? Why?"

Krishna Chatterjee drew himself up on the little hard chair behind the cluttered desk.

" Inspector, it is professional ethics."

Ghote gaped.

"But I must have that address," he said.

"I am sorry, Inspector. But absolute confidentiality is the core of the social workers' code."

"But I need that address. It will almost certainly result in the arrest of a major criminal."

"Inspector, I think you do not understand."

"I most certainly do not understand."

"Inspector, it is like this. We have to establish a relationship with our clients. It is of the utmost importance. Crucial, I might say. And to do this it is essential that they can give us their entire and complete trust. So, they must believe that we would not in any circumstances betray anything we have learnt from them."

"All right," Ghote said. "Let this boy believe that. Let him believe anything you choose to tell. But give me that address."

"No. Most regretfully, no."

Ghote felt a pure, burning rage sweeping a clear path before it.

He turned without another word and strode along the narrow book-lined room towards the square of dull red cardboard indexes with their neat rows of little brass handles waiting to be jerked open. He could see the single letter "T" down towards the bottom right-hand corner of the array.

As he reached out to it, the little Bengali's plump hand banged hard across the front panel.

"Inspector, I will not let you."

Mr. Chatterjee wriggled round till he was between Ghote and the wall. He stood upright. The sweat was gleaming on his forehead.

Ghote stood looking at him.

Then he abruptly turned away.

"Very well, Mr. Chatterjee," he said, "if you wish to impede a criminal investigation."

"Inspector, it is a matter of the utmost regret. But, I am sure you will appreciate that a principle is, alas, a principle."

He stayed standing in front of the square of red indexes. Ghote, without another word, stamped out.

And, no sooner had the door of the little office swung to behind him than he took to his heels. On tiptoe he ran out of the big front door, past the corner of the house, through the wilting bushes of the shrubbery and round to the place where Mr. Chatterjee's narrow window looked out on to a prospect of greenery.

There he waited in the deep shadows, with the broad leaves of a hibiscus dappling the sunlight on his face.

He did not have long to wait. A bell sounded fiercely from inside the house. Mr. Chatterjee, whose studiously bent back Ghote had been watching as if mesmerised, pushed himself back from his desk. He looked at his watch. Through the small opening between the two frames of the window Ghote could even hear him say to himself "Tut, tut."

Then he got up and with complete unconcern waddled happily away.

Ghote let one whole minute pass while he considered the strain of almost wild determination Mr. Chatterjee had so unexpectedly shown himself capable of. That and the ease with which the little Bengali could be deceived.

Then he strolled out of the bushes, put his nails into the crack between the two window frames and prised them easily apart. He swung his leg across the sill, ducked his head through and stood up.

He crossed to the set of indexes, reached out for the handle of the one marked "T," flipped through the cards and came across the neatly written name "Tarzan" in no time at all. He read rapidly through the notes written underneath, keeping an ear cocked for noises on the far side of the door, and found that they told him nothing new. Except for the last item. The scrupulously printed address, the simple name of a coastal village and its nearest little town and the terse instruction "Hut nearest sea." He read this twice over and had it by heart. He closed the index, crossed to the window, slipped out, turned and pushed the two frames gently together again and dusted off his hands.

"Nice work, Inspector."

It was the voice of Edward G. Robinson. It could be none other.

Ghote wheeled round. The boy was standing among the bushes in much the same place that he himself had stood to watch Mr. Chatterjee. He must have seen everything.

"What—what are you doing here?" he shouted.

The boy had the grace to look put out.

"I can explain, Inspector. I can explain everything."

Ghote breathed a secret sigh of relief. Perhaps the boy had not understood what he had seen. With luck he had even succeeded in putting the boot on the other foot. The boy was going to be the one to do the explaining.

Ghote advanced towards him with heavy tread.

"Well?" he said. "Let me hear it, and it had better be good."

"I was making sure you didn't steal anything, Inspectorji."

Ghote dived forward, his hands reaching out.

And it was all he could do to save himself from falling head foremost into the soft earth clutching at nothing. From round the corner of the bungalow came a happy laugh.

"And you did not steal."

"I would hope not," Ghote muttered.

"When you could have had a good haul. Not very clever, Mr. Inspector."

: : : :

Yet, some four hours later, approaching the place where the boy Tarzan had his home, Ghote reflected that perhaps after all he had not had such a bad haul. He had got the link he needed in the chain which might well in the end put Amrit Singh behind bars for a good long time on a gold smuggling charge. And that was more than a little.

With a faint frown of uneasiness, he recalled a certain Inspector Patel, a preventive officer of the Customs. He had met him some time ago at a conference on the very subject of gold smuggling, and he had a distinct feeling that he ought to have informed him of what he had learnt about Amrit Singh. This was the sort of thing that made for a lot of bad blood between a State service like the police and a Central one like the Customs.

He shrugged.

After all, it was vitally important to him to be the actual person who put the big Sikh away. Unless he could get him on a major smuggling charge, D.S.P. Naik would want to know why he had not charged him with the murder of the always enigmatic figure of Frank Masters. And doing that was something Ghote was still determined to avoid.

He looked round.

He had come a good distance, some twenty-five miles or more from the centre of Bombay, first by a slow, crowded suburban train and then in an aged tonga drawn by an aged horse. In front of him lay the sea, the wide sweep of the Arabian Sea stretching out into the far, hazy blue distance. Between him and the water's edge was a length of muddy sand littered here and there with the debris of the ocean, shells, sea-smooth stones, the skeletons of fish. Directly behind him was a deep green tangle of lush vegetation, sucking rich life from the low swampy ground.

Ahead he had just made out the dark mounds of a number of huts clustered at the point where the sand gave way to the matted vegetation. They must be what he was looking for. In one of them Tarzan's family would live, the oldish father, the woman Mr. Chatterjee had called the Paramour and one other son, a young man of eighteen.

Ghote advanced carefully, keeping under the shade of the ragged palms at the top of the grey beach. A big bird with long trailing legs and widespread white wings suddenly rose up in front of him and lazily ascended into the pale blue sky.

He felt out of place. His shoes were thick with mud and his legs dragged.

He looked at the little village with its scatter of beached

boats again. Beyond it the shore curved to form a wide creek. In the distance he could see an immense, low railway viaduct cutting across the soft, muddy landscape. He wished he was on a train there, heading steadily and directly back to the city.

But ahead of him lay his only hope of gaining enough time to break the dilemma of whether Krishna Chatterjee or Amrit Singh had been the one to open with a protective piece of cloth the jar of arsenic trioxide in the dispensary hut and tip out some of the contents. If he could only get enough here to hold the Sikh on that major smuggling charge, he would have bought himself just so much extra time. And then he would press and press until at last something cracked and down went one side of the balance once and for all.

He saw now the value of the terse instruction "Hut nearest sea" on Mr. Chatterjee's precious index card. In all the collection of huts, each constructed in almost exactly the same way out of mud bricks slimed over with a greenish growth and precariously roofed with palm leaves, one stood out by being built a good ten yards nearer the wide expanse of the sea than any of the others. And, sure enough, just outside it stood two figures corresponding to two of Tarzan's family, a small wiry man of about fifty and his sturdy young son. They were methodically at work repairing a net hanging between a pair of tall bamboo poles. From time to time the young man straightened his back and turned to gaze out to sea. Once he caught hold of his father by the elbow and pointed to the far horizon where a small smudge of dark smoke showed a distant steamship heading south for Bombay Harbour.

The old man looked at the smoke impassively, glanced up at the sun as if to tell the time and went purposefully back to his net-mending. Ghote wondered whether the Paramour was inside the hut. The old man must have hidden qualities, he thought, to have acquired a mistress when his own appearance and demeanour were so unpromising.

He looked round at the rest of the village noting everywhere the signs of poverty. A youngish woman emerged from one of the huts and came over towards the old fisherman. Ghote looked at her closely. Would she be the Paramour? She wore her sari tucked up hard between her legs in the fisherwomen's fashion so that it showed every outline of her whipcord body. She walked with a decided sway. Ghote found his thoughts beginning to wander.

The woman said nothing to the two men at their net but went through the gap in the tumbledown little fence surrounding the hut, stooped and entered. The inspector wondered whether the time had not come to approach.

Suddenly from inside the thin-walled hut there came a deep burst of laughter. The young woman came hurriedly out clutching a borrowed wooden bowl and an instant later another woman followed her. She was enormous. A great round, shiny face presided over a pyramid of contented chins, which in turn capped a huge wobbling torso culminating in a vast rounded belly and huge shaking hips. And it was immediately apparent from the comfortable way she looked about her that it was she who was the mistress of all she surveyed, the Paramour.

She went over to Tarzan's brother and said something which evidently she found colossally amusing. She jabbed the young man in the ribs to emphasise the humour of the situation. His ribs were well-covered: they needed to be.

At last she decided that her joke had been well and truly dealt with. Still chuckling subterraneously she turned back towards the hut. Ghote broke from cover and approached.

They watched him coming with frank stares. He stopped and asked if they had a young son who had run off to Bombay.

"Oh, that boy, that boy," said the Paramour, lifting her great pudgy arms in a gesture of despair. "What has he done now? There is a devil in him. I know that. A devil, a real devil."

She clapped her thickly fat hands to her massive sides and snorted with laughter.

"Well," Ghote said, "I will not hide from you that he

is causing us a lot of worry. I have come from Bombay to see if I can find the cause."

The Paramour was still laughing at intervals.

"Oh, the cause is easy enough to know," she said. "It is that devil in him. I tell you when first I came to this man——"

She halted herself, waddled heavily over to Tarzan's father and slapped him tremendously on the back. The little wiry fisherman took no notice at all, simply making use of the interruption in his twisting and tying of the threads of his big hanging net to glance once again at the position of the sun in the sky and then at the little lapping waves of the sea as they advanced slowly up the muddy beach.

"When I first came to this man," the Paramour went on, "I took that boy to my heart. Everything of the best I gave him. Milk he had to drink, meat to eat. Never once did I beat him. And you know what he did?"

She swung round on Ghote.

"He tried to run off."

Ghote looked serious. But seriousness was foreign to the Paramour. Abruptly she burst into new guffaws of laughter.

"To run away he tried," she shouted. "And his brother I had to send after him to bring him back, holding his ear."

The thought convulsed her. Her massive sides shook like jelly, her enormous thighs wobbled, her immense bosom heaved in and out.

The brother turned from the net-mending to confirm her story.

"Yes," he said with laboured earnestness, "he ran away from a good home. Of course, I had to bring him back."

He stood thinking for a little.

"I held his ear very hard," he said.

This was a new and delightful matter of amusement to the Paramour. She positively stamped on the loose, greyish sand under her feet in an ecstasy of mirth.

Her little spouse turned and looked at her without moving a muscle of his face. Then he glanced once more at the thin scummy line of the advancing tide and from that to the long curving black craft that lay pulled up on the beach in front of their hut.

"But later the boy ran off again?" Ghote asked.

"Oh, he ran off," said the Paramour, grinning hard. "This time he had reason. After being good to him had been so badly repaid, I started to beat him."

She looked down at her massive forearm.

"I beat good," she said.

She began to titter again.

Unexpectedly Tarzan's father left the half-mended net and came up to Ghote.

"You go," he said.

Ghote looked at him. His face was so unmoving that he could hardly believe he had spoken the two abrupt words.

He did not repeat them, but the jerk he gave to his head was eloquent enough.

"Soon I will have to be off," Ghote said easily. "But first I must learn some more about this boy. Did he have friends in the village, for instance?"

The fisherman turned away and went over to his son. He muttered something that Ghote could not catch and both of them looked out to sea with shaded eyes.

Ghote turned to the Paramour.

"What about the friends?" he said.

She shrugged her huge, well-padded shoulders.

"It is easy to have friends," she said. "You make a joke. They laugh. You laugh. You have friends."

She gave Ghote a hearty slap on his back and burst into a fountain of deep chuckles.

Ghote forced a smile to his lips.

"Does the boy ever come home nowadays?" he asked.

Before the massive Paramour had time to reply, the fisherman again came up to Ghote. This time he pointed in a totally unmistakable way.

"Go. Now."

Ghote nodded and smiled.

"In a minute. In a minute I go. But first it is most important for me to know whether the boy ever comes back here. You know, that is a very important sign to us. Whether the runaway still feels a liking for his old home at times."

The fisherman turned to the Paramour.

"Tell," he said, and jerked his head towards the lean black shape of his boat.

The Paramour raised her two hands in the air.

"He is going fishing again to-day," she said. "Oh, ho, the poor man. Twice in one day sometimes he has to go out on that terrible sea to support his family. And the day after to-morrow is Holi. He will not go to sea on such a holiday, so there is a day lost. And we need money to buy the things for the feast. That is why he must go out to-day again. The poor man, the poor man."

She cascaded into a shower of deep, guttural giggling.

"Ah, it is a hard life," Ghote said.

"Oh, hard, hard, very hard. Before daylight they go out and now they must go again. The catch this morning was so poor, so poor."

She turned a happy smiling face towards the vast spread of the ocean.

Out of politeness, Ghote looked too. And then something distinctly odd caught his eye. The whole beach in front of the little village was littered, he saw, with dozens of tiny fish. Here and there a big seagull would fly up from the sea, sweep gently down and pick one up in its beak. But it was obvious that the birds, bobbing contentedly on the little chopping waves, had had their fill that day. And the litter of fry round Tarzan's father's boat was every bit as noticeable as elsewhere. He had had no poor catch that morning. That was certain.

"Perhaps," Ghote said, "you could tell me the names of the boy's friends in the village here. Often, you know, a boy will tell his friends more than he will tell anyone else."

He slipped a notebook from his pocket, turned over the

pages, perched on a post in the tumbledown fence and sat looking up expectantly.

The fisherman gave his son one short glance of baffled fury and then resumed his habitually dour expression.

The boy came heavily up to Ghote.

" It is not right to come asking questions of poor people," he announced.

Ghote looked up at him.

" But this is in the interests of your brother," he said. " Do you not want to help? I think you could tell me a great deal of what I want to know."

" He ran away," the young man said. " He left his good home. He ought to be put in prison."

He turned on his heel.

His father glanced at him and then looked over at the boat. They went down to it across the soft, unwetted sand of the higher shore and began making sure they had everything needed to put to sea. Ghote turned to the Paramour again.

" Now," he said, " there is no hurry. You think about that boy. Think who used to play with him on the shore. And then one by one tell me the names as they come into your mind."

She grinned and shook her head.

" Oh, I have better things to do," she said. " There is the meal to get for these men. They are always hungry, always eating."

She laughed.

" Then they will not be at sea long?" Ghote asked.

" Long? Long? Who can tell? Who can ever tell with a fisherman? He sets sail when the sea is calm and in a moment the sky darkens and the wind blows, the whirlpools come and he is drowned."

This thought was too much for her composure. She roared with elephantine laughter, bent forward and doubled up as far as her vast bulk would allow.

Ghote waited.

The two men by the boat, without exchanging a word,

began suddenly to push the narrow craft through the sand towards the lapping wavelets. Ghote kept his eyes on the great laughing woman.

"Now you must tell me the names," he said loudly.

The boat had grated its way to the edge of the sea. The fisherman and his son ran round to the stern and bent low to shove it harder.

Ghote leapt to his feet. Still clutching his notebook, he sprinted over the loose, slippery sand.

The boat was afloat now. The fisherman scrambled in over the side. His son stayed at the stern pushing with all his might, the dark greenish water up to the backs of his knees.

Ghote reached the water's edge. He plunged in, shoes and all.

The boy gave a final, wild shove and flung himself into the boat at the back. It glided easily forward over the little chopping waves. Ghote waded on, leaning against the heaviness of the water all around his legs.

He flung himself almost full length. One outstretched hand just made contact with the rough edge of the little vessel at the side somewhere near the prow. He flung his notebook in with the other hand and heaved with all his strength.

The fisherman came towards him along the length of the narrow, swaying craft. Ghote managed to get his other hand on to the boat's side. The fisherman stooped and lifted up a heavy wooden gaff. He leant over Ghote's tightly clutching hands and brought the wooden handle chopping hard down on Ghote's fingers.

Ghote tightened his grip.

His legs were clear of the bottom now. He gave a terrific jerk with them and felt himself shoot through the water. He heaved hard and got his head up to the edge of the little boat, which leant deeply over towards him.

"Let go, let go," the young man shouted. "You will sink the boat. It is wrong to do that."

"I am coming with you," Ghote gasped out.

"No," said the fisherman.

"I am coming. Help me in or I will upset the boat."

He tugged down on the edge of the frail craft as hard as he could. Underneath him he felt the water slipping past his soaking trousers, tugging and pulling.

XII

Suddenly Ghote felt the tugging strain on his arms cease. The unsmiling fisherman and his tubby, self-righteous son had grasped him under the armpits and were carefully easing him over the side of their frail craft. He had won.

Once he was aboard and the danger to the narrow little boat had been averted, the two fishermen let him flop like a sodden sack down near the prow and turned their backs on him. For some minutes he was content that they should do so. He wanted only to be left alone. If he could just have time to ease the wrenched muscles of his arms and sides, he felt, nothing else mattered.

But soon he began to feel better and started to look about him. The fisherman had by now hoisted their tall, thinly triangular white sail, patched here and there with old flour sacks. The wind was beginning to fill it out and send the little boat skimming through the slightly choppy sea, heading out away from the creek and the fishing village towards the distant blue line of the horizon.

Ghote noticed his notebook lying in the bottom of the boat near three plump pomfret left there after the morning's catch. He gently pushed himself off the hard beams of the thin gunwale and reached for it. It was soaked with cold, salty water but looked as if it would be salvageable. He pressed the covers together so that a thin stream of water, slightly blue from ink that had run, trickled out. Then he pushed the wet mass into his pocket, where it thumped heavily against his side.

He lay back and thought.

At least he had achieved his first object. He had stuck close to the two fishermen at what was obviously the start of a trip to pick up something smuggled. The signs had been too plain to be anything else. The trip out to sea at this time of day when the routine was to leave before dawn and come back on the wind that could be relied on to sweep in from the sea during the morning. The two men's obvious keenness to leave at a certain time and to have got rid of him before they went. No doubt some sort of rendezvous had to be kept. The patent excuse of needing extra money because the morning's catch had been poor when these three plump evidently eatable fish had been actually left in the boat.

So now the task was to watch the two of them like a cat to see what it was they had come out to sea to do. One thing was in his favour already. Evidently the old fisherman had decided that in spite of his presence the rendezvous must be kept.

Ghote stretched forward and began trying to wring the heavy seawater out of his trouser legs. In the stern of the narrow boat, cleaving its way swiftly through the little waves, the two fishermen talked together in muttered voices over the long steering oar. Ghote pretended not to notice. It would be hopeless to try to overhear them. The thing to do was to lull their suspicions.

He sat up straighter. The fresh wind, laced with spray, chilled his face. He envied the close-fitting caps the other two wore.

"Well," he said in a loud voice, "I think it is most important to have an idea how a boy like your son would earn his living."

From the other end of the long, narrow boat the old fisherman looked at him sourly.

"Yes," Ghote went on, shouting a little in case his words were being whipped away by the breeze even before they reached the stern of the skiff, "Yes, someone like me has to know just what it feels like to work the way the boys we help will have to."

He warmed to his theme.

"When I saw the very hut the boy lived in," he said, "I realised already much more about him. The damp walls, the palm leaves on the roof. Do they let in the rain?"

For a little he thought his question was going to go unanswered. But the lure of all this pity was too much for Tarzan's brother.

"Yes," he said at last, making his way forward a bit, "always the rain comes in when it is heavy. But we have no money for a better roof. We work so hard. We get up while it is still dark and set out to sea, and then the merchants give us so little for our catch. It is not fair."

Ghote edged along the boat towards him. At the stern his father, taking no notice, threw out a long baited line and watched it unblinkingly.

"This is what I want to hear," Ghote said. "I want to know the way you live. To see how to help your brother. That is why it was so important for me to come out to sea with you."

The young man nodded gravely.

"That boy," he said. "He must not be helped. He has run away from home when he should be working with us. He should be sent to prison."

"But no," said Ghote loudly, carried away by his role as social worker. "That is not the way. When a boy runs off from home, we have to ask what made him do it. To see if we can put that right."

The runaway's brother looked at him solemnly.

"The boy is bad," he pronounced. "He left us. We have to do the work. And we have so little money. Even this boat may be taken from us for the money we have borrowed. He should be locked up."

He tilted his chubby chin and looked away out to the far horizon. In the distance the faint blur of the smoke from the steamer Ghote had noticed before was still visible. The old man hauled in his line. A pomfret was jerking and wriggling on the end of it. He tugged it off the hook and flung it forward.

"Or he should be well beaten," the young man added.

Ghote found nothing more to say.

For some while Tarzan's brother sat where he was, evidently waiting for some further understanding comments on his lot from this heaven-sent professional sympathiser. Ghote let him wait.

Eventually the youngster seemed to realise that the source had dried up. He gave Ghote a sudden glare and made his way, swaying slightly to the narrow boat's motion, to throw out a second line beside his father's in the stern.

He put his head close to the old man's and indulged in a long muttered tirade.

The old man turned and looked at Ghote along the length of the frail boat. He seemed to be weighing him up.

Ghote looked down at the sea slipping past the sides of the craft. A big patch of yellow, sun-bleached seaweed slid up, swept by a yard or two away and slowly disappeared.

The choppy waves began to grow higher and the boat dipped and rose with an unpleasant, regular motion.

The boy put his head near the old man's again and added something to what he had been saying before. It was obviously a forceful plea. The old man shrugged his shoulders and seemed unable to make up his mind. He brought in another flopping, fat pomfret.

The boy added one more sentence. And then brought his clenched fist sharply upwards in an unmistakable punching gesture.

Ghote was unable to prevent himself looking hastily all round. They were far out to sea now. The low coast was barely visible behind them. Beyond it the distant, jagged outline of the Western Ghats could be seen dark grey against the blue of the sky. Ahead and to each side the sea stretched blankly and ominously out, flecked here and there now by a white cap of a wave. Only on the far distant horizon was there a sign of human life, the last tiny smudge of smoke from the rapidly disappearing steamship.

Ghote looked along the length of the skiff at the two fishermen squatting together in the stern. The boy was fattish, but hefty. His father, though lean, was wiry and had a decidedly ugly look to him. If it came to a struggle, the odds would be very much on their side. And even if he won, he would still be left with two prisoners to keep subdued, miles out to sea in a boat he had no notion how to sail. He felt sick.

The son had caught a fish now. As soon as he had dealt with it and baited his line again he once more urged some action. The old man took another searching look at Ghote. The inspector felt very sick. The sweat rose up on his brow in spite of the salt spray which was coming more heavily off the bobbing waves with every moment that passed.

Suddenly Ghote realised that he felt sick for a very good reason. The little boat was bouncing on the waves with altogether too much speed. Much though he wanted to outstare the two fishermen in the stern he had to let himself look downwards into the sea for a moment's respite.

A bladdery, iridescent Portuguese man-of-war sailed by right under his nose, its evil purple filaments trailing out behind. Ghote closed his eyes. But the image remained. He was sick.

He forced himself up and glared down the boat at the two others.

Only to see in the eye of the impassive old man a glint which was purely and unmistakably sardonic. He nudged the boy and said something terse. The boy looked down the skiff at Ghote. He burst out laughing. The old man said something more. Suddenly he leant his whole weight against the long steering oar. The little craft veered swoopingly. Ghote felt burning hot all over. The boy roared with laughter. His father swung the boat back to its former course.

But only for a moment. For what seemed after this an eternity to Ghote he swung the tiny vessel to and fro so that it dipped and plunged like a wild thing. Soon Ghote had to lean over the side again and be even more sick. By the end of it he hardly knew or cared where or what he was. And all the while the old man went on impassively fishing, cynically, it seemed, tossing the gaping mouthed catch up the boat towards Ghote.

He stared dully at their great, staring cold and horrid eyes. In the rigging of the slim mast the freshening wind whined and sang.

Suddenly the boy grabbed his father's arm and pointed away to his left. The old man stopped swinging the boat. He stared in the direction the boy had pointed, shading his eyes with a lean hand. The easing of the tossing motion revived Ghote a little. He looked at the two of them in the stern with the dispassionateness of an extremely distant observer.

And then at the very back of his mind a tiny signal started up. This was what he was here for. Not simply to fight against the overwhelming sickness and misery that had invaded every part of him. But to pursue a police investigation.

With an effort that brought the sweat back to his forehead in huge drops he forced himself round to follow the line of the old man's concentrated gaze.

At first he could see only the hateful dark sea with its ominous lacing of white crests. Then suddenly for a second's glimpse he made out something else. A tiny orange speck.

He let himself slump back on to the bottom of the boat again.

Under his veil of misery he forced himself to think. There could be no doubt that the orange speck he had seen was what the two of them in the stern had been looking at. What would it be? The orange was the colour of rescue dinghies he had seen being used as swimming rafts up at Juhu Beach sometimes. The colour was one that could be seen from the maximum distance.

And then he had it. The steamer he had noticed before.

Someone on board had dropped the gold to be smuggled off it attached to a float in that bright orange. It was the task of the old man and his son to pick it up.

No wonder the Customs people had not had much success rummaging ships when they had rounded Colaba Point to the south and come up into Bombay Harbour.

Abruptly the little boat began to swing and swerve again. Ghote looked up. In the stern the two fishermen were looking at him intently. And he could not look back. He let his head sway forward and was terribly sick once more.

It was about this time, he later worked out, that they had picked up the orange float. He had had a glimpse of it, in fact. Or had he imagined it? An oddly-shaped balloon of tough orange cloth, like a huge drop of liquid the wrong way up. He certainly had not simply imagined the length of thin cord and the quite small package tied to it. They had dropped the incriminating orange bag over the side and the sea had sucked it down, but the fine line they had kept. It would be useful for catching fish. And might have come from anywhere.

What had happened to the package? He had not seen it being undone. Tacking their way shorewards again with the bobbing little craft dipping and swinging if anything even more wildly than before, he had done his utmost to watch this part of the process. But the odds were against him. He had to fight the drain on his strength. He had to see, if he was to see, without letting them realise that he had. It would still be quite easy for them to attack him in this state of weakness.

So he had missed getting even a glimpse of the little bars of gold. He just had to assume their existence.

As they neared the shore the wind backed and they got a good run in. In the little boat's stern they seemed to have decided that Ghote was no longer a danger. They let him lie in the prow, looking backwards to the wide sky and the dark sea. They made no further attempt to swing and sway the boat.

He began trying to work out how to catch the two of

them red-handed. It was obvious that on his own like this he was not going to be able to impound the whole vessel when they touched the beach. He would have to rely simply on keeping his eyes wide open. But he reckoned that he had the advantage of surprise on his side. The fisherman and his son thought they had been too clever for him. Well, they would see.

He sat trying to regain his strength.

Above him the narrow white triangular sail was stretched taut to the wind. The boy got up and untwisted a rope. The sail quivered and a series of horizontal ruckles slid down it. Then, quite quickly, it collapsed into the boat. The momentum carried them smoothly forward. It was a neat piece of seamanship. The skiff came up to the low slope of the beach with its speed dying gently away and touched bottom as softly as a falling leaf reaches the ground.

The boy jumped out. He caught hold of the worn wood of the bow beside Ghote and ran sharply forward. Underneath them the sand grated harshly. Then the skiff stuck fast. From the family hut the Paramour came waddling hastily to meet them, laughing contentedly to herself. On her head she carried a big, flat basket wider at the bottom than the top.

"Did you like your trip to sea?" she greeted Ghote as he scrambled out on to the warm, blessedly firm sand. "I am glad to see you back safely."

She dropped the basket on the sand and laughed with her head thrown back.

Ghote looked at her angrily.

"Oh, there are many whirlpools out there, and dangers," she said.

Her stepson picked up the basket and held it in his outstretched arms just at the edge of the boat. His father caught hold of a couple of the fish lying in the bottom of the boat and lobbed them neatly by their tails one after the other into the basket. Ghote watched, his eyes darting from the man stooping down to pick up the fish to the boy standing holding the broad basket. One by one the fish swung gleaming through the air and landed with a smack on the others already in the basket. Not one seemed any different from the next.

At last the old man straightened up. The boy put the basket on his head and set off across the sand with its litter of broken white shells, ribbons of seaweed and little humps of wormcasts. He was heading for the curing yard at the far end of the cluster of shacks that made up the village.

Ghote watched him go.

XIII

When Tarzan's unsympathetic brother had carried his flat basket of plump fish past the palisade of the curing yard and out of sight, Inspector Ghote swung round to the old man sitting impassively on the edge of his beached boat, beginning to gather up the stiff folds of the sail into neat coils.

Ghote let him finish the task. Then he moved in confidently.

" I would like to see the three fish still at the bottom of the boat," he said with quiet triumph.

For a moment the old man crouched in front of the fish braced for combat. But Ghote knew he could not lose now.

" They are my fish," the old man said.

" I want to see them," Ghote replied implacably.

" They are for us to eat only."

" You can eat them after I have seen them."

" Who are you that you should see my fish?"

The stony-faced old man began looking up towards the huts as if he might summon his neighbours to help defend his private property. Ghote darted forward, dipped agilely into the boat and seized one of the fish.

He squeezed it hard.

And felt nothing.

He pushed the old man back and grabbed the other two fish. He thrust his fingers down their gullets.

Nothing.

He stepped back. The old man took a short knife from his loincloth and in a single swift jerk ripped open the first fish from mouth to tail.

Mockingly he presented the two pieces for Ghote's inspection.

Ghote hung his head. Cheated, and so easily. He looked over at the curing yard. Villagers were coming and going from it in a regular procession. Some carried bundles of dried fish on their heads. Others swung baskets by their sides. Tarzan's brother strolled back to the family hut, empty-handed.

He could always arrest them still. He could swear to having seen them behaving suspiciously at sea. But with no actual gold to prove his claims he would have a hard time getting a conviction, let alone being able to touch Amrit Singh. With such a doubtful case against them, the old man and his son would never even consider turning approvers and giving evidence against the big Sikh.

He had failed. He would be unable to get the Sikh on a smuggling charge. His orders to arrest him for murder and work up the evidence afterwards stood.

No, he thought obstinately, he would at least see Krishna Chatterjee once again. He would try his squeezing process at least once. He would give himself twenty-four hours more. Not a minute above that. And then he would go the whole hog, pull in Amrit Singh, bring every pressure to bear on the boys to say the right things in court. Be a complete D.S.P. Naik man.

: : :

Ghote decided to play it tough.

He had Krishna Chatterjee brought down to headquarters. After all, the social worker was no Amrit Singh. He would hardly stand up to rough treatment. The threat of it, or even the hint of it, might still change everything.

Before his victim was due to arrive he set about making a few preparations. He pulled his squat, little spare chair out from its place against the wall and set it very carefully in front of his desk. He went round to the other side and sat down. He leant forward to judge the distance between himself and anybody sitting on the little chair.

He came to the conclusion that the gap was a bit too wide and went round the desk to make a final adjustment.

There was no harm in a policeman having finer feelings, he told himself, but that did not mean he had to be soft. Far from it. Real softness was as much going too far with witnesses as not going far enough. The right thing, the truly tough thing, was to judge the amount to a nicety. This was the real world where people acted. They did things. It was necessary to do things back to them to set the balance right again. But the whole art was to do just what was necessary and no more.

He turned the heavy, squat chair a few degrees round so that it would be a strain on anyone sitting on it to look directly at the occupant of the desk.

After all, if Krishna Chatterjee had indeed been driven by some inner urge to poison Frank Masters, then he had laid himself open to whatever sort of treatment he might get. He had put himself in the wrong. And if that meant being pretty tough to him, it was the kindest thing in the end.

A scutter of movement caught the inspector's eye.

He turned round. The little lizard had once again got itself caught in the glass-fronted bookcase. Ghote shrugged. Some creatures would never learn. He went round to his own side of the desk again, sat down, opened the bottom drawer and took out a wad of clean paper. He looked at the pencils in the enamelled brass tray in front of him. Some of them seemed a bit blunt. He took a little bright purple plastic pencil sharpener from the deepest corner of the bottom drawer, where he kept it to stop it being pinched, and set to work.

A few minutes later he heard the tread of heavy boots on

the corridor floor outside. A sharp but respectful knock sounded on the door.

" In," he called.

It was Krishna Chatterjee, escorted by two constables.

" Wait outside," Ghote said to them briskly. " You may be needed."

The two big men with their shining brass buttons and heavy highly polished boots saluted smartly.

Ghote watched them go and then turned back to his pencil sharpening. Krishna Chatterjee, round-faced, round-shouldered, stayed where he was by the door watching him. In the bookcase down in the corner the little lizard flung itself wildly at the unyielding glass.

At last Ghote glanced up.

" Sit down," he said. " Please."

Krishna Chatterjee came forward and sat on the heavy chair, having tried unsuccessfully to shift it slightly first.

" Good after——" he began.

Seeing that Ghote was busy down behind his desk restoring the plastic pencil sharpener to its hiding place, he stopped. Ghote took a long time tucking the little purple object safely away. It would do the talkative Bengali the world of good to have to sit for a little with no one to speak to.

At last the inspector swung suddenly up.

" Well," he barked, " have you thought better of this ridiculous nonsense?"

Mr. Chatterjee leant forward, twisting round uncomfortably.

" Inspector," he said, " I very much regret, but I have nothing more to tell you. I admit that for reasons I thought good I entered the dispensary on the evening Frank Masters died. I admit I obtained the key from Mr. Carstairs by using what amounted to threats. But I must insist on keeping the reasons for that visit strictly confidential."

" You must insist?" Ghote said, leaning back so that Mr. Chatterjee had to twist forward even more to keep his face in view, " you must insist, and what right have you to insist on anything at all?"

Mr. Chatterjee looked very pained. His big, almond-shaped brown eyes went liquid with hurt.

" Inspector, I had hoped you would respect my decision. I assure you it is one that is totally inevitable. Totally."

" Nothing is inevitable when it gets in the way of a police inquiry," Ghote said. " We have ways of removing inevitabilities, Mr. Chatterjee."

He glanced over the little Bengali's head at the door of the office where he had ordered the two enormous constables to wait.

Mr. Chatterjee wriggled round in the heavy little chair to follow the direction of his glance. The big, brown eyes widened in fear.

" Yes," Ghote said, " we have ways. So I suggest you think again, Mr. Chatterjee. Do some very hard thinking. And very quick thinking."

He swung himself suddenly forward across the narrow, lined and ink-blotched desk, bringing the legs of his tilted chair down on to the floor with a jarring bang.

" Now," he said, " when you took the poison from the jar what did you keep it in on your way up to the house?"

Opposite him, not eighteen inches away, the round face of the little social worker went suddenly flabby.

He stammered for an answer but could find nothing to say.

Ghote never for half a second took his eyes off him.

At last the little Bengali managed to stutter out a reply.

" Inspector, you must understand this. I am not telling you any lies. Perhaps it would have been altogether less distressing if I had. But I have a constitutional objection to falsehood. So, when because of Frank Masters I am obliged not to inform you of certain matters, there is nothing I can do but fall back on silence."

He twisted round even farther in the squat, heavy chair. His eyes shone with trepidation.

"Inspector, spare me," he murmured in a voice that could be scarcely heard.

Ghote knew that this was the moment he should act. Even the reference to never telling lies alerted him. That way lay thoughts of doing evil that good might come. Now was the moment to leap up and stand over the fundamentally timid Bengali and shout and shout until he got a confession.

But something else Mr. Chatterjee had said had set up a sudden long echo in his mind.

He leant a little more forward.

"For Frank Masters?" he asked. "You are keeping silence for him? Tell me what it is about him that makes you do that?"

Mr. Chatterjee looked up. His big eyes had a faint gleam of hope in them. Reprieved.

"Yes," he said, "it would have been more satisfactory perhaps not to have referred to this. But it is the strict truth."

Ghote pressed the palms of his hands down on the blotched surface of his desk.

"All right," he said, "but what was it about Frank Masters that made you do that? What was his secret?"

A look of staring dismay suddenly appeared on Mr. Chatterjee's face.

"His secret——" he stammered

"Yes," Ghote said, his voice almost at a shout, "what is this secret of his personality that made him so different from all of us?"

The dismayed look faded from the Bengali's round face. He coughed a little primly.

"Oh yes, that," he said. "Well, you might put it that it existed only to a certain extent. Frank Masters was unlike us, certainly. We are not all immensely wealthy men, and we do not give up all that wealth in a crusade in a foreign country. That is true. But on the other hand, Frank Masters was in many ways all too like us. That is to say, all too human."

He came to an end and sat contemplating the humanness of Frank Masters with a woebegone expression.

"All too human?" Ghote said at last. "Please explain that a little more."

Mr. Chatterjee looked up.

"In certain ways his very wealth was a disadvantage," he said. "He was apt to prefer to be kind rather than to be strictly useful, and his money frequently gave him the opportunity to smother up any unfortunate results of too much kindness by the exercise of further acts of generosity. And at this stage on many occasions a certain lack of interest would manifest itself. He failed to follow through."

Mr. Chatterjee pronounced these last words with great sadness. Ghote nodded sagely.

"Yes," he said, "you can often do more harm than good that way. People like that should not really be allowed to interfere in other people's lives."

"No. You are wrong. Quite wrong."

Ghote jerked back in astonishment. In the big, almond eyes of the little Bengali there shone fire.

"No," he repeated, "you are quite wrong. Frank Masters did good. That we must never forget. He set out to use his wealth to do good to others, and this he did. Whatever else we reproach him for, this blots out everything."

He breathed rapidly.

"After all," he went on, "he had no need to spend his money on us, and live a life that was relatively austere. Decidedly a life that was relatively austere."

He sat looking straight forward at the wall to Ghote's side. His big eyes were moist.

Ghote puffed out a long breath.

"I dare say there is something in all that," he conceded.

He pulled himself together.

"However that is not the point. We are not here to discuss the charitable activities of Mr. Masters. We are here to discuss his sudden death."

He glared fiercely at Mr. Chatterjee.

"His sudden death and the part you played in it."

Mr. Chatterjee slid round again to the uncomfortable position in which he could look Ghote straight in the eye.

"Inspector," he said, "I must repeat that I played no part at all in Mr. Masters's death. It was the last thing in the world I would have wished to have occurred. The absolutely last thing."

"That will not do," Ghote shouted.

But it was too late.

Mr. Chatterjee sat serenely now on the heavy chair. During his summoning up of the spirit of his former chief Ghote's threats had lost their power over him.

"That will not do at all," Ghote repeated. "I must have answer."

"I regret that you have had such answer as in my power to provide."

The little social worker looked modestly down.

And Ghote let him go.

When the door had been softly shut he sat there contemplating bitterly the course of the interview. To begin with, he had puffed himself up with all those thoughts about being tough. And little Krishna Chatterjee had shown him what real mental toughness was.

For a moment he speculated on whether this display of inner unshakeable resolution put the little Bengali more definitely into the murderer class. He decided that it did not. Certainly, this was the sort of force that could have led him to an altogether unlikely ruthlessness. But the mere possession of it did not necessarily mean that he was bound to have killed Frank Masters. Amrit Singh, if it came to that, possessed beyond question the ability to kill.

The scales were still level.

The thought of Frank Masters plunged Ghote into deeper gloom. He had actually been so foolish as to abuse him, to sit there and utter statements about preventing people like him interfering in other people's lives. How could he have done it? In face of an example of real goodness like that? Mr. Chatterjee was right to have snubbed him.

He bunched up his fist and banged it down on the pile of untouched white paper in front of him. The dull, padded sound of the blow reverberated quietly through the small room. Down in the glass-fronted bookcase the lizard was stirred to a fresh frenzy of ineffectual scuttling.

Wearily Ghote got up, took a piece of the paper, went over to the corner and hoicked the little beast to freedom once more.

: : : :

Shortly afterwards he went home. There was no point in staying in the office. At any moment D.S.P. Naik might come in and start asking awkward questions. Home was safe.

Home was delightful. He found Protima in a very good humour. His son was being extremely serious and well-behaved, which in a replica of a man only a quarter lifesize he found always so absorbing that for a time nothing else seemed to matter.

He relaxed. Frank Masters might have been murdered in circumstances which were still almost as mysterious as when he had been assigned to the case, but that could wait. The impression he had at last begun to gain of the murdered American as a human being, and one whose very existence posed problems in behaviour almost too big to deal with, might be still heavily present in his mind, but at least it could for a few minutes be pushed into the background. To be a father and a husband and nothing else was important and right. Ghote watched his son and talked in a low voice to Protima about the events of her day at home.

"But you," she said at last, "what have you been doing? Your clothes? How did you get them into that terrible state? When you came in they looked as if you had been wading through the sea in them."

So Ghote was gently urged back into being a policeman. He told Protima, in brief outline, about how he had hoped to catch Amrit Singh as a smuggler and about how he had failed, leaving himself faced as inexorably as ever with his dilemma about Amrit Singh and Krishna Chatterjee and the D.S.P.'s almost inescapable order.

Protima promptly justified his former reluctance to tell her about his work by getting the situation typically wrong.

" But why cannot you arrest Amrit Singh?" she said. " He was the one who poisoned your Frank Masters."

" But he did not," Ghote replied. " Not necessarily. I explained to you. Both he and Krishna Chatterjee admit going into the dispensary where the poison was. Both swear they did not take it. Either could be telling the truth. And while I know for a fact that Amrit Singh has killed three people himself at least, I am also sure that someone like Krishna Chatterjee could push himself to the extreme of murder. It balances up."

" Then you do not want to believe Amrit Singh killed Frank Masters?"

" It is not a question of what I want to believe. It is question of simple logic."

An unexpected stain of dark anger appeared momentarily on the smooth stream of his tranquillity.

" Logic," Protima laughed. " It is no good talking your logic this and your logic that. You know I never understand such things."

She made them sound as if they were all right for little Ved, solemnly bringing dishes of pickle in from the kitchen for their evening meal, but not really worth considering above that level.

" But you cannot escape logic," Ghote said, his voice suddenly rising.

Ved looked up but said nothing.

" Oh, I can escape it very well," said Protima, undisturbed. " You must not let such things worry you."

" But I have failed to find who killed Frank Masters."

" All right. You must ask yourself who killed him. Was it Amrit Singh, was it Krishna Chatterjee, was it that Dr. Diana?"

Ghote's fury boiled over.

"How can you be so stupid?" he shouted. "I tell you it could not possibly be Dr. Diana. She does not come into it at all."

Protima gave a little toss of her fine, long head.

"Well," she said, "from what I have heard about the way she talks to you, I think it must be her. But enough of this nonsense. If I do not go to kitchen now, we will have no food to-night."

And she went.

Ghote stood in the living-room looking at the empty doorway, oblivious of Ved arranging the pickle dishes with great exactitude.

"Dr. Diana has absolute alibi," he said into space. "For all the time when the poison was stolen she did not have a key to the dispensary. That is a fact."

From the kitchen came the sound of a pan being put on the gas-ring and its contents being stirred briskly. Ved went back in to fetch another pickle dish to complete his display.

Ghote marched up and down. He began to feel hot and uncomfortable even in his fresh clothes. He slumped down on a rattan stool in the corner and fanned at himself furiously.

Protima came back in calmly carrying the food with Ved and his final pickle dish in the rear. Ghote glowered at them and stayed where he was.

"Well," Protima said, "the meal is ready. Are you going to eat?"

Ghote did not reply.

"Come, why are you sitting like that?"

"It is hot."

"Then take some water to drink. It has been standing in the big clay jar. It is quite cool."

Ghote got up and helped himself, dipping a brass tumbler into the big pot. He drank.

"Cool," he said contemptuously.

"Well, it is cool as water can be kept without refrigerator."

"Refrigerator. Refrigerator. There you go again. Always dragging it in. Always nagging about it. Always hinting."

It was the signal for battle.

But Protima, with that contrariness that was both the bane and delight of her make-up, refused to fight. Instead she was all sweetness.

"No, you are wrong," she said. "Really, I do not always go on about the refrigerator. Or if I do, it is joking only. Yes, I would like, I admit. But if we have not got the money, then we cannot have one. I know that."

And, as was almost always the case, she melted Ghote completely.

"But you will get one one day, soon even," he burst out. "I meant to keep it secret. I have been saving."

It was true. He had been saving in secret. Whenever Protima had talked about how wonderful it would be to have a refrigerator he had taken good care to laugh at her, to ask how Indian women had survived so many centuries without such objects, to say that at his present rate of pay such luxuries were unthinkable. But some time before he had been unable to resist setting aside a lump sum in back Dearness Allowance that had unexpectedly been paid him. It had made a start and bit by bit he had added to it. Now, although the refrigerator was still a good distance away, the sum in the Post Office account he kept for it, his refrigerator fund, was of a respectable size.

Protima came running up.

"You have been saving? In secret? Oh, my husband, such a deceiver he is. Oh, you funny man, you good man. How much have you saved?"

"Nearly five hundred rupees."

"Five hundred rupees. Five hundred rupees. But that is wonderful. How clever to get so much together and never hint at it to me."

Never, thought Ghote a little wryly.

Protima laughed tenderly.

"And you are so silly, too," she said. "When you have

saved that much money there is no need to go any longer without refrigerator. It can be bought on easy terms."

She came up to him and stroked the back of his head with a long, slim, fine-boned hand.

"Oh, Mr. Practical," she said. "With his logic here and his logic there. Sometimes you must think of how things really are in the world. To-morrow you can get the money and we will go to the Hiro Music House shop and make the arrangements. We can have proper cold drinks to-morrow night even."

"I will see," Ghote said.

He felt suddenly shy about the whole transaction.

"But the next day is Holi. It would be nice to have cold drinks for the holiday."

"I may be too busy," Ghote said with a trace of irritation.

"Then we will wait. We have waited so long, two days more will not matter. Straight after Holi we will go."

"Yes."

XIV

Next morning as soon as the big Post Office in Frere Road was open Ghote drew out the whole sum in his refrigerator fund. He found that it actually just exceeded the five hundred rupee mark.

"With accrued interest," the elderly, delicately-spectacled clerk explained gravely.

Ghote waited while his pass-book was ceremoniously ruled up.

He sighed. He had wanted to let the money grow and grow till he had accumulated every one of the 1,090 rupees which the refrigerator he had his eye on would cost, excise duty and taxes apart. But these he generally contrived to leave out of his calculations.

Carefully he fitted the crisp new notes away in an inner pocket. And as he did so an alarming diminuendo of thoughts spiralled through his head. That it was wonderful to have actually got hold of so much money; that life with a refrigerator in the house would be like them having a whole series of gifts; that there were many people much less lucky than this, like the gang over at the Masters Foundation, saved from the misery of the gutters only by chance, or the people of the fishing village, always on the edge of disaster. Then the thought came that Frank Masters would have gone to the aid of the village if it had happened to come to his notice; and then that to a villager five hundred rupees would seem unattainable wealth; then that Protima did not know exactly how much he had saved; and next that he ought to devote at least some of this wealth to helping the wretchedly poor people he had been brought into contact with; and finally that he should go out to the village as soon as possible and give Tarzan's family a generous present.

: : • : :

He had meant to decide on the way exactly what the appropriate sum was, whether it should be as much as fifty rupees or whether less would be fair. But instead he found he could think of nothing but that by going off on this jaunt he was avoiding doing his duty over Amrit Singh.

All the way through the flat, dreary, crowded stretches of North Bombay, past the tall mill chimneys and the squalid shacks between them, he cursed himself for not simply arresting the big Sikh. He might not be the toughest man in the force, or the cleverest, or the biggest pusher, but at least he did his duty. Always. As laid down. Until this business.

It was the thought of Frank Masters, the good man, that had done it, he reflected. If this investigation had been into anybody else's death, perhaps he would have felt able to accept his orders and carry them out to the end. Afterwards someone else, someone senior, could take the responsibility if the orders had created more harm than good. And if improving the evidence like that put Amrit Singh in a cell for a really long time, well, that was where Amrit Singh ought to be, and everybody knew it.

The stations along the way were slowly ticked off—Matunga Road, Santa Cruz, Ville Parle, Andheri, Goregan, Malad, Kandivlee, Borivli. He found the same old tonga and weary horse as he had used the day before and made the same uncomfortable trip to the point where the road to the sea became a mere path. Blackly he ploughed along the muddy strip of sand towards the village, keeping just in the shade of the matted tangle of vegetation springing from the marshy land at the highest point the tide reached.

Because there could be no doubt about one thing. If ever anybody was a bad person, a man content to live well at the expense of anyone he could bully or bang money out of, it was Amrit Singh. And he was a proven killer, too.

Ghote stopped.

Ahead of him, standing casually behind a thick sprout of growth at the foot of an old, leaning, battered palm, there was a figure in a heavy red and blue turban with a white shirt and tight whitish trousers kept up by a broad sash. A Sikh. You could tell a mile off. But more than any Sikh, surely.

Over the soft, grey sand Ghote advanced carefully, noiselessly.

Yes, there in front of him, spying over the village in much the same way that he himself had done the day before, was Amrit Singh. In the flesh.

Ghote glanced round. There ought to be a police shadow somewhere in sight.

He could see no one. He decided to plunge into the dank vegetation behind and try to work round Amrit Singh in a half-circle to see whether he had been properly followed or not. If he had been let off the hook, someone ought to pay for it. It was not so often that they had the big Sikh where they wanted him, and after that long afternoon tracking him down in Morton Road no one should have let him get away.

When he got back to the office he would . . .

He pulled himself up. Surely this was just the result of thinking that Amrit Singh's shadow would see Inspector Ghote miles from his proper territory at a time when he should be answering his D.S.P.'s queries back at headquarters.

But there was no one to observe such curious behaviour as it turned out. Almost an hour later when he had emerged on to the grey sands again after completing his slow, careful half-circle he was convinced that if anyone had been tailing Amrit Singh they had let him get right out of sight.

He quickly looked along the beach to the tongue of jutting vegetation where he had left the sturdy Sikh. He had had glimpses of him often enough while he was manœuvring round, but he had not seen him for the last few minutes. He was still there, only sitting comfortably at the foot of the tree now.

The inspector drew a deep breath of relief.

He looked over at the scatter of palm-leaf thatched huts and the palisaded curing yard. Outside most of the huts the women sat or stood in little groups. Many of them were preparing food. Children ran about on the greyish sand, except for a group of girls busy stringing flags on lengths of cord in preparation for the Holi holiday next day. Evidently the men were still at sea. Was Amrit Singh waiting for their return? He certainly seemed in no hurry to move.

Quite suddenly Ghote decided to tackle him. This time the advantage of surprise would be on his side. He smiled quietly.

A few steps along the soft, yielding sand and he was within easy speaking distance. Amrit Singh was looking out to sea. Plainly he had no idea that anyone was so near to him.

Ghote spoke softly in a voice which would just reach the big Sikh.

"Amrit Singh, why did you kill Frank Masters?"

Amrit Singh leapt up. His right hand reached swiftly down to the bulge in his cummerbund.

"No," said Ghote. "No guns. You do not think I would come out here without saying where I had gone, do you?"

"A gun, Inspector?"

The tall Sikh laughed. But for once without conviction.

"No," said Ghote, "this is not the time for shooting. This is the time for answering only. Why did you kill Frank Masters?"

"Inspector, you know that I did not," Amrit Singh said.

The words were delivered flatly, as a matter of mere form.

"I know that you did," Ghote said. "You took the powder from that green glass jar. You put it in the curry on the serving table by the open window of the tiffin room at the Foundation. Why did you do it, Amrit Singh?"

But he had overplayed his hand.

"Inspector, I did not take any poison. I did not know it was powder even. Or that it was kept in a green glass jar."

Ghote thought of the smashed fragments of the little brown jar the arsenic trioxide had been in. If the jar had not been broken, would they after all have got a trace of one of Amrit Singh's prints off it somewhere? Or would it have been a latent impression from Krishna Chatterjee?

He felt the initiative was slipping away.

"Inspector."

Ghote looked quickly up at the big Sikh. Unexpectedly, his voice did not contain the familiar broad hints of irony. For once he did not seem to be playing with his interrogator like a jungle cat. He seemed ill at ease.

"Well," Ghote snapped, seizing on the first thing that came into his head to gain himself the upper hand again, "well, what exactly are you doing here? Is this a bazaar for a poor travelling salesman to display his goods?"

And he seemed to have made a lucky hit.

Amrit Singh looked nervously at the collection of patched, dank, greenish huts with the women in their tightly wrapped saris squatting outside them.

"Inspector," he said, "we are friends, are we not? And it is strange for friends to meet here."

"Never mind about friends," Ghote said. "What are you doing here?"

"A man may travel where he wants," Amrit Singh said. Again he lacked real conviction.

"He may travel where he wants, but he should be able to say why he is there," Ghote stated.

"Look, Inspector, between friends," Amrit Singh began again.

"Between a policeman and Amrit Singh," Ghote said.

The Sikh ploughed on.

"Inspector, I am a poor man. You are a poor man. Between poor men there is always friendship."

Suddenly Ghote remembered the five hundred rupees in his pocket, and why it was that he had come out to the village. To see whether there was something someone not really poor could do for people in real danger of having just nothing to eat if precarious luck turned only a little against them.

He looked past the Sikh's broad frame down towards the cluster of flimsy huts. The group of girls rose to their feet at just that moment and carried a long string of pathetic little flags towards the curing yard.

Amrit Singh, who had been looking at Ghote trying to assess his reaction to the general propositions he had been putting out, gave up and launched into a more direct approach.

"Inspector sahib," he said. "I am poor. I know it. You know it. Poor as can be. But just to-day, as it happens, I have a little money. I have been lucky in selling some things. I know I ought to use the money to pay off the heavy debts I have, but I am ready not to. For a friend."

"What about the huge sum you made at the Masters Foundation?" Ghote said, trying for another lucky shot.

"Inspector, no huge sums have I made. I am a poor man, the poorest of the poor. But to-day I have a few rupees, perhaps even a few hundred rupees, and if you like I will share them with another poor man who is my friend."

"Are you trying to bribe a police officer, Amrit Singh?"

"Inspector, that I should do such a thing. I am trying to share my luck only. And I am remembering a friend who only two days ago was talking about such a thing as a refrigerator."

The Sikh decided that he had advanced enough counters for the time being. He waited to see if they were taken up.

And Ghote, standing in front of him, his eyes unmoving, keeping the questioning firmly in his own hands, felt his heart patter hard.

A refrigerator. How had the Sikh happened to hit on that, of all things, to propose as a bribe?

Perhaps he had let something of his private life appear when Amrit Singh had been talking to him in the compound at the Masters Foundation. He must watch himself.

His silence had the happy effect of forcing the Sikh to go yet another stage onwards.

"Ah," he said, "there are many refrigerators, but why should not poor men like you and I have one? It would cost not very much money. I saw yesterday only a fine refrigerator in the paper. And it would cost only one thousand and ninety rupees."

Again he waited, with so much more bait economically laid out.

"If you are offering me the price of a refrigerator to forget I have seen you here," said Ghote levelly, "then you can stop right away. I will take no bribes."

"Inspector, think of your wife when you go home and say a refrigerator is coming by the next delivery. Or when you show her the very notes that will buy one. One thousand rupees, Inspector."

The Sikh's hand slipped between the folds of his broad sash. Ghote had little doubt that somewhere there he had notes to the value of a thousand rupees, and beyond. He thought of the notes in his own pocket, and of what they were intended for.

"You are generous," he said to Amrit Singh. "But then when your money has been taken from other people only, you can afford to be generous. If it had been truly your own, would you give it to others? And out of true kindness, like Frank Masters? Or would you keep every anna?"

The Sikh evidently understood that this was a really final answer. His dark eyes suddenly glowered with rage.

Ghote tensed slightly, expecting violent action.

But he got only violent words.

"Give? Kindness?" said the tall Sikh with deep contempt. "What man would look on you as a man if for no reason you gave? Money is not a plaything to be handed to children only. If a man has got money for himself, then he knows it is worth something. He does not go here and there giving."

From the emphasis he put on this last word, it was plain that Amrit Singh had a very different outlook on life from that of Frank Masters.

"You would be twice the man you are if you had given a tenth only of what Frank Masters gave," Ghote said sharply.

"Frank Masters."

The Sikh spat into the slimy earth at his feet.

"I know all about Frank Masters," he said. "Why did he have to come all the way to Bombay to rule other people's lives? Are there not poor people in America for him to play with? But, no, he has to come here to make himself feel good. Only in India can he find the very poor and get the most for his money. For a few annas here he can make a poor boy do just what he tells him, and can say to himself that he has changed a life."

Ghote felt that he wanted to protest but could find nothing to say.

"Oh yes," the Sikh went on, "if you want to find a really bad man, look there. There is someone who, just to feel happy himself, will make someone else change his whole life, will make him go where he thinks it is best for him to go, do what he thinks is best. And not even to get money. But just so that he feels good with himself. If I had my way

Frank Masters and all his sort would be dropped into the Harbour with a good rock tied to their legs."

"So that was why you killed him?" Ghote said.

But he knew that the question was only a hasty jibe. His real answer was going to be in deeds not words: he was going to give every anna of the five hundred rupees to the fisherman's family. To make it up, in a way, to Frank Masters.

Only one thing stopped him from running down straight away to the huts and shouting for the great fat Paramour.

That was that he did not want to let Amrit Singh go. More than ever now he wanted to make sure he could have him pulled in at any moment. An idea occurred to him. Swallowing his anger, he made himself speak casually.

"Well, perhaps you are right," he said. "Frank Masters was certainly very rich."

"And very bad," said Amrit Singh determinedly.

"And yet you and I are far from having his money," Ghote went on.

He positively saw the spark of hope light up again in the Sikh's dark eyes.

"Yes," the tall man said, "we are poor."

Ghote sighed.

"But we can be friends," Amrit Singh said. "And what money we have we can share with friends as friends. And friends can help each other. They can keep quiet about some things sometimes."

"Perhaps," said Ghote.

Amrit Singh dug his hand into his sash again.

"No," Ghote said. "I will think. It is wrong."

Amrit Singh shrugged his broad shoulders.

"Can I see you somewhere later? To-morrow?" Ghote said.

Amrit Singh calculated for a moment.

Then apparently he decided to make the best of a difficult situation.

"I shall be at Morton Road early to-morrow," he said.

" Then perhaps I shall see you," said Ghote.

The tall Sikh did not wait to exchange pleasantries a moment longer. He had got as good a bargain as he could hope for, and in an instant the thick swamp vegetation swallowed him up. Ghote caught one quick sight of the red and blue turban, and no more.

He turned towards the huts of the village.

Outside Tarzan's family hut now the Paramour was sitting cross-legged. Between her enormous rounded knees, straining tight the cloth of her sari, there was a big bowl in the bottom of which she was pounding something. Her great forearms, whose flesh pressed hard against the dozen thin glass bangles she wore, were working rhythmically bringing a pestle down and down with terrible heaviness.

When Ghote's shadow fell across her she looked up. The moment she saw who it was she laughed till she shook.

" Have you come looking for that bad son again?" she said.

" I have come because of what I saw yesterday," Ghote replied.

The remark evidently seemed to her even richer in humour than her own question. She roared and gasped with laughter.

" What you saw yesterday," she got out at last. " Or was it what you did not see?"

Ghote ignored all this.

" Yesterday," he said, when he thought she would hear him, " yesterday I saw how difficult it was for you to live without being a prey to evil men. And that is why I have come back: to offer help."

" Oh, it is difficult to live," the Paramour agreed. " In a few days we have to pay money back on the boat, and it is not there. We save nothing. The men will not do it. You know what they say? That because a fisherman lives by robbing the sea he cannot save what he makes."

She giggled softly, almost to herself.

" But you see how foolish this is," Ghote said. " You

are a woman of authority. You must make them put away a little when the catches are good."

The giggling became a frank laugh again.

"All right," Ghote said, "I understand your difficulties. And I am prepared to help you start again. This is what I will do."

He put his hand into his pocket and pulled out the tight bundle of notes. For an instant the fat woman stopped laughing completely. Her eyes went wide.

Then she lowered them to look at the handful of pounded spices in the big bowl and giggled modestly a little.

"I want you to take this money," said Ghote. "It will pay off much of the debt on your boat. Then your catches will bring you a proper livelihood, you and both your step-sons. But you must promise you will make them save when they do well, so that they can last over a poor catch without borrowing again."

A podgy hand reached upwards towards the roll of notes he held.

"Will you promise?" he asked.

"Oh, sahib, I will promise. Such wealth. Such goodness. Sahib, I kiss your feet."

Ghote thrust the money into her fist.

But he could not help noticing that she made no move to kiss his feet in actuality. Instead she shoved the notes down into her enormous bosom and stayed with her head lowered.

Ghote decided that it would be best to leave at once. He turned and marched off through the yielding grey sand along the top of the beach. He tried to analyse his feelings. They were confused, but seemed mostly to be stirrings of disappointment. He had certainly not felt a great surge of happiness at the moment the notes had left his hand. But there had been something in the way the big podgy fist had enveloped them that had disconcerted him.

He turned and looked back.

It came as no real surprise to see that the enormous

Paramour was sitting there visibly quivering, even at this distance, with great tides of irrepressible laughter.

: : : :

The journey back to Bombay was terrible. To begin with, Ghote found when he got to the end of the muddy path through the swamps that there was no tonga waiting at the start of the road. Amrit Singh had commandeered it. The extra walk to the railway station took him hours. The sun beat down. The dust rose up. His left heel began to throb where it had been so jolted at the Morton Road place. He felt abominably tired.

Then he had an interminable wait for a train, and, once it had come progress was hardly faster. The stations crept by—Borivli, Kandivlee, Malad, Goregaon, Andheri, Ville Parle, Santa Cruz, Matunga Road. At last they pulled into Churchgate Station. It was by now late in the afternoon.

Standing in the station concourse, buffeted by people hurrying by in all directions, mostly carrying, it seemed, huge bedding rolls, Ghote stood and tried to make up his mind what to do. A red-shirted coolie with three battered cardboard suitcases under each arm banged into his back.

Should he go to the office even at this late hour? What would he say if the chaprassi on duty in the entrance gave him a message that D.S.P. Naik had been asking for him all day? How could he possibly tell him that he had spoken to Amrit Singh and had not arrested him? There would be certainly no point in confronting the D.S.P. with the question that reared up in his own mind at any and every opportunity. If he said to him " Which of them did it? Which?" he would be told pretty sharply not to talk such nonsense.

And it was possible the D.S.P. was really right.

A man wheeling a low barrow neatly piled with dozen upon dozen of sticky-looking cream horns scraped its edge all the way across Ghote's shin bones. Ghote stepped sharply back and banged into an elderly, bespectacled traveller nursing a big earthenware drinking water jug.

Some of the water spilt. The eyes that looked at Ghote through the spectacles were infinitely reproachful.

Ghote strode away.

There was no point in going home. Although he hardly dared put the thought into words the suspicion was beginning to lurk somewhere in his mind that he had been a colossal fool to give all that money away. It would need a great deal of explaining.

He tried thinking about Frank Masters to counteract these thoughts. After all, when Frank Masters gave huge sums away nobody put it in the papers that he was a fool.

And with the memory of Frank Masters back again came the question: Which of the two? Which?

Ghote decided to go to the Foundation once more. There was nothing to be done there, but at least he would be near the source of it all.

: : : :

Before he got to the big, old bungalow in Wodehouse Road he became involved in another incident of the sort which, it seemed, had dogged him ever since he had first been put on the case.

His bus stopped a little north of the Foundation and he was walking abstractedly along towards it, past the Catholic cathedral, past Stranger's Guest House, past the Y.M.C.A., when an abrupt contortion in the traffic stream beside him caught his eye. He looked round.

Standing half in the deep storm gutter, half in the roadway itself, were the boys of Edward G. Robinson's gang. Their heads were bent in a tight circle and evidently some deeply secret negotiation was going forward. The passing traffic was swerving sharply to avoid them and an occasional driver with an unusually tender social conscience broke the silence-zone rule by giving a quick toot of his horn as he passed. But the boys ignored it all, even the rackety van Ghote saw at that moment positively brushing the back of Edward G. Robinson's tattered black jacket.

With a sigh Ghote walked over. He caught a glimpse of a couple of old fruit juice bottles half filled with reddish brown liquid. He did not need to ask what this was: too much bhang processed from hemp leaves into a sweet drink had come under his eyes in the past for there to be any doubt. However in the quantity the boys had, though illegal, it was much less dangerous than standing in a busy roadway.

"Hey, you," Ghote shouted.

The boys looked up. Edward G. stuffed in a leisurely way the bottle he had been holding into the one remaining practical pocket of his battered jacket.

"Hi," he said.

Ghote looked at him sternly.

"That is no way to behave," he said. "You are causing traffic congestion and also risking injury."

The boys looked at him in silence, all except Edward G. himself who showed true leadership by taking absolutely no notice whatsoever.

But Ghote was in no mood to appreciate such qualities. He felt a spasm of sharp irritation and stepping forward caught hold of the boy's arm and shook it hard.

Edward G.'s appallingly crinkled face remained eloquent with total boredom.

"Listen to me," Ghote said with all the emphasis he could put into the words, "listen to me. This is dangerous. Do you want to see one of you getting killed?"

Edward G. turned right round to face the inspector and put a friendly arm round Tarzan's bare shoulders.

"This one's pretty dumb," he said. "He could go all right."

XV

To Inspector Ghote's surprise, in spite of Edward G. Robinson's limited attitude to road safety, a minute or so later the boys began to drift back into the half-heartedly cared for front garden of the Masters Foundation. But beyond this concession they ignored him and wandered over to settle down contentedly under the shade of a peepul tree. Tarzan swung easily up into the branches and hung upside down above the others like a half-naked, wiry bat and the two bhang bottles appeared again.

Ghote looked at the group for a moment and then turned and faced the steps of the Foundation and the tall front door.

Faced them without pleasure. The fact was that he was still entirely undecided about what he would do. Whom should he ask to see? There was really no point in questioning anybody. He had asked everything long before. He had seen every cranny in the big bungalow. He had made every test he could think of, taken every measurement.

As much to force himself to come to a decision as for any other reason, he went up the wide steps at a run and put his forefinger firmly and definitely on the bell push.

But he still had time to make his decision and unmake it. The die was cast, but the dice was still toppling over and over with its number yet to come up. He seized on the notion of asking to see Krishna Chatterjee again. It was all that was left: battering away at an unyielding surface in the mere hope that in spite of all the signs something would crack, that little Mr. Chatterjee would let something slip and settle it one way or the other. Either the killer, or the innocent one.

The bell remained unanswered. Ghote decided not to press it again. There might still come to him a last-minute flash of inspiration for some other way of breaking the dilemma.

"Hey, mister, what you going to do?"

He recognised the voice without needing to turn round. Edward G. Robinson again. As usual hitting the nail exactly on the head and driving it painfully home.

"Come on, mister, what you going to do in there? Who you going to see? Going to make the big arrest?"

Ghote decided to turn round.

From the slight height of the doorstep he looked over at the group under the peepul tree. They were happily and completely at ease. One of the bhang bottles was just finishing its round. It had come to Tarzan. Ghote watched fascinated for a moment as the boy contrived to take a long, cool swig of the sticky liquid while still remaining hanging from his branch. Then he turned to Edward G. Robinson's wrinkle-interlaced face. It semaphored an expression of simple, impudent questioning.

"What a police officer is going to do at a private institution can be of no possible concern to you," Ghote said in a loud and clear voice.

"If the police officer is going to bully poor old swallow-all Chatterjee it is of concern," came the reply.

Edward G., expert in film American, had also caught the inspector's tone, to a nicety.

Ghote bit his lip.

"If I wish to question, I shall question," he said. "Mr. Chatterjee, or anyone else I like."

He saw that Tarzan was flapping his arms up and down in a highly agitated way. Another comment. And, true enough, it was the way he felt.

Edward G. took a lazy swig of bhang. He was lying on his back with his left knee raised and his bare right leg swinging idly across it.

"Listen, mister," he said, "why you bothering about this case any more? So you ain't cracked it? So what?"

"So the death of the great benefactor of the children of Bombay is still a mystery," Ghote answered. "Does that mean nothing to you? You would not be here at this moment if it was not for Frank Masters coming from America and spending his money to help you. You."

He came down two of the steps and glared over at the reclining form of Edward G. Robinson across the hot afternoon sunshine.

"Mister, did you ever think I might like not to be here?" Edward G. said, gently twirling the bhang bottle. "Did you ever think I might want to sleep on the pavement instead of in that great, big, warm and dry house?"

He squinted through half-closed eyes in his wrinkled old man's face at the solid whiteness of the bungalow behind Ghote.

"What nonsense is this?" Ghote replied.

He came right down the steps and strode across to the idle group under the peepul.

"What nonsense is this?" he repeated, facing them. "Are you hungry? No. Are you wondering every day whether you will starve to death before long? Or catch some illness? No, you know you will get treatment here from the money that good man did not hesitate to give."

"You know what he felt when we got better?" Edward G. said.

He drained the last of the bhang. There was a rustle of protest at this from the other members of the gang. Edward G. ignored it.

"You know what good Frank Masters felt when his good money had saved our lives?" he asked Ghote. "He felt 'I have got another boy to be mine for ever.' He felt mighty fine."

The cowboy drawl might have come from the lips of the Lone Ranger himself.

Ghote drew breath to reply. What infernal impudence, he thought. What gratitude. The man who had come from America to look after these boys, and had got killed for his pains. And now this. All right, he would tell them a thing or two. It was all very well for a thug like Amrit Singh to put out opinions like that, but for a boy, a mere boy, and one who had actually benefited from Frank Masters's great kindness. It was appalling, truly——

He stopped himself.

What was he doing? Dictating what someone else should think.

Just because the boy had expressed an opinion that did not echo the respectability of every schoolmaster that had ever lectured a delinquent, he was accusing him of all the crimes in the book. And it was not even as if the picture of Frank Masters he had put before the boy was a true one. It did not square up really with what he had learnt from Krishna Chatterjee. It was almost as distorted as Amrit Singh's view of him. Or, come to that, as the view Dr. Diana had put when he had questioned her about Frank Masters in her English-looking room in this very house.

No, he would stop it.

He looked down at the boys.

"If you go on drinking bhang," he said, "in the end you will suffer worse than any pleasure you get. But perhaps you knew that."

He turned and walked back to the front door. His ring on the bell had remained unanswered. He climbed the steps and rang again.

"Well, mister, what you going to do?" Edward G. sang out.

Ghote turned round.

"I am going to investigate a most curious discrepancy," he said.

: : : :

As Inspector Ghote approached the dispensary hut, where he had been taken by the solemn, weighty bearer who had eventually opened the door to him, he found that the burst of courage and curiosity that had sprung up in him at the moment he had realised there was a curious discrepancy to investigate was oozing fast away.

Dr. Diana, he said to himself, Dr. Diana. Was he really going to tackle her successfully? Would he actually manage to make her account for the fact that she had praised Frank

Masters to the skies while Krishna Chatterjee, apparently with the best of intentions, had painted a very different picture when he had been questioned at headquarters?

He licked his lips and contrasted the two portraits that had been given to him.

Little Mr. Chatterjee had convincingly spoken of the man whose immense wealth was a disadvantage leading him all too often to be kind rather than useful, a fallible mortal subject to mortal failings such as gradually declining interest in the face of un-success. Dr. Diana, on the other hand, had talked about a man who saw what was to be done and did it. She had said Frank Masters was no sloppy sentimental fool.

And somehow, Ghote realised now, what she had said had not rung true. It had been too much delivered as a challenge. While Mr. Chatterjee had seemed to speak with instances in mind.

Ghote was aware that he had failed to answer Dr. Diana's challenge. Probably he had not realised earlier that the two views of Frank Masters were in such contrast because he had been hiding from himself this very failure.

The bearer threw open the door of the hut, the rough wood hardly measuring up to the treatment.

"Inspector Ghote, Bombay C.I.D.," he announced, apparently unconscious of the fact that the last time he had used such words had been to usher in Ghote to the dead body of Frank Masters.

Ghote, well remembering the first occasion, stepped inside. Once again Dr. Diana had her back to him. But this time she was not standing looking fixedly into the mirror on the cupboard face. She was bending over the sink in the corner with a whimpering eight-year-old boy propped up on one knee.

She glanced round for an instant.

"Oh," she said, "you again. Well, you can see I'm busy."

"I regret," Ghote said. "I was not informed you were engaged."

Dr. Diana turned the high chromium tap of the sink on full blast.

"When one of the kids gets bitten by a piedog," she said, her voice for all its clarity hard to hear above the spluttering of the water, "I don't get time to go round warning everybody I'm too busy to bother with trifles."

"I perfectly understand," Ghote said. "I will return when you are free."

"Oh, no, stay now you're here," Dr. Diana answered. "You can talk to me while I see to this chappie. I dare say I'll be able to spare you enough attention."

She turned back to the boy.

"Here, let me look again," she said. "Now. Steady on."

The boy's whimpering became louder.

"What do you want anyhow?" Dr. Diana called over her shoulder.

Ghote hesitated. Was he really going to let her get away with giving him the fag-end of her attention like this? And then he decided that he was. He would not let a sense of his own dignity interfere on this case.

"I want to talk to you about Mr. Masters," he said.

"No," said Dr. Diana. "That doesn't look too good to me."

Ghote realised that she was not talking to him. He waited.

"Here," the doctor went on, "let me see the finger."

She glanced round at Ghote.

"Thought we'd been into all that," she said.

She took hold of the boy's hand, bent low over it and put the blood-covered finger to her lips. She sucked hard.

"Yes," Ghote said. "I thought that also. But a certain discrepancy has come to light."

Dr. Diana took her mouth away from the boy's finger, and spat slappingly into the sink.

"Discrepancy?" she said contemptuously, as she put her lips to the small brown hand again.

"Yes, discrepancy," Ghote replied firmly.

The single note of contempt had done its work. In a moment all the courage that had seeped away, and the curiosity, sprang up again. He went on.

" You told that Frank Masters was never kind only. You told that he saw what had to be done and did it. I think that was not true."

Dr. Diana spat out another mouthful of the boy's blood She spared time to give Ghote a steady, appraising look before she bent to her work once more.

Ghote waited.

At last Dr. Diana took her mouth off the boy's finger again. She examined the wound.

" Yes," she said, " that looks a bit more like it. Now, come over here."

She led the boy, moaning quietly to himself and shaking a little, over to the glass-topped table.

" Stand there a moment," she said, turning to the cupboard with the mirror front.

As she opened it and ranged over the rows of bottles, jars and packets inside, she gave Ghote her answer.

" All right. I dare say I did gloss over one or two things. I can't see that it matters."

She found the bottle she was looking for and put it on the table. She turned back to the cupboard.

Ghote ignored the fact that he was having to speak to her white-coated back.

" I am investigating Mr. Masters's death," he said, with an edge of controlled anger. " And when I ask questions about him I expect to get told the truth."

Dr. Diana turned slowly back. She was holding a blue paper packet of cotton wool. She looked at Ghote expressionlessly.

" Yes," she said at last, " yes, I see that I shouldn't have done that."

She pulled a lump of cotton wool off the roll from the packet. Then she went over to the table and tipped a plentiful quantity of mercurochrome on to the neat wad she had made.

"Now, laddie," she said, "I'm afraid this is going to hurt."

She reached down and picked up his hand.

The boy looked up at her with wide eyes. His teeth were chattering hard.

"Then I would like to hear from you what Mr. Masters was truly like," Ghote said.

The boy screamed as Dr. Diana firmly pressed the red-soaked pad on the wound.

"Frank?" she said when the boy was quieter.

She took a dressing from the cupboard and began strapping it round the boy's finger. Ghote watched. And waited.

But for some time Dr. Diana was too occupied to add anything more. She finished tying the dressing into place, took a hypodermic from the cupboard and went quickly into the inner part of the hut.

For an instant Ghote wondered whether he should follow her. But he recollected the grilles on the windows and the fact that there was no other door to the whole hut and decided to stay put. Dr. Diana returned a second or two later. The hypodermic was half full. She went up to the boy.

"Now, nearly finished," she said.

Ghote could not help noticing that, though brusque, her voice was clearly comforting. The boy looked up at her, still shaking.

"Have to get an anti-rabies shot into him as quickly as possible," Dr. Diana said.

She addressed her remarks to the top of the glass-covered table but Ghote interpreted them as a sort of apology for not answering more quickly.

He stood looking at the fine, gleaming needle held steadily in the thin flesh of the boy's arm while Dr. Diana firmly squeezed the shot home.

"There," she said, taking the needle out, "now we'll just put you down somewhere comfortably and then you'll begin to feel better."

With one swoop she picked the feather-light boy up and deposited him on the hard, white examination couch. Ghote wondered if it had been used since Frank Masters's body had been removed from it. Dr. Diana took up a coarse, red blanket from the foot of the couch, shook it out and placed it over the boy.

"That'll warm you up," she said.

She turned to Ghote.

"Well now, Frank. As he really was. I suppose you have a right to know."

She went over to the sink, stooped, picked up a small kettle from underneath it and filled it with water. Not until she had taken it to the electric boiling ring in the inner half of the hut did she give Ghote her full attention.

"I've a notion," she said, "that you got your picture of Frank from that credulous idiot Krishna Chatterjee."

Ghote kept his face blank.

Dr. Diana grunted a half-laugh.

"All right, protect your sources of information. I don't mind. But let me tell you one thing. Chatterjee is a nice fellow and all that, but he's simply too good. It isn't that he won't see people's faults, but by the time he's finished finding excuses for them he's forgotten the faults are still there."

Again Ghote made no comment. Dr. Diana, hands thrust into the patch pockets of her white coat, went on.

"Did he tell you that Frank was a damned bad administrator?" she asked. "If he did, I bet he found so many excuses for not doing administration that in the end you thought it was a positive virtue to go about wasting what resources we have."

"Being a bad administrator is hardly a grave fault," Ghote said. "I am not going to be satisfied so easily, you know."

Dr. Diana's eyes flashed.

"I wasn't trying to fob you off, as a matter of fact," she said. "When I make up my mind to tell someone something, I tell them. So you can just listen."

Ghote made no reply.

"No," Dr. Diana went on, "I'm not making out a lack of administrative talent is a crippling moral defect. What I am saying is that Frank was not only a bad administrator, but that he wouldn't realise it. He thought that whatever way he tackled something was the right way."

"And you found this out when he left you in charge and went to the Punjab?" Ghote asked.

"I'd suspected it for years. But, yes, when he went sidling off to his mystics I realised just what a mess he had made. He was a poor judge of character for one thing. The way he let himself be deceived by that rogue Amrit Singh was a positive scandal."

"Amrit Singh?" Ghote said.

Dr. Diana looked at him.

"Oh, don't get so excited," she said. "Everybody knows you'd like to pull in Amrit Singh for this. But if you do his lawyers will have him out in no time. And well you know it. After all, you haven't got cast-iron proof, have you?"

"Where did you hear this?" Ghote snapped.

Minute by minute he felt himself being pushed back on to the defensive, and he resented it.

"My dear man, surely you realise everything you've done and said here has been watched over and talked over till we're sick of it?"

Ghote knew it only too well. With the eyes and ears of the clients everywhere he could expect nothing less.

"Whether we shall take action against Amrit Singh is a matter for us," he said. "What I want to know is what were Mr. Masters's relations with him."

"Practically non-existent," Dr. Diana answered. "What could they be? Amrit Singh hung around here because he had dealings with some of the boys, as you'd expect. And Frank saw him, and let himself be charmed. Typical of him. But I put all that right when I found out what was happening."

"So," Ghote said, "this is a very different Frank Masters I am hearing about."

Dr. Diana gave him a still scornful look.

"Well," she said, "you didn't think I was going to let Frank down if I could help it, did you?"

"No, perhaps not," Ghote replied. "But now you cannot help it."

"No. Very well then. What else can I say to blacken him? That he was selfish? Well, that's certainly true."

"Are you saying that he did all this just for his own sake?"

Ghote gestured round at the walls of the hut in their dazzling white paint, the medicines in the cupboard, the boy quietly lying on the hard couch.

Dr. Diana puffed out a sigh.

"To tell you the truth," she said, "I honestly don't know. Who does? About someone else? On the whole I think his motives were mixed. Some days whatever he did was to make Frank Masters feel good. At other times, well, I can't say."

She treated Ghote to a sort of grin.

"It made life pretty difficult, you know," she said.

Ghote hardly heard. A terrible thought had struck him. He had been building up in his mind an ideal of Frank Masters. Dr. Diana's words had shown him that it was not at all like the truth. And yet, on the strength of this ideal, he had been so stupid as to give away five hundred precious rupees. How could he have been so utterly foolish? Krishna Chatterjee had spoken of Frank Masters as a man who did good, certainly, but he had at the same time painted him as human. It was only hearing him abused by someone as calmly unscrupulous as Amrit Singh that had turned the balance in the end.

Ghote saw now that it had been a gesture of sudden revulsion to thrust all that money into the podgy hand of the Paramour, a silly and impulsive gesture. And in making it he had given away every anna he had scraped together to get his own wife something she had wanted for years.

"I—I have to go," he said abruptly. "Yes, I must go now. Thank you for your help. But I must go."

Dr. Diana was looking at him wonderingly as he hurried out.

"You could have had some of the coffee I was making for the boy," she said.

XVI

One thought tapped away inside Inspector Ghote's head as he ran off through the big garden of the Masters Foundation. Perhaps it was not too late. He had given the Paramour the five hundred rupees only that morning. She would hardly go hurrying round to the money-lender to pay off the debt on the boat right away. Money-lenders were not that popular.

So she would still have the rupees.

And from the way she had taken them, he would have every right to demand them back. She had shown no gratitude. All right, she would lose the money.

It was with this idea lodged solidly in his mind that he arrived in the hurly-burly of Churchgate Station again and set about finding a train to take him back. As he scanned the timetable and ran to make inquiries here and there the same thought kept hammering away in his head. It is not too late: she deserves to have to pay the money back.

And there was no train.

He could hardly believe it. He repeated his round of inquiries but had no more success. While he had been talking to the boys outside the Foundation and seeing Dr. Diana in the dispensary time had passed. Then the trip across the city, though short, had been more than usually bedevilled with traffic hold-ups. And there it was. No train going out that far till early next day.

He thought of hiring a car but then remembered that after all the following day was Holi. There was even less chance of the Paramour handing the five hundred rupees over to a money-lender in the middle of all the festivities. He decided to get out to the village as early as possible next morning.

He spent a miserable evening. He did not dare go home till late in case there was talk about the refrigerator. He dared even less go to the office in case orders were waiting for him to get in touch with D.S.P. Naik. In the end he went to a cinema. The amorous intrigues of the film failed to grip. The music grated on his nerves. He left before it was over.

: : : :

Next morning when he arrived, hot, sweaty and unoptimistic, at the village he found it looking very different from his previous visits. The overlying atmosphere of poverty had been temporarily swamped in an uprush of holiday gaiety. On the greenish, decaying walls of the huts bright, crudely coloured banners reflected the equal brightness of the sunshine and rippled happily in a strong breeze coming saltily off the sea. From the masts of the village boats, beached high and dry to-day on the soft sand, fluttered gay pennants, long and twisting, or stubby and forcefully patterned. More streamers and banners decorated the tall net-drying poles.

On the beach in front of the huts a positively enormous bonfire had been built. Ghote wondered for a moment how a community of such poverty could have gathered together the great pile of broken wood, discarded household objects, substantial pieces of furniture and even boat oars that made up the bulk of the merrily crackling blaze with its attendant circle of children, now excitedly jigging up and down, now suddenly solemn in front of the glowing heart of the fire.

But he had no time for idle speculation.

In all the stirring jubilation he was faced with the awkward business of broaching the reason for his visit to Tarzan's family. The evening before, during the slow unwinding of the colourful love epic in the cinema, the notion that the Paramour had somehow forfeited any rights to the five hundred rupees had finally faded away in the harsh light of reality. He had handed the money over: he wanted it back. That was what it amounted to. He wanted it back because he had parted with it under a false impression. Frank Masters was not the person he had thought. The family had not been entitled to the money.

Even the very altered atmosphere of the village could not rob him of this cast-iron resolution. Even the sight of the family themselves standing outside their hut, on the verge of entering into the general jubilation, could not kill this.

One glance at the Paramour however was enough to make Ghote dismiss her as the best one to approach straight away. Her natural jollity had already so blended with the gaiety all around her that he doubted whether it would be possible to communicate at all. Tarzan's brother, standing jigging a little in time to the rhythmical drumming coming from the far side of the great fire as if he knew his duty in times of merriment, he reserved as a last hope.

He concentrated on the father. Certainly the old man seemed impervious to the increasing noise and excitement. His face was as absolutely impassive as ever. His arms were folded indomitably across his ribby chest and he stood, legs just a little apart, still as a statue.

Ghote went up to him.

"Good morning, good morning," he said cheerfully.

He looked back over his shoulder at the revelry behind him.

"Happy holiday," he added.

Tarzan's father moved his eyes. He looked at Ghote. But his expression did not alter.

"Well," Ghote said, "how are things with you to-day? The village seems to be very happy. I hope you feel your troubles are a little less?"

He thought he had succeeded in bringing the subject of the five hundred rupees neatly to the fore.

Tarzan's father looked away.

Ghote tried again.

"This is not a day for the money-lender to come round, is it?" he said.

He laughed.

The laugh ended up on a cracked note he did not like. And Tarzan's father ignored it all.

"So you have not had to pay off your debt yet?" Ghote said, feeling the time for delicacy had come to an abrupt end.

"Our debt?"

The Paramour had evidently been more attentive to the conversation than her lolloping half-dance to the drumming rhythm had indicated. She turned round now to Ghote, still dancing and still smiling with as much all-embracing benevolence as ever, and put out a podgy finger to dig him in the ribs.

"You have come to see us paying our debt with that money?" she asked.

"Yes. No."

"To-morrow. To-morrow. Perhaps later. This is no day for debt paying. *Holi hai.*"

Ghote felt obliged to smile and even essay a slight dance step. And, in fact, he did already feel suddenly much more light-hearted.

So the debt was unpaid. Then the five hundred rupees were still safely tucked away somewhere. Though it was not going to be easy in the middle of dancing, smiling and shouting "*Holi hai*" to broach the delicate core of the problem.

Ghote tried.

"No, no," he said. "I did not come to watch such a thing. I would not do that."

"You came for Holi?"

The Paramour seized him with two solid, chunky hands and swung him three times round to the beat of the drums.

"No, no, no."

Ghote managed to break free. He thrust his face close to the Paramour's bouncing, jiggling fat orb. He spoke sharply and clearly, and with a touch of desperation.

"I came to take back the money, some of the money," he said. "For a little while. I find I need—— I must have it. I must have the money back. Now."

The grin across the Paramour's huge face split into an enormous crease, deep pink, dotted and littered with stumps of white tooth, wide as a crater.

"You want the money back now?"

"Yes, yes. I am sorry. I do. It is most urgent. I will talk about it later. After this . . ."

He looked past the great wobbling bulk of the Paramour at the festivities on the sand in front of the village. They were really beginning to warm up now. The drums were beating madly and almost everybody had joined in the dance.

"It is gone. All gone. Gone."

"Gone?"

Ghote felt a great cold wedge of ice descending crushingly down on to him.

"What do you mean gone?" he said. "Where has it gone?"

It was the Paramour's turn to wave at the rising tide of celebration on the sands. The high-piled blazing fire, the teams of musicians, the flags and banners everywhere, the fireworks screaming up into the blue sky, the food clutched in happy hands, the bottles waving high above heads.

"It has gone for Holi," she said. "Such a Holi the village has never known. It has gone to honour the great Krishna. Every anna."

Ghote turned slowly away.

The sight of that huge face, stupidly happy, reasonlessly gay, maddened him. She had spent every anna of his five hundred rupees in treating the whole village to a wildly extravagant fiesta. Every one of the rupees that at least ought to have gone to make the family's whole life easier by lifting the crushing burden of their debt. Gone. Spent. Going up in smoke.

No wonder the big fire had been blazing so merry on such a fine assortment of rubbish. When money was being thrown about in that way, anyone would be willing to sacrifice a dilapidated piece of furniture or even an oar past its prime.

Waves of pure rage swept through and through him as he marched away.

And quite suddenly, approaching the swirling crowd of merrymakers on the sand, his mood changed. The rage fell apart to leave a hard residue of bitter determination. Never again was he going to set himself up to help or judge other people. They had their lives to lead: he had his. And he knew too what the life he had to lead was. The life of a policeman. Doing his duty as he should. All right, so D.S.P. Naik was prepared to tell plain lies to improve the case against Amrit Singh. Well, he was probably correct. After all, this was the formed opinion of a respected and senior police officer. Who was Ganesh Ghote to go setting himself up against that? No, from now on he would do his duty as it was put to him. And first of all he would go and pull in Amrit Singh. On the murder charge. And the moment he had seen him safely behind bars he would go out to the Masters Foundation, get hold of those damned boys and see that they came into line. He would get up such a case against Amrit Singh that the D.S.P. himself would not be able to better it.

Round him the excited holidaymakers suddenly whirled. He found himself in an instant surrounded by smiling, smiling faces. Everywhere bodies jerked and swayed in dance. In his ears shout after shout, "*Holi hai, Holi hai, Holi hai*" rang and echoed. Fireworks fizzed and banged right, left and centre. Their smell mingled dramatically with that of a hundred sweaty bodies. For a few moments a broad-shouldered fisherman stood pressed close to him, his head thrown back and his mouth opening and shutting rhythmically in the words of a song of consistent and remarkable lewdness.

Krishna and the milkmaids, Ghote thought sourly, hemmed in and pressed upon from every side.

And then the real business of the day began. With a

multitude of high, screaming whoops the saturnalian colour throwers came roaring into the fray. With big, crude syringes they sprayed long, drenching streams of coloured water, red, yellow, blue, high into the air and down on to one and all. Other swooping troops puffed huge clouds of pink and purple powder at anyone and everyone, but especially at anybody in the least way high and mighty.

And in all the simple village throng, who looked higher or mightier or more worthy of drenching and powdering than Inspector Ganesh Ghote, C.I.D.? Tossing powder by the handful, squirting ink by the bicycle pumpful, they came at him from every side. In seconds he was wet through, red wet, blue wet, yellow wet. And on to the wetness the coloured powders, pink, turquoise and orange, clung and smeared. He put his head glumly down and pushed forward. Dancing bodies bumped him, hands seized him and whirled him bouncing round. The drums beat in his ears, and everywhere the faces were smiling, smiling like maniacs.

I have deserved this, he thought. This is a fit punishment for coming here with my money and telling people how to live their lives. Exactly fit. They have taken my money and used it to buy all these pots of powder and buckets of dye and they have jumped on me and put me down to the lowest level of the low. Well, there it is.

Buffeted and banged, swung and tossed, he endured it till at last he found himself quite suddenly ejected from the whirling crowd.

He staggered a few paces clear and stopped to draw breath. He flapped at his multi-coloured clothes in an ineffectual attempt to get them looking a little more presentable. Then he gave up. He would have to go home looking like this, and that would be the crowning blow of his punishment. He looked round to see where he was and how he could get to the inland path without going through the crowd again.

And just twenty yards away he saw Amrit Singh.

This time the big Sikh was doing more than spy over the village. He was down on his hands and knees round at the back of the palisaded curing yard scraping up the soft muddy earth with his bare hands like a dog.

An energetic and extremely purposeful dog.

At once Ghote realised what it was that he must be doing. The patch of earth he was working at was clearly marked out by lying in the exact centre of a triangle formed by three singularly ugly, stunted and battered banana palms. If ever there was a place to bury something in the sure hope of digging it up again, this was it. And what had anyone here to bury that Amrit Singh would want to dig up but gold?

He had caught him in the very act.

Ghote stood where he was, poised. Surely this must be it? He would get Amrit Singh now, get him for smuggling. Fair and square. And after that he could see once more what he could make of the mystery of Krishna Chatterjee.

The big Sikh's broad back lifted and from behind the heap of dark earth he picked up a small but heavy bundle wrapped in a piece of dirty coarse gunny. This was the moment.

Ghote ran forward silently across the soft, dry sand.

And something—a scatter of little sharp-beaked paddy birds, a fleeting shadow—warned the Sikh. With half a glance behind he was up and off, his long legs striding out, heading down the gentle slope of the seashore, out and away by the quickest route that came.

Ghote ran. He felt his legs moving swiftly under him. He would do it. In spite of whatever unlucky accident had warned the Sikh he would catch him.

But one thing he had forgotten.

His own appearance. The multi-coloured fool. Flashing down towards the distant sea, covered from head to foot in a dazzling array of the brightest shades, with the strong sun catching every colour and the breeze sending every loose end flying, he was a sight to catch the eye of even the most absorbed Holi reveller.

There was a sudden, sharp, directed roar of laughter, and then the crowd closed in on him again.

He was caught by both hands, flung round in circles, jumped high, swung low, sluiced once more from chunky syringe and venomous bicycle pump, sloshed and soaked from bucket and jug, puffed and dusted again, green, blue, yellow and above all red. The very air he breathed was smoking with colour.

There was nothing he could do. All the while he kept thinking of the big Sikh, striding out across the beach with the heavy package in the dirty, earth-stained sacking clutched firmly to his chest. And taking with him that sudden, last delusive hope.

As abruptly as he had been caught up the capricious crowd let him go.

Dazed and half-blinded he took a few drunken steps clear of the noise and wild movement. One idea he had kept in his head. Amrit Singh had been running towards the sea. Hardly looking where he was going he set off at a loping run down the gentle slope of the grey sand.

At last he found himself well clear of the revellers, dodging through the scattered groups of narrow beached fishing craft lying careened over to one side or the other. He stopped for a moment and looked both ways along the shore.

Amrit Singh was there.

His tall figure, a single lone presence on this day of mass celebration, could be distinctly seen making its way along the edge of the sea over to where the sluggish creek broke the low coastline. And he was walking. He thought he was safe.

Ghote set out in pursuit, cutting straight across the grey sands to head off the Sikh following the shore line. He wondered why Amrit Singh had not taken the same short cut.

And then he knew. Abruptly his feet began to sink in soft, wet, rippled sucking sand. Should he go back? To retrace his steps and then go round the long way would mean that he would almost certainly lose sight of Amrit Singh. And above all he must stay where he could see him. If the Sikh stopped to bury the heavy little package again while he was unobserved all would be lost.

Ghote decided to plunge on. A little crab scuttled across the wet sand in front of him.

He cursed himself for not having noted that wet gleam as the Sikh must have done. But there was nothing he could do now. Supposing the water-saturated patch got suddenly deeper? People were sucked to death in places like this.

And then he was out.

The sand under his soaked and heavy shoes was suddenly firm. Wet still, but hard now, almost like a cement floor. He began to run.

He found himself moving easily forward and smiled a little to himself, thinking he was not as out of training as D.S.P. Naik had supposed. Tramping the hot, crowded and hard streets of the city was probably every bit as good for the stamina as playing games of hockey. Even if it lacked the same touch of glamour.

He moved swiftly forward, almost as if in a dream. And everything began to take on a matching dreamlike quality. Behind him the sound of the Holi revellers was faint now, shrill, musical and distant. The pounding, brutal noise of reality had simply been left far behind. Above the solid black smudge that represented the dancing crowd he saw, when he glanced for a moment over his shoulder, a light, fabulous and unlikely cloud of pinkish red, the dazing, dazzling powder of a short time before. And, turning back, ahead of him walking with his head down and arms still clutching tight the heavy little bundle, was Amrit Singh. On the smooth, caked sand Ghote's heavy shoes were making no noise. As if still in a dream he let his legs stretch out in a quiet increase of pace and a second later launched himself almost gently through the air.

His arms closed hard round the tall Sikh's legs. And he had him. Gold-handed.

:: ::

But he never got Amrit Singh safely behind the locked door of a C.I.D. headquarters cell. At the railway station he enlisted the help of the local police to make sure his hard-won captive, for all that by then he was being held at his own gunpoint, did not succeed in making a break for it. It was a sensible precaution. But it was Ghote's undoing.

As he stepped out of the train at Churchgate Station he was greeted by the immaculately white-clad form of Inspector Patel of the Customs. In the sudden realisation of the contrast between his own clothes after the Holi assault on them and the Customs man's spotless appearance he even almost forgot the existence of Amrit Singh, handcuffed firmly to his wrist. But Inspector Patel could plainly think of nothing else.

"Well, well," he said, giving Ghote a quick, piercing look from his thin, chopping blade face. "This is a very unfortunate business indeed."

Ghote looked at him. His bewilderment must have been all too obvious.

"This business of arresting the man yourself for a purely smuggling offence," Inspector Patel explained painstakingly.

"I had the gold put into the safe at the chowkey where I took him first," Ghote said.

"Yes, yes," said Inspector Patel. "I dare say that can be put right. But you cannot expect this other business to be forgotten just like that. You had no right to do it, you know. No right. Not for a purely smuggling offence."

And so it was that Ghote, stained and spattered from his encounter with the celebrating villagers, had to stand mutely among the noisy crowds at Churchgate Station and watch Inspector Patel, in the full glory of a properly entitled Customs officer, lead away the faintly sardonic figure of the notorious Amrit Singh.

Suddenly he thought of the refrigerator fund and what it had been spent on. His world looked very flat.

: : : :

He waited till late that night to make his apology to

Protima. Longer than this he felt he could not put it off. It must be done that day.

But the day could be prolonged.

They were sitting outside in the yard at the back of the house. Already it was beginning to feel a little cooler.

"We could sleep now," Protima said.

"Just a few minutes more. It is only now that it is pleasant."

"And to-morrow? Are you going to be fresh to-morrow if you have such a short night when for once you do not need to?"

"To-morrow will be different," Ghote said.

To-morrow you will know that your cherished plans for the refrigerator have fallen to pieces, he thought.

He said nothing more.

From the neatly shaped, heavy bulk of the neem tree nearby came the muffled cheep of a sleepy bird. Ghote sighed.

It was true, it was pleasant out here at this time of day. It was cool. It was calm. Everything was peaceful. You could put everything finally into its place, if you wanted to. Except, perhaps, that some things would have to be looked at before they were put away, and . . .

So in the end it was Protima who brought up the subject of the refrigerator fund.

"To-morrow," she said. "To-morrow will be a great day for me. Can you get the money out early?"

Ghote took a breath. One. Two. Three.

"There is no money," he said.

"No money? But you told——"

"There was. There was. I did. But—— But I have done a very silly thing. I have given the money away."

"You have given away five hundred rupees?"

Protima was too astounded, it was obvious, to keep the sheer incredulity out of her voice.

"Yes," Ghote said.

His disappointment at not having the confession received with more understanding put an edge on his voice.

"Yes," he repeated with a touch of bravado, "I have given away five hundred rupees."

Protima rose to her feet like a sudden whirlwind.

"Who have you given it to? How could you give away so much? Have you no thought of your family even?"

"Whose money was it?" Ghote shouted, suddenly swept right away. "Who earned the money? Who saved it up? If I had said nothing you would never have even known there was five hundred rupees."

"That has nothing to do with it. There were five hundred rupees. Five hundred rupees. And you gave them away. Gave them."

"What do you mean that that has nothing to do with it? It has everything to do with it. I have just explained. As far as you are concerned the money simply does not exist."

"Oh, I know that. It does not exist indeed. You have given it away."

"That is not what I meant at all. Not at all. Why can you never understand a simple piece of logic? If I had given the money away, of course it would exist. But I was saying that it does not exist. As far as you are concerned."

"Have you or have you not given the money away?"

"I told you I had given it away."

"Then what do you mean about 'if you had given it away'? You have. You have given away the money that was to buy me a refrigerator. After all the years when I needed one so much, when it is the day before we get it, you give the money away. My money."

"Your——"

And he stopped himself. He took a deep breath and told himself that he was in the wrong. He had given the money away. Protima was right to be angry. But how to tell her what had happened to the money after he had given it away?

"Listen, my little one," he said.

This was almost his last card. The special term of endearment he kept for her. The expression that meant so much because it was so plainly not really true. The tall, invariably elegant Protima, fine, chiselled, fiery, was never anyone's " little one." Except his. It was his right.

" Listen, my little one."

She stopped. She stood looking at him, even though it was with smouldering, guarded eyes.

" I can explain everything. It was all the fault of this damned case."

She seemed restive at this and he hurried on.

" Look. It was. I tell you it was having to think all the time about such a person as Frank Masters. I saw him as a man of such generosity, coming to this country from the luxuries of America, devoting his time to caring for the vagrants that most of us do nothing about. I began to think about what sort of person he must be, and what sort of person I was."

" And so you set up as a little Frank Masters of your own and gave away my refrigerator money?"

He would not be roused.

" Yes, I did. That is what I did. And only afterwards did I begin to find out what Frank Masters was really like."

" What?" she exclaimed. " His death was caused by something bad he had done? Underneath all the while he was——"

" No, no, no. It was not that. Frank Masters was not a bad man. But he was not the all-good man that I thought either. I found that out in the end. He had his faults. And one of them was even giving away too much."

Protima was looking doubtful now. He stared at her intently.

" Listen," he said, " that is what my mistake was. I tried to be like him, and instead of doing my work I began thinking about whether I was a good man or a bad man. And—— And there is worse."

" What worse?"

" What happened to the money after I had given it to the poor family of fishing people who needed it to pay off the debt on their boat."

He was whispering now.

"They took the money," he went on, "and they spent every anna on celebrating Holi. It all went up in smoke. Down to the last pie."

And Protima threw back her head and laughed.

He sat where he was on the rattan chair with the sagging arm and looked up at her. In the faint light he could see her neck, smooth and columnar, as she laughed and laughed with her head back and her whole body shaking.

"Oh, Mr. Policeman," she gasped at last. "Mr. Policeman, what a judge of character you are."

"If it comes to a criminal . . ."

He had begun stiffly, but he could not keep it up. In a moment he too was shaking with mad outbursts of laughter.

From the open window of the house behind them came a plaintive voice.

"What is it? Why are you laughing?"

Ved.

"It is all right," Protima called. "It is just your father. He is such a funny man."

No reply came. After they had stood in silence for a little Protima walked softly into the house. She came out again almost at once.

"Asleep," she said.

She looked at Ghote down her nose, her eyes sparkling a little.

"You with your difficult case," she said.

"But it is difficult," Ghote said.

"When you have arrested Amrit Singh with smuggled gold on him?"

"Yes. I know that. But still I am just in the same position as before over the Masters affair. Certainly Amrit Singh would say nothing more to me all the way back in the train. And I suppose he will never say anything."

"Does it matter now?"

"But of course it does. The situation is exactly the same as before. Frank Masters started to be sick soon after he ate a beef curry. He was poisoned by arsenic trioxide.

Arsenic trioxide was stolen from the dispensary at the Masters Foundation just before the meal. Only two people went into that dispensary, both of them without any right to, Amrit Singh and Krishna Chatterjee. It rests exactly equally between them."

"But just because Frank Masters was sick," Protima said, "why should it be poison? I think you are quite wrong about that. Little Ved is sick sometimes, and no one says it is poison then."

Ghote sighed deeply.

He knew there was never any point in going over such details with Protima. She might be wonderful when you had made a terrible mistake, but she lacked any powers of logical reasoning.

"Well?" she said in face of his sigh and silence. "Well, is that not right?"

Ghote shook his head.

"No, I am afraid it cannot be that," he said.

"But why not? Are you saying that Ved has been poisoned so many times? I think you policemen need to come and do a woman's work in the house."

"No," Ghote said. "I have explained everything."

"But I have told you that children get sick for all sorts of reasons. That was something you forgot."

Suddenly Ghote felt nettled.

"I did not forget," he said sharply. "Just, please, leave police work to me and I will leave house matters to you."

He saw that Protima was ready with a reply. As she invariably was. And he made up his mind that he would not hear it. This was his business.

He jumped up and walked quickly into the house, his head tilted up proudly.

But, once out of Protima's sight, he checked himself. His old fault again. And it was at that moment that he solved the Masters case.

XVII

Inspector Ghote's first action was to go as fast as he could through the city centre and out to the Masters Foundation. There he found that he had arrived in the middle of a serious crisis. As he stood just inside the tall front door, pausing for a moment to set in his mind the final details of his plan of campaign, there came hurrying past the obsequiously bent form of the podgy, shiny-skinned cook. He went at a half-run, bare feet pattering on the floor, towards the door of the staff tiffin room. At it he stopped, groaned heart-rendingly, ducked his well-greased head even lower and entered.

A waft of cooked-food smell, rich and spicy but with a tang of the burnt about it, came out. Ghote realised that he had arrived at the time of the evening meal. He thought for a moment and decided that this suited him pretty well.

He saw that the cook, in his worried haste, had neglected to close the door completely. Quietly he walked across and stood listening.

It was not difficult to make out what was going on. Just as he approached, Dr. Diana's clear English tones rang out.

"You know what I've had you called in here for?" she was demanding.

"Oh, yes, memsahib. Know very well," came the cook's soft reply.

"All right, my lad. Let's just hear what. If you know so well."

"Oh, memsahib, is my disgraceful cooking."

"Yes, it is your disgraceful cooking. But don't think you're going to get away with all those apologies this time. I want to know just why your cooking's so disgraceful."

"Very bad cook, memsahib."

"Come on, that won't do at all. Why are you bad? Tell me first exactly what was bad about the food to-night."

"Don't know, memsahib. Just appalling all round, memsahib."

"No, it was not."

"No, memsahib?"

"No."

"Cooking good, memsahib?"

"No."

"Oh yes then, cooking very bad. Sorry, memsahib."

"I asked you just what it was you had done wrong to-night. I am not interested in how bad you want to make yourself out to be. I simply want to know what you did wrong with the food we are attempting to eat now."

"Yes, memsahib."

"Well?"

The cook evidently could think of no way of abasing himself in a manner that would please Dr. Diana. He remained silent.

After an ominous pause Dr. Diana's voice floated coldly out again.

"You know that this cannot be allowed to go on, don't you?"

But it was not the cook who answered. Instead Ghote recognised Fraulein Glucklich's curiously accented English.

"Dr. Diana," she said sharply, "I think you are forgetting something."

"I tell you one thing I cannot forget. I cannot forget the interminable series of utterly disgusting meals I have had to put up with here. And nor do I think the whole blame should be put on the cook."

"No, indeed it should not. That is precisely what you are forgetting. If the cook is bad, I would remind you, it is because the late Herr Frank, whose *purusha* has passed on in the great *samsara*, deliberately chose a bad cook."

"All right," Dr. Diana came back icily, "he did choose the cook. But then it's simply time you and everybody learnt that Frank's choices are no longer binding in this establishment."

Even from where he stood in the quiet hall Ghote could hear Fraulein Glucklich's gasp.

"That is certainly a very true observation."

It was Krishna Chatterjee intervening now.

"Certainly a most true observation," he repeated. "But on the other hand, there can be no doubt that an institution that bears the name of Frank Masters is bound, at least temporarily, to pay due attention to the practices observed in his lifetime. Perhaps, however, there is a solution to the problem that would heed the wishes of all parties to this unfortunate occurrence. What I mean to say is, is it not possible to arrange for some instruction for this poor fellow?"

Ghote waited in some apprehension for Dr. Diana's answer to this. But the reply when it came arrived from elsewhere. From the unexpected voice of Sonny Carstairs.

"I think Dr. Diana's right," he said. "It's all very well remembering Mr. Frank and all that. But we know who's in charge now, and a jolly good job she's making of it."

Now it was that Dr. Diana spoke.

"Yes," she said, "it's obvious some people know who's in charge now. But don't think fulsome praise is going to do you any good, Sonny, my lad. One slip in the dispensary, and you're out. I promise you that."

Sonny Carstairs laughed.

In spite of everything Ghote felt sorry for him.

But Dr. Diana had not finished.

"Come on," she said to the still silent cook, "I asked you for an explanation of what went wrong with your *vindaloo* to-night. I am still waiting for it. And I warn you that I shall not wait long."

Ghote decided that the moment had come. He stepped into the open doorway.

"But I must ask you to wait at least a little, Doctor," he said.

His entrance certainly created its sensation. The podgy, glistening cook, crouching hypnotised almost under Dr. Diana's wrath, positively jumped. Sonny and Krishna Chatterjee sent their chairs scraping back. Fraulein Glucklich violated her studious *sannysini's* calm with a little squeak. And even Dr. Diana looked distinctly surprised.

"What the hell are you doing here?" she said abruptly. "Can't you see we're in the middle of a meal. Really, we must be given a bit of peace sometimes, you know."

"I regret," Ghote said quietly. "But I have come on very important business."

"That's as may be," Dr. Diana replied. "But I can't see that any business of yours can be so important that you have to come barging in here without so much as being announced."

"Perhaps not," Ghote said. "But my business is important. You see, I know now who killed Frank Masters."

"Do you indeed?" Dr. Diana said. "Well, you'd better get on and arrest them."

She turned her chair slightly so that she was facing squarely in the direction of Krishna Chatterjee.

Ghote did not pretend to be ignorant of what she meant by the move.

"You think I have come to arrest Mr. Chatterjee?" he said.

"Well, you'd hardly come to our tiffin room to arrest Amrit Singh," Dr. Diana replied.

"And supposing I want to arrest neither of the gentlemen?"

"Don't be a fool, man. We all know what the situation is. Vague threats like that will get you nowhere. The poison that killed Frank was put into the curry he ate in this very room. It was stolen from the dispensary not an hour before. Two unauthorised persons entered the dispensary, Amrit Singh and Chatterjee here. You have come to us, so I suppose it's for Chatterjee."

"Certainly I have succeeded in working out why Mr. Chatterjee went into the dispensary," Ghote said.

Sitting in front of his neglected plate, Krishna Chatterjee stirred uneasily.

"If I had listened to everything I had heard with an open mind," Ghote went on, "I would have known long ago."

Dr. Diana glared at him. He hastily continued.

"It was just a matter of connecting three things. That Mr. Chatterjee greatly respected the late Mr. Masters in spite of what he knew were faults in his character, that the boy Edward G. Robinson boasted to me that he could tell a good story about why Mr. Masters was supposed to have hidden some gold in the dispensary, and thirdly that he cheekily referred to Shri Chatterjee as a 'sucker'."

The little Bengali's big eyes looked up at Ghote with dawning realisation, and a sudden tinge of laughter.

"Yes," Ghote said, "I believe Edward G. must have told you Frank Masters had lost his money and was smuggling gold, and you believed it and tried to hide the fact from the world."

"My dear sir," said Mr. Chatterjee. "And you are telling me that the whole business was a pure fabrication? I am most extremely relieved. Something like that could do incalculable harm."

He blinked two or three times.

"Of course, I very much doubt whether I would have gone through with it," he added. "To the bitter end, you know."

"Well, Inspector, what are you doing here, then?" Dr. Diana said abruptly. "Why aren't you rounding up Amrit Singh?"

"We have him in prison awaiting trial already," Ghote answered.

"Then it was him?"

"No."

"But——"

"Dr. Diana, you said just now that the poison that killed Mr. Masters was put in the curry he ate. How can you be sure of that, may I ask?"

"Because on your own admission he was proved scientifically to have eaten that curry shortly before he died," Dr. Diana answered carefully. "Because he was full of arsenic trioxide. Because the symptoms set in at just the right time."

She looked at Ghote with all the certainties of science itself behind her.

"The symptoms appeared," Ghote answered calmly. "But what caused them? Was it arsenic trioxide? Or was it just an ordinary emetic, Doctor?"

Dr. Diana's eyes went wide.

"What do you mean?" she said.

"I mean that, if the curry had contained not poison but a simple emetic which anyone could obtain, then Mr. Masters need not have been poisoned at dinner when he had the beef curry you ordered for him. He could have been poisoned afterwards. At a time when there was nothing to stop you getting hold of the arsenic, Doctor. When you had sent Mr. Carstairs here away to call the police. Then it was quite simple to take the powder from the dispensing room next door and to offer poor Mr. Masters a drink. From a doctor's hands."

Ghote kept his eyes firmly on her. There could be no doubt she was hearing the truth.

She stood up slowly.

"Yes," she said, "it seems I wasn't as clever as I thought. My congratulations, Inspector. But you do see that I had to do it, don't you? He was going to take his money, lock, stock and barrel, and spend it on a pack of mystical Tibetans. All this was going to be allowed to drop. Just like that."

She looked round, seeing through tear-blotched eyes the workings of the big house beyond the four walls of the tiffin room, the steady rescuing of the almost hopeless flotsam of the big city's pavements, the doing good.

"I could have made something of this place," she said.

: :   : :

Just as the blue Dodge truck took Dr. Diana off to headquarters dusk fell. Ghote stood on the Foundation steps enjoying for a few moments the ending of the day's glare. He breathed deeply. There was nothing to stop him relaxing now. The rest was routine.

"So you finally got her," a familiar voice said in his ear.

He noticed the shapes of the thin, wiry bodies emerging once more from the darkness.

"Yes," he said, without looking round, "she has been arrested."

"Just the sort of dirty trick you get with a policeman," Edward G. said.

"Dirty trick?"

Ghote wheeled round and glared furiously into the upturned, crinkled face.

"She fought to keep all that money from going to those stinking holy men," Edward G. explained.

Ghote looked at him in astonishment.

"You knew that?" he said.

The boy sighed in the darkness like an exasperated schoolmaster.

"I told you," he said, "we need to know what goes on. We need to."

"And you knew that she was the one who sent the message to bring Amrit Singh down to the dispensary at the right time?"

Edward G. laughed.

"She reckoned he was safe to get off at the trial," he said. "She reckoned all those lawyers would do it."

"She was probably right," Ghote said.

The boy grunted contemptuously.

"Just like a social worker that idea," he said. "You ever think what would have happen if we'd said we did see him steal the poison?"

Ghote peered down at him. In the gloom it was difficult to make out the expression on the wrinkled, wry, old man's face.

"Still," the boy added, "you were pretty clever to catch her."

Ghote felt a ridiculous sense of having received an accolade.

"Thank you," he said. "But you should never forget that the police are not always stupid. Sometimes by sheer hard——"

He pulled himself up sharp.

"Or the least," he said, "we have wives who cannot be tricked."